# A COLD MONTANA CHRISTMAS

## CHRISTMAS

### A CROSSFIRE CANYON NOVEL

## MINA BECKETT

CURTISSLYNN
PUBLISHING

A COLD MONTANA CHRISTMAS

A CROSSFIRE CANYON NOVEL

*A Cold Montana Christmas* is a work of fiction. Names, characters, businesses, places, events, and incidents are either the products of the author's imagination or used in a fictitious manner. Any resemblance to actual person, living or dead, or actual events is purely coincidental.

Copyright © 2021 by Mina Beckett

ebook ISBN: 978-1-7375127-0-7

Print ISBN: 978-1-7375127-1-4

Published by CurtissLynn Publishing

Cover and internal design by Shiver Shot Design

Editing by The Killion Group, Inc.

# ALSO BY MINA BECKETT

**Books by Mina Beckett**

***Coldiron Cowboys series***

*The Cowboy's Goodnight Kiss*

(ebook prequel novella only available on Mina's website)

*The Heartbreak Cowboy*

*The Fallen Cowboy*

*Breaking the Cowboy*

***Rough Creek series***

*A Cowboy Charming Christmas*

***Coming soon in the Rough Creek Series***

*Hollywood Cowboy*

***Crossfire Canyon series***

A Cold Montana Christmas: A Crossfire Canyon Novel

For more book news, visit minabeckett.com

# BLURB

*Love is rekindle and a cold Montana Christmas becomes a second chance for two star-crossed lovers.*

Eight years after Post-Traumatic Stress Disorder destroyed his marriage and nearly took his life, all ex-Marine Colton Ritter has left are summers with his son and his family's sprawling ranch, the Lucky Jack. When his father dies and leaves the ranch's future in the hands of Colton's estranged wife, Lauren, Colton knows he has one chance at saving everything he holds dear.

Loving the cowboy was never the problem. Learning to live with the soldier who returned from war was, so the stipulation of her father-in-law's will is nothing short of insanity. But living at the ranch for a year may be the only way she can save her son's inheritance from being auctioned off to the highest bidder.

Like the five generations before him, the Lucky Jack is in Colton's blood, and Lauren knows he'll do anything to protect it even if it means breaking her heart again.

# FOREWORD

I adore writing second chances, so I purposely wrote Colton and Lauren Ritter into the story when I drafted *The Heartbreak Cowboy*. The first two books in the *Coldiron Cowboys* series touched on the couple's problems, but the heart of their breakup was a mystery. Colton and Lauren were high-school sweethearts who, because of his deployment overseas and the effects of Post-Traumatic Stress Disorder, weren't able to develop their relationship as a husband and a wife. I wanted to give them that while giving readers a moving love story.

I hope you enjoy *A Cold Montana Christmas!* It's the first of many stories planned for the *Crossfire Canyon* series.

# CHAPTER ONE

COLTON RITTER RESTED HIS SHOULDER AGAINST THE knotty cedar post of the cemetery entrance. Once tall and sturdy, its weak form now creaked against his weight.

His dad, Jack Reid Ritter, had taken a similar stance against the hoary post years ago as he tried explaining his grandfather's death to Colton.

*Son, there are three forces in life a man can't understand. The weather, the heart of a woman and death.*

Colton lifted his eyes towards the snow-covered crests of the Big Belt Mountains and welled his lungs with a deep breath of frigid Montana air.

He'd been seven when his grandfather died, but he recalled the time distinctly. The bite of the cold wind as it swept through the cemetery and the unfamiliar ambiance of grief surrounding his dad was a memory Colton would never forget.

Faint lines had furrowed through his dad's brow as he fought back tears and lost. With icy rivulets streaking down the hard planes of his weather-worn cheeks, his red-rimmed eyes had searched the cold horizon.

Now at thirty-six Colton wasn't any closer to understanding the weather, the heart of a woman, or death, but he was feeling the full measure of those tears, the soul-shattering grief, and the bone-crushing weight of loss as it threatened to buckle his knees. And like his dad, Colton couldn't find any justification for the demise of a great man as his gaze roamed the same snowy vista for solace.

Major, his dad's twelve-year-old German Shepherd, sat beside Colton. Positioned with a straight back and attentive ears, the dog peered at the horizon as if he were pondering the same sort of questions about life and death.

Colton pulled a hand from his coat pocket and gave Major's head an affectionate rub. The dog responded with a low-pitched whimper, flopped down on a patch of dead prairie grass, and rested his head between his outstretched paws. A long and woeful moan followed.

Major hadn't left Colton's side in days. The dog looked unsettled and Colton wasn't sure which one of them needed comforting the most, him or Major.

Colton shivered inside his coat as a gust of wintry air swept through the cemetery. The wind carried with it the distinctive fragrance of ponderosa pines, Douglas fir, and the crisp clean scent of approaching winter. The scattering of snowflakes that had been falling for most of the morning whirled around him and settled to the ground. He could hear the clashing waters of Whiskey Creek as it cut through Crossfire Canyon and the unmistakable call of a hawk as it circled around him in search of prey.

Colton loved this land. The Lucky Jack Ranch was as much a part of him as the blood pumping through his veins. There were perils to ranching, especially in the bitter winter months of Montana. Both animal and man could freeze to death in a matter of minutes.

He knew that all too well. He'd almost lost his life and

his horse, Boaz, on a wintry morning that started out much like this one; with the weight of the world resting heavily on his shoulders and the confusion of unanswered questions banging around in his head.

Other seasons were no less hazardous in this often-harsh landscape of mountains, canyons, and endless sky. But for Colton, the rewards outweighed the risks.

The land helped to ease his mind and cure whatever was ailing him. But today his heart was hurting in a way it never had before. Nature couldn't assuage a sorrowful heart.

The crunch of footsteps on the frozen ground behind him jerked him out of his reflections. It took but a second to identify the swift but feathery tread as his mother's.

He heaved in another sharp breath and expelled it in a short, exhausted way that made her lay her hand on his arm.

"I needed a minute," he explained, his withdrawal from the gravesite. He was handling enough grief, and there had been too many onlookers with grief-stricken faces.

"I figured as much," she said.

Most of Crossfire Canyon were gathered for his dad's funeral, and several of his friends from Texas had made the trip to pay their last respects. "The old man would've loved the turnout."

His mother chuckled despite her grief. "Yes, he would have."

Sue Ritter was a strong woman. Braving twenty years of marriage with a combat veteran was no minor accomplishment. And neither was remaining friends with him after they divorced. His dad's diagnosis, the hospitals, the doctors... the last hours were hard for her.

Colton knew his mom and dad had never stopped

loving one another. His mother hadn't cried crocodile tears when his dad breathed his last breath. Instead, she'd cradled his callused hand in hers and said her goodbyes as he drifted into eternity.

"A storm is coming," she said now, her eyes surveying gray clouds that were rolling close to the mountain tops. They were a clear sign snow was on its way.

He covered her hand and gave it a gentle squeeze, his gaze dropping from the mountains to the Jeep driving up the long road leading to the cemetery. He didn't recognize the rental vehicle, but he knew who the driver was.

It had been eight long years since his wife had taken their son, stuffed their clothes into her old Toyota truck, and driven away from the Lucky Jack. Colton hadn't forgotten a single thing. The taste of her lips, the sweet attar of her skin... the blood oozing from her forehead and the fear in her eyes as she'd scrambled to get away from him.

When the Jeep stopped near the other parked vehicles and the door opened, Major lifted his head and let out a bark.

Colton straitened, the nervous fluttering in his stomach growing stronger. "I wasn't sure she'd come."

"How could you think that?" his mom asked, her tone scolding. "Jack Reid was like a father to Lauren."

That was the truth. Despite his stern exterior, Jack Reid Ritter had had a tender heart, and he'd loved Lauren like a daughter. "I don't think he ever forgave me for her leaving."

"Don't say that. In your father's eyes, there was nothing to forgive. He loved you both." She patted his arm. "And he never took sides with what transpired between the two of you. He understood how hard marriage was."

Hard wasn't the word.

Colton had gone through war, witnessed the death of his team, suffered life-threatening injuries, and endured countless hours of surgeries, therapy, and counseling. But marriage was, by far, the toughest thing he'd ever tackled. And he'd failed miserably at being a husband.

Their son, Little Jack, nearly ten and hardly "little" anymore, hurried to where Colton was standing. "Is that Mom?"

He gave his dark head a rub. "I think so, buddy."

Their son had flown to Montana with Sue so he could attend the funeral. This was Little Jack's first experience with death and Colton hadn't seen him shed a single tear about the loss of his grandpa.

That worried Colton.

When the Jeep door opened and Lauren stepped out, the nervousness in his stomach twisted into a knot.

Major's tail wagged and he let out another bark.

Colton never expected her to set foot on Ritter soil again. But here she was, walking up the small incline to the cemetery, closing the distance between them.

She was wore black boots with a modest heel and a long gray skirt. Her hair, the color of wheat, was braided and hung over one shoulder.

Lauren was a resplendent light, full of warmth and love that he yearned to hold in his arms again. But his greatest fear was that time had slipped from his grasp.

Halfway across the cemetery, she halted, tucked her chin into the fur collar of her black downy coat, and braced herself against a hard blast of frigid wind. She staggered and nearly lost her balance.

Colton wanted to rush to her side and catch her before she fell, be the man she'd wed. A husband she trusted, but he thought touching her, for any reason, would be a mistake.

"Go," he told Little Jack with a pat to the back. "Help your mother."

The boy and Major shot off like a rocket, leaving Colton with nothing to do but stuff his sweaty hands into his coat pockets and wait.

Lauren's lips split into a broad smile when she saw Little Jack. He hadn't recognized how much their son had grown until he saw him standing side-by-side with her. The crown of his head was nearly to her shoulders.

Little Jack wrapped his arms around his mother's waist and held on tight. The boy loved being a hero, like Colton had at that age.

He prayed every night that his son would grow out of that vain need and that he wouldn't grow up to be like him or his dad. Every aching night he lay in the bed he and Lauren once shared and prayed his son's life would differ from his own, that his path would take him in a different direction, away from the military, and that if he found love, he wouldn't let it slip through his fingers.

Colton shifted his stance, his heart reeling from the loss of his dad and the remorse for decisions he'd made early in his marriage. Watching the two of them walk across the field with the backdrop of the ranch house and mountains behind them was a surreal moment for Colton. Everything he held dear was in that frame.

His wife, his son, and the Lucky Jack Ranch.

An unexpected sense of dread lurched inside Colton's chest. He quickly shrugged it off, attributing it to grief.

With his ears up and his tongue hanging from his mouth, Major waited for Lauren's attention. When he didn't get it, he barked. She crouched down to scratch his ears. "There's my good boy." After she'd given Major a thorough greeting, she rose and went to Sue for a tight, consoling hug. "How are you holding up?"

"I'm numb," Sue confessed with a dull whisper against Lauren's ear. "And I pray I stay that way until after the funeral."

Lauren nodded and closed her eyes, sending tears down her cheeks.

Colton's throat tightened. He hated watching his wife cry but took comfort in knowing that this time, he hadn't caused it.

When Sue drew back, Lauren wiped her face and reached for Little Jack. "And how about you, young man?" she said, addressing him with a sympathetic and motherly smile. "How are you doing?"

His left shoulder cocked up and dropped. "Okay, I guess."

She enveloped him in a hug, her face crumbling as she consoled him. Little Jack's chin quivered and his mouth twisted with a silent cry. Grief was ruthless and only time would heal the wounds of death. Until then, all they could do was tenderly guide the boy through it.

When the tears subsided, Lauren kissed the top of Little Jack's head and gently handed him off to Sue. Together, they walked towards the gravesite, leaving Colton and Lauren alone.

A gaggle of snow geese flew across the sky and filled the air with coarse honks and high-pitched quacks. After the noise passed, a forbearing silence settled around them.

Lauren stayed where she was with her feet planted on the snow-covered earth and her feelings hidden behind a stony visage as she fixed her eyes on one of the old tombstones.

Major assumed a neutral spot between them and waited. Turning his head from side to side, the old dog studied Lauren, then Colton.

Colton didn't have an answer for the curious dog. He

didn't know why she'd stayed behind, but he was damn happy she had. Any time with her was a gift.

He tried dislodging the lump from his throat so he could speak. He'd make sure it was nothing challenging, a simple, "Hello Lauren. I'm glad you're here" or maybe something about the cold wind or the bad weather that was coming. But when he opened his mouth, nothing came out. All those years of rehearsing what he wanted to say, and he couldn't muster a single syllable.

*That's probably for the best. When you talk, she cries.*

True, but standing in the cemetery like a dimwitted jackass wasn't helping either of them. But his only alternative, as he saw it, was to walk away. He wouldn't do that. He'd keep his mouth shut and let whatever was happening play out.

It seemed simple enough, but nothing about their relationship or lack thereof was simple.

Seconds ticked by without a word.

Colton shifted his shoulders, hinging more and more towards blurting out that greeting. He wondered how silence could be so complex, concrete, and heavy, yet so translucent and elusive. But this was no time to delve into the complexities of the past or present state of their marriage, whatever that was.

Together but apart?

United in matrimony but separated by thousands of miles for years?

Finally, Lauren raised her head to put her gaze on the mountains and sighed heavily. "Colton, I–ah…" Her warm breath clashed with the freezing air, forming a vaporous veil around her face. She swallowed and swung her tear-filled gaze to his.

When he'd heard Lauren planned to make the funeral, he'd been nervous. Since their separation, he'd only seen her face-to-face a handful of times and each time ended with her bursting into tears and running for the nearest exit. She never approached him and never ever made eye contact with him, so locking eyes with his wife after eight long years was like being hit with a charge of electricity.

"I'm so sorry for your loss." More tears came. "I wanted to come sooner. But Jack Reid told me not to."

Colton had been on the opposite side of the room when his dad took that call from Lauren. He hadn't agreed with his dad's decision, but he'd respected it. "He loved you, Lauren, and he wanted to spare you the pain."

She forced another swallow, nodded rigidly, and bowed her head, then turned and walked towards the gravesite.

Colton stood there for a few more minutes to compose himself. When he was sure he had the tears under control, he removed his Stetson, and he and Major joined the mourners near the flag-draped casket.

Jack Reid had buried three brothers, a mother, and a father in this ground. When he found out the cancer was terminal, he'd planned every detail of this day because knew how hard it was for a son to bury his father and how hard it was to steel your shoulders against a force you couldn't control.

The words spoken by the reverend faded into the background, and Colton's thoughts once again centered on his dad. There was so much he wanted to say to his dad and so many holidays, birthdays, graduations, and occasions where the great Jack Reid would be missed.

Colton was a grown man with a son of his own, a rancher with thousands of acres under his direction, and a war-marred Marine. But a part of him was still that little boy looking for answers.

He felt a hand on his arm and looked down to see Mia

standing beside him. Composed and proud as only a Ritter could be, she gave his arm a squeeze.

She was a lovely young woman with stunning features, dark hair and eyes, wide cheekbones, and a sweet, sweet smile.

Overcome with joy, his dad hadn't needed proof that Mia was his daughter, but Colton had stubbornly held on to the obvious fact that among those beautiful facial attributes there wasn't a trace of Jack Reid anywhere.

But Colton couldn't deny the proof supplied by DNA testing. And he didn't want to, not anymore. Two years since she'd bounced up the drive in that old jalopy with wild claims of kinship. At first, he'd detested the very sight of Mia, but now, he couldn't imagine his life without her. He and his half-sister had grown close and would need each other now, more than ever.

He wrapped an arm around her shoulders and gave her a hug. "We'll get through this."

"I know," she whispered back, laying her head against his chest. "I just can't believe he's gone."

Neither could Colton. Even though he'd known months before that this day would come, he hadn't been able to come to terms with the fact that his dad was going to die. He wasn't ready to say his last farewell.

Family and friends gathered closer and waited as the honor guard removed the flag-draped casket from the hearse and brought it to its resting place over the grave. Colton and the others took their seats, and Reverend Mitchell prayed.

Mourners stood for military honors. At the command, Colton raised the fingertip of his right hand to his brow for a final salute to his dad. The clear and lonesome sound of the sole bugler pumping out taps echoed through Crossfire Canyon.

Colton braced himself for the twenty-one-gun salute. Certain noises and odors were still triggers for him. The sound of fireworks, the malodor of burning rubber or gunpowder, and sudden bright bursts of light used to send him into a paralyzing state of anxiety and fear.

But Colton had learned to work through it. He reminded himself that he wasn't in any danger. This was a cemetery, not a combat zone. He was aware of his surroundings and planted in the present. This was a military tribute to a great man and Marine.

Both Colton and Mia jumped when the rifles fired, a normal and involuntary response. She reached for his hand and held on through the folding and presentation of the flag.

# CHAPTER TWO

*THE LUCKY JACK.* LAUREN MUSED LISTLESSLY AS SHE braked near the gravel in front of the ranch house and shoved the rental into Park. There hadn't been a damn thing lucky about the place for her.

But God, how she'd loved the ranch.

She and Little Jack were the first to leave the cemetery after the service was over. But the front lawn of the ranch house was quickly filling with heavy-duty trucks and rusty four-wheel-drive vehicles.

When Colton's red Ford rolled to an easy stop near the edge of the porch, Lauren tried fortifying herself against what was to come. She didn't want to go inside, didn't want to cry and run away as she had in the past. Barging through the door and throwing divorce papers in his face would be rude and provoke a scene. She preferred this to be cordial and as painless as possible.

He opened the driver's door, planted a boot on the gravel, and stepped out. The black wool coat he wore molded to his formidable shoulders, reinforcing his muscular build and strength.

Seeing him had never gotten easier, though, logically, after eight years of separation, it should have.

Lauren loved him. That hadn't diminished.

Her heart would always ache for him and for the life they could've had together.

"You okay, Mom?"

Her hands tightened around the steering wheel. She prayed Little Jack wouldn't notice how they trembled and mustered a gentle smile for her son's sake. "I'm fine, honey. It's just been a hard day." *And it's about to get a lot harder.* She watched Colton escort Sue and the dark-haired woman she'd seen him with at the gravesite from his truck to the house.

Lauren had never had cause to be jealous. Colton had been a devoted fiancé, and she'd thought, a faithful husband. *But he's not your husband.* And, biblically speaking, he hadn't been her husband in over eight years.

"That's Aunt Mia," Little Jack offered before opening his door.

The Ritter clan was considerable. Jack Reid had several brothers and sisters. Colton had dozens of cousins strewn across Montana, but he was an only child. How dare he cover up his relationship with the woman by lying to their son! The simmering suspicion in Lauren's chest boiled to scorn. "Aunt Mia, huh?"

"That's what Dad said. I'll see you inside." He hopped from the Jeep, ran up the steps, and met Sue at the front door.

Lauren had wrestled with her decision, but after seeing Colton with Aunt Mia, she was sure that a divorce was the right thing to do.

But it didn't feel right. Nothing about this felt right. *You knew this wouldn't be easy. Pull yourself together and get it done*, she heard Big Tom Briggs say like he had a hundred times over the course of her childhood. But this wasn't like falling off your bike or not getting picked for the cheerleading team.

This was a divorce. The end of what had been a wonderful and happy marriage. The finality of it meant her marriage would be over and not just resting on a rear burner. She'd held her ground for a short time and thought she was prepared to fight for her husband and her marriage.

But in the end, she'd run away from both.

A divorce was an admission that she'd lost that fight. She'd broken her commitment to help Colton heal from his mental and physical wounds. The memories, the nightmares, and horrors of Post-Traumatic Stress Disorder. She'd lost her marriage because she'd been too weak to hold on. With that belief came more guilt.

Lauren closed her eyes, feeling the impact of her cowardliness sweep her back to that dreadful early morning phone call. She could see Sue's white face as she'd melted to the floor and hear the tremble in Jack Reid's voice as he'd delivered the grim news that Colton had been discovered half frozen in a snowdrift a mile from the house.

The odds that it had been an accident or poor judgement was remote. He was a seasoned rancher with years of experience hiking, fishing, hunting, and camping in the wilderness. He would have never gone out with a blizzard coming.

She opened her eyes and sighed heavily.

After Colton shut the door, he walked around to the other side of the truck. His movements were smooth and confident, like a mountain lion prowling through the wilds of Montana. His thighs - clad in dark denims - were as powerful as they'd been the day he returned home after being released from the hospital. He seemed as perfect as a man could be, whole and unaffected by war.

Lauren knew better. She saw his jaws tighten as he rubbed his left hand before reaching for the door handle. The bullets had ripped away more than flesh and muscle. They'd stolen a part of the Colton she'd fallen in love with. The sweet man who was always optimistic and happy. What remained was an angry, brooding man who never laughed and scarcely spoke. So while she appreciated the outward appearance of the man who was legally her husband, her heart ached for the man she'd lost and for what they could have had together if she hadn't given up and walked away.

Colton held the door open until they'd all entered, then stepped inside and closed it. The same way he'd shut her out after he'd returned home. No talking. No communication, just silence and seclusion. Today, he hadn't looked up or so much as glanced Lauren's way since she'd offered him her condolences at the gravesite. Why would he when a pretty woman was clinging to his arm?

They would never be the happy family she'd dreamed they would be. Her heart ached for that loss, provoking a sob. She let out a jerky breath and her eyes stung from the threat of tears. But the part of her that was Big Tom Briggs refused to let her emotions escalate into a self-pity party. "You will not cry."

She grabbed the large manila envelope from the back seat and shoved it in her oversize bag before she stepped out of the Jeep and walked to the house.

Lauren paused at the front door, took a deep breath, and stepped inside. Funeral goers were chatting quietly and helping themselves to comfort food prepared by people of the Crossfire Canyon community.

It was the second day of December, but a large white

ceramic turkey gobbler proudly maintained his place at the
center of the dining room table. An array of pumpkins and
fall foliage decorated the counters and the old antique
china cabinet Lauren picked up at a ranch auction the year
she and Colton wed. Aesthetically, the house was warm
and inviting, but Colton didn't have an ounce of decorating sense. The tasteful Thanksgiving decorations were a
woman's touch.

It seemed Aunt Mia had excellent taste in style
and men.

Fighting bile, Lauren took off her coat and hung it on
one of the wooden pegs near the door.

Jack Reid and Sue resided in Texas when Colton was
born and divorced when he was a teenager. Jack Reid
came home to the Lucky Jack to help his last surviving
brother with the family ranch.

Sue remained in Texas. She'd established her own business, a bridal boutique, and she'd done well for herself.

The ranch house harbored too many reminders, Jack
Reid had said, so he'd built a log cabin on the north side of
the property.

Lauren and Colton started their married life in the
warm and comforting atmosphere of the old two-story
ranch house. She'd seen such possibilities in it, and she'd
put her heart and soul into making it their home, a home
where their children and grandchildren would grow up.

Everything was precisely the way she remembered it.
Hardwood floors, worn slick from generations of Ritters,
stucco walls and handmade furniture constructed sturdy
and designed for large men and practicality rather than
style. The unique blend of cedar, rain-soaked earth, and
Jack Reid's imported cigars lingered in the air.

Lauren adjusted her grip on the bag and struggled to
keep her mind focused on why she was here. But she

couldn't keep the memories from flooding in. Good and bad.

Her gaze shifted right into the living room. Little Jack took his first steps in there. With chubby, wobbly legs, outstretched arms, and a smile that could outshine the sun, he'd staggered straight into her arms.

Colton carried her over this very threshold three days after they said I do, the day they'd returned from their short but passionate honeymoon at Jackson Hole.

For a second, she was that bride again in love and floating high, innocent to married life and naïve about the challenges of being a soldier's wife. Nothing went as planned. Colton left for boot camp a few months after they moved into the ranch house, and everything went downhill from there.

She harnessed the feeling, plummeting back to earth and reality with a hard jolt that shook her already frazzled nerves with the intensity of a minor earthquake.

The early years of her marriage were lonely and mentally exhausting. But she'd held on, believing that once Colton returned home from deployment, life would be better. She'd had such high hopes and dreams then.

But she'd watched helplessly as her expectations slowly crumbled around her. When she left the Lucky Jack Ranch, it set in motion the final demolishing blow that left their marriage in ruin. She was tired of stepping over that heap of old rubble and guilt. It was time to build something new. After today, she'd never be in the house again. Her marriage was over and she had to accept it.

Lauren walked down the hallway and into the large kitchen and dining area where most of the mourners gathered.

Cowboys, some she knew rode for the Lucky Jack, eyed her peculiarly. The Boss's Wife might as well have been tattooed across her forehead. A few, when they realized they were gawking, jerked their eyes away. Others kept gawking, with wide eyes and open mouths. Some people Lauren recognized from neighboring ranches, others were strangers to her. It was most likely that some of those unfamiliar, well-to-do faces belonged to Colton's new business associates and friends.

She knew from Sue that he'd taken over the ranch operations years before Jack Reid became ill and invested a substantial amount of money in bovine embryo transfer to increase calf production. The venture paid off. The Lucky Jack Ranch had tripled in net worth and was in several northwestern newspapers and country-wide ranching magazines.

Little Jack was sitting at the table with three of the younger cowhands. He looked at home around them, smiling and talking as if he were already one of the boys and none of them seemed to mind that he was younger.

Her son had his grandfather's easygoing personality and loved spending time at the ranch. Lauren wasn't begrudging of that. She was happy he had a good relationship with his father. It was something she wished she'd had as a child and as an adult. But steel was a hard metal to forge, and she'd given up on ever changing Commander Thomas David Briggs.

Though Jack Reid and her father were both military men, they were cut from a very different cloth. Her father handed out orders, and he expected them to be followed to the tee. No mistakes. No failures. He didn't understand that raising a child wasn't like running a Navy battleship.

Jack Reid believed that for a child to grow, it needed room to fail. For Lauren, being a military brat without permanent roots and used to living on bases, the great expanse of the Montana mountains and sky overwhelmed her. She'd been a newbie to ranching. Jack Reid taught her how to ride, corrected her mistakes, but always cheered her on. He'd taught her how to open and close gates without dismounting, cross creeks, and how to navigate steep terrain. He'd even given her roping lessons.

The last time she saw him, he'd accompanied Colton to Texas for a charity event. Jack Reid had pulled up a chair and made himself comfortable. They'd laughed, talked, and caught up on her years away. Before he and Colton left, he'd hugged her tightly, called her his daughter, and made it clear that she was always welcome at the Lucky Jack.

Lauren had wept when Sue told her about the cancer and prognosis. Six months, if he was lucky. He'd lived five. She regretted not coming to see him. Mostly, she regretted she hadn't had a chance to say goodbye or let him know the positive impact he'd had on her life.

Jack Reid was a wonderful father and his son's rock. He'd been there through the surgeries to repair Colton's hand, the physical therapy, and the downward spiral of Post-Traumatic Stress Disorder. The outbursts, the shouting, the nightmares, and flashbacks...God, those days had been horrible. But Jack Reid hadn't wavered. He's seen war and what it could do to a soldier, mentally, physically, and emotionally. But he'd held on and done what Lauren couldn't.

The love between father and son had been stronger than that of a husband and wife.

Lauren maneuvered her way through the people, smiling with cordial words when one spoke to her but not stopping to talk. She was on a mission to find Colton.

She scanned the room and saw him talking to McCrea Coldiron, his best friend since childhood. McCrea's parents, Hardin and Belle, McCrea's brother Jess and his wife, Mallory, were standing near the fireplace talking with Sue and Aunt Mia.

The Coldirons were good people and from the same small Texas town Colton was born and mostly raised in, the town where Lauren currently lived. McCrea's mother was on several of the town committees that Lauren oversaw, which meant they worked together regularly.

The Coldirons were also founding members of the Promise Point Foundation. The equine rehabilitation program was a vital part of Colton's recovery and was something both he and Lauren worked religiously to support.

Did Belle, or any of the others, know about Colton's affair? Lauren wanted to crawl under a rug and hide. But that wasn't an option, so she got a firm grip on her pride and walked toward her husband.

# CHAPTER THREE

"ARE YOU SURE?"

"I'm positive," Colton answered. "Three have gone missing within the last two months."

The Lucky Jack was an extensive enterprise handed down through five generations. It started out small, but over the years, Jack Reid gained more acreage and established a profitable cattle production business, encompassing thousands of acres.

Colton had made changes since taking over the operation of the ranch three years ago. He'd started by moving calving season from early spring to early summer which resulted in healthier calves, less supplemental feed consumption, fewer man hours, and higher profits. Then he'd invested in bovine embryo implantation to ensure the production of high-quality calves. He'd discovered the first embryo missing before his dad moved into hospice care.

"Have you talked to the authorities about it?"

McCrea was Colton's closest friend. The man who'd found him and saved his life on that snowy, ill-fated morning eight years ago. The morning after, Lauren left the Lucky Jack. He was the only person Colton trusted with the news of the theft. "When I learned they were missing, I phoned the sheriff's department and changed the lock."

"And? What did they say?"

"They opened an investigation, but we're keeping the theft under our hats."

"Don't want to spook the culprit, huh?"

"Something like that," Colton answered. "No one is exempt from the suspect list."

"You think it's one of the new hires?"

"Maybe," he answered, even though his gut feeling was telling him otherwise. He had a short list of who the thief might be. At the top was a man his dad had trusted. Colton hoped he wasn't right.

He was about to refill his cup when he saw Lauren. Like a magnet drawn to true north, he watched her hurriedly make her way through the guests.

His stomach knotted.

McCrea glanced over his shoulder to see what caught Colton's eye. "Have you talked to her?"

"No, not really," he answered, watching Lauren. Without the bulk of her coat, he saw the defined outline of her feminine form.

The knot in his stomach loosened and slid lower.

Ah, there it was. Desire, an ache for his wife he hadn't soothed and probably never would.

When he'd come home from the hospital, he'd tried so damn hard to make love to her the way he had before, putting her pleasure before his own. But he'd felt so damaged inside and out that he couldn't bear to touch her. The disappointment in her eyes the last time he'd tried and failed had ripped his heart out. Living with half a hand was nothing compared to living with sexual dysfunction.

But right now, nothing below his belt showed signs of impairment.

Colton shifted positions to hide his arousal. Being noticed in a crowd such as this for a hard-on would be embarrassing as hell.

McCrea bit into one of Mrs. Wilhite's homemade brownies and chewed. "They've moved into a new house."

Everyone needed their own space and Little Jack was getting older, which meant he'd require less supervision. But after years of living with his mom, Lauren had decided she wanted to move out? The abrupt move made Colton uneasy. "Mom said it was closer to work."

"Yeah." McCrea's eyes went to the cup in his hand. "It's a few blocks down from City Hall."

Shortly after the separation and her move to Texas, Lauren enrolled at a community college, earned an associate's degree, and thereafter earned a bachelor's degree. She was hired as an executive assistant to the mayor after graduation.

To hear his mom tell it, Lauren practically ran the town. Colton knew that was an overstatement, but she was working long hours since the mayor's stroke three months ago. "How's Harry?"

McCrea shoved the rest of the brownie into his mouth and chewed. "The stroke paralyzed his left side. The road to his recovery will be a long one, and he won't be coming back."

Colton's mom hadn't said a word about who was in charge now that Harry was incapacitated. "Harry had what, two years left in office? Who's taking his place until the election?"

McCrea shifted his weight from one boot to another, clamped a hand over the back of his neck and rubbed hard. "The town council appointed someone."

Someone? Why was his friend being so evasive? "Who?"

"Jonas Ward."

Colton thought for a second, then laughed when he placed the name. "The Jonas Ward from elementary school?"

McCrea looked less amused. "The one and only."

The Ward family was in the aviation business, with a substantial amount of money. Jonas was never reluctant about letting people know he was a rich kid. "Is he the same snot-nosed brat he was in elementary school?"

"No. Well, not in public, but I hear he's a real bear to work with."

An acute case of indigestion started simmering in Colton's gut. Some men in power preyed on female employees. He wouldn't let his wife be harassed; separation be damned. "How's Lauren dealing with that?"

McCrea gave him a sideways glance. "You could ask her yourself."

"We both know what happens when I try talking to her," Colton said, chancing another look at his wife. McCrea's wife, Eleanor, had snagged Lauren as she walked by, and the two were now engaged with baby Samantha, the couple's third child.

"Write her a letter, send her a text or an email —"

"Answer the damn question." Lauren sent him short, to-the-point texts about Little Jack periodically. But the subject was always about their son. They were never more personal than that. He'd tried once, but she'd ignored him.

"Ah, hell, Colton." McCrea swore and pinched the bridge of his nose. "You know Lauren. She can tame the wildest beast."

"A bear? A beast?" He scowled. "Do I need to straighten this guy out?"

"Jonas isn't the wafer-thin boy with glasses and starched polos you remember from elementary school. He's ditched the glasses, stands six-one and is about two-hundred pounds of solid muscle. He's into kickboxing and all that judo crap women find irresistible," McCrea lifted the cup to his lips, but stopped to add, "And he's newly divorced."

Colton wasn't a runt. At six-three and a hundred and ninety pounds, he wasn't afraid to go head-to-head with any man, beast, or bear. "A divorced kickboxer?"

"Yep." McCrea rocked back on his boot heels and shoved his bottom lip out, mulling over the information he'd told Colton. "It burns like hell when that green-eyed monster bites into you, doesn't it?"

"Yeah, it does," Colton agreed without pretense because there was no use pretending the scorching sensation inside of him was a brewing case of diarrhea. It was full-blown jealously, and while both could produce a pile of stink, only one could damage his already troubled marriage.

If he marched into the mayor's office, blaring out accusations and slinging punches, his chances for getting Lauren back would be zero, so he needed to get a grip on his emotions. He'd be calm and level-headed about the way he approached her and her boss, the beastly bear.

But he couldn't rein in the jealousy. And he couldn't help but question her faithfulness after all this time.

Harry Barnes, the former mayor, was in his sixties, partly bald and hunchback. Lauren was sharing office space with a well-built, recently divorced kickboxer. "Should I worry?"

"About what?"

"Lauren sleeping with her boss."

"Lauren? Having an affair? Hell, no." Rebuke

furrowed a sharp crease through the center of McCrea's forehead. "You know she'd never do that."

Did he? They'd been separated for a long time, and a woman had needs that might overpower loyalty and marriage vows if a man was seductive enough.

"Get that notion out of your head," McCrea ordered, before turning around to watch the three of them. "That's not to say the men around town don't try. They do, but she doesn't waste any time setting 'em straight. Some apologize when they see her wedding band. Others couldn't care less. She keeps to herself and has a small circle of friends."

Lauren had an outgoing personality. That hadn't changed when they'd moved to the Lucky Jack. She liked people and crowds and had tried to connect with the people of Crossfire Canyon.

He imagined her life in Texas to be full of activities, office parties, and evenings with friends, but according to McCrea, she'd isolated herself. She had to be lonely and tempted to accept an invitation to dinner and a movie — or maybe more — with any of the men who'd asked her out.

Could Colton blame her for wanting male companionship? No, but in his book, solitude wasn't a reasonable cause for cheating on a spouse. His life was solitary, but he wasn't searching for a woman to warm his bed. And he never would as long as he was a married man.

The thought of Lauren being with another man was eating him alive. But when he looked at her, his anger, summoned by jealousy and an invented affair, abated.

What the hell was he thinking? His wife wasn't having an affair, nor would she betray his trust.

"Something has changed though." McCrea's observation punched through Colton's unsettling notions and snapped him back to the conversation. "What's changed?"

"Her eyes. Something about Lauren's eyes has changed."

Colton noticed melancholy in her eyes when she spoke to him at the cemetery, but given their past, he'd chalked it up to present company and all that.

McCrea snapped his fingers. "I've got it. Remember Nugget?"

It took less time for Colton to establish the woolly rodent from their third-grade class than it did for him to remember Jonas. "Yeah, so? What about him?"

"That's it."

"What's it?"

"Lauren looks as miserable as that caged hamster," McCrea said as he tugged the waistband of his jeans higher and adopted a smug smile, like he'd explained the enigma of the Bermuda Triangle.

His best friend was comparing Lauren to a rodent. "Well, that's a shitty analogy."

"Okay," McCrea answered dryly, his head bobbing like a crass dashboard ornament. "Lauren is like a caged bird who has lost its will to fly. Is that poetic enough for you?"

"Yeah, yeah." Colton held up a hand. "I get it."

His wife was miserable because she was living in the confinement of their long-distance marriage. God, he wanted to change that, make her happy again, and replace that lost look in her eyes with life. But how was he going to do that?

"Look at that." McCrea bumped him with an elbow and nodded towards the women. Lauren clapped the baby's chubby hands, causing Samantha to let out a giggle and a squeal. "She's so good with kids and such a good momma."

Colton would never deny that. His wife was an excellent mother. "Little Jack's lucky to have her."

McCrea frowned and pushed a finger into Colton's chest. "So are you and it's a damn shame she doesn't have more babies to play with."

Having stated what he wanted to about the matter, he walked across the kitchen to join the women.

∼

COLTON PUSHED FROM THE DOOR FRAME AND STEPPED TO the coffeepot sitting on the counter to refresh his coffee. He stared out the window, reflecting on what his friend had said.

He didn't have Lauren and at the pace their reconciliation was advancing, he never would. The silence wouldn't last forever. At some point, he knew she'd give up on their separation and divorce him.

And she had every right to.

Colton learned she was pregnant via a phone call, and his mom had been the one holding her hand in the delivery room when Little Jack was born. He'd missed so many milestones with his wife and son.

He didn't want to miss any more. He was tired of being miserable and he was tired of waiting for the right time to make his move toward atonement.

He'd only agreed to a split because he'd needed time to get his head on straight, and he'd been terrified of what might happen if Lauren and Little Jack came back to live with him at the ranch while he was in counseling. He'd intended it to be a temporary fix, something that would help save their marriage and last only a couple of months, not stretch on for years.

He'd thrown himself into the ranch and into raising money for the Promise Point Foundation. Before he knew it, years had passed.

Colton watched Little Jack and two other boys run across the yard to the corral. He and Lauren came to an arrangement early on in their separation about sharing custody of their son. He lived and attended school in Texas with Lauren. But in the summer, he resided at the ranch with Colton. They rotated holidays and his birthday.

It would have been nice to have Christmas with Little Jack this year, but he wasn't going to ask Lauren to make an exception or swap turns. His son would fly back to Texas with Lauren and Sue tomorrow, which meant Colton would be spending the next couple of weeks by himself, save for the cowhands and Major.

Mia would drop in to check on him and stock the cupboards, refrigerator, and freezer to make certain he didn't go hungry, and his mom would be back for Christmas.

But when the holidays were over, he'd be alone again.

Before Mia arrived, Colton devoted his evenings to playing cards or watching television with his dad. But when the cancer took hold, Mia moved into the cabin to take care of Jack Reid. Soon, his dad was too sick to visit and the emptiness of the old ranch house had echoed with loneliness.

Colton's mind and body had adapted to working from sunup to sundown. He was frequently so exhausted by the end of the day that he'd skipped dinner and a hot shower to pass out on the bed. While he didn't mind the labor, he couldn't tolerate spending the rest of his life alone.

"Colton."

Lauren's soft voice called out from behind him. Startled, he pivoted on a boot heel. There she stood, exquisitely feminine and delicate, like she had the first time he saw her.

Caught off guard and uncertain of what he should say,

he held his cup up. "Coffee? It can walk to Billings on its own, but it's hot."

"No," she replied, her voice carrying a slight quiver. She was holding on to that mammoth purse as if it held top-secret government intel. "I need to speak with you."

He shouldn't have taken another sip of coffee because the sup he had in his mouth took a wrong turn and caught in his windpipe. He coughed to clear his airway and choked out, "You want to talk?" just to make sure he'd heard her accurately. "To me?"

She glanced around the crowded kitchen, then tucked a loose strand of hair behind her ear. "Alone."

The only downstairs room which would grant them privacy was the den, the place Lauren had found him that last tragic night before she left, soaked in sweat from another nightmare, confused and raging.

"Is the den —"

"That's fine," she stated, and headed in that direction.

Colton would have sacrificed his good hand for the opportunity to talk to Lauren, but he also couldn't discount the murderous glare in her eyes before she marched off.

He set his cup on the counter and followed. As they walked, his mind was quickly overwhelmed with all the things he wanted to say to her. Words that vanished from his memory at the cemetery surged forward. Years and years of apologies and regrets tumbled over and over in his mind. A mass of words perfectly honed from practice.

Lauren walked straight into the den, swung around, and waited for him to close the door. When he did, the murmurs of the people outside faded, and they were once again standing in silence.

He never thought he'd be this nervous around Lauren, but he was. Sweaty palms, unsteady hands, and a dry mouth. "Would you like me to take your luggage upstairs?"

*Luggage? There's a conversation starter, genius.*

"No. I've made arrangements at the Travelers Inn in town," she informed him. "The lawyer's office is a short stroll from there. We'll be going as soon as the reading of the will is over."

"Oh," he said, shoving four fingers into the front pocket of his jeans. Again, there was silence. He was lousy at conveying his feelings. His words always turned out wrong and jumbled. He hoped they wouldn't. Just once, he wished he could get out what he needed to say.

Lauren brushed a trembling hand across her forehead. Her cream-colored skin was without a single blemish except for the scar over her right eye.

A wound he'd given her.

He'd put her through hell the months after he'd come back from Iraq, and he was so damn guilty about what he done that night—the wailing and the roar of confusion in his head.

The ghastly nightmares Colton had of his unit being picked off one by one had hounded him for years. Night after night, Ray and the others had come for him like the grimmest of reapers, slashing away his sanity and blackening his soul with remorse. In the early years of his struggle with PTSD, those nightmares had been so tangible, he hadn't been capable of discerning what real and what wasn't.

He hadn't meant to push her into the desk. He hadn't meant to harm her. Remorse draped over him like an icy garment as images of that night flashed in his head.

Lauren's bare feet, red from searching for him in the snow. *"It was just a dream, Colton. Everything is going to be okay."*

*The cold steel of the revolver in his grip. "No! It's never going to be okay! .... Get out! Leave! Now!"*

He closed his eyes, struggling to unseat his mind from

what had happened, to what needed to happen. He wanted his wife back, and he'd do whatever it took to make that happen.

There were hundreds of ghastly memories floating around in his mind, but the one of Lauren's head crashing into the desk was the one that haunted him the most.

It had taken months before he could talk about what had transpired the night she and Little Jack had left the Lucky Jack. His therapist had told him he couldn't blame himself, that his conduct had been triggered by Post-Traumatic Stress Disorder. He accepted that now, but he wasn't any closer to forgiving himself for what he'd done. He'd made the woman he'd vowed to love, and protect, bleed.

Though she showed no signs of fear, he wanted to recreate that sense of security she'd had with him before that night. It was important that he reassure her he would never hurt her in any way ever again.

"Lauren, there are so many things I need to say," he began. His throat constricted. "First and foremost, that I'm sorry for pushing you–"

"This isn't easy for me," she cut in and reached inside her purse for a large manila envelope. She held it out to him. "I know the timing is off, but this needs to happen."

He peered at the envelope, understanding that the impending doom he'd sensed at the cemetery had nothing to do with his dad's death and everything to do with Lauren and this moment.

Hesitantly, Colton took it, flipped open the top, and slipped the papers out.

# CHAPTER FOUR

Colton's heart sank. "You want a divorce?"

His question brought about a transformation in her face. The murderous glare melted away. Her eyebrows sloped up obliquely and her chin quivered as she choked out, "It's time, Colton. Aunt Mia is proof of that."

Aunt Mia? "What does Mia have to do with you divorcing me?"

Lauren was on the brink of tears. "Does everyone know?"

He didn't have a clue what she was talking about. "Know what?"

"I just don't understand how you could lie to..." Her voice broke. "To our son about your mistress."

Mistress? It dawned on him that she thought Mia was his mistress. "You want a divorce because you think I'm having an affair?"

"You were expecting me to condone it?" she asked hotly.

He thought about inspecting the den for hidden cameras because this had to be a joke. But judging from the woundedness in his wife's eyes, it clearly was not. "Oh, Jesus," he said, swiping a hand over his mouth. "I thought you knew about Mia."

The dam burst, expelling a well of tears over her bottom lids. "If I had, you'd have gotten those divorce papers a lot sooner."

This was serious. He had to explain. His marriage depended on it.

"Look," he said, stepping from behind the desk to approach her. "I've done things and said things I can never take back. I hurt you and there's no excuse—"

"You're still hurting me, Colton," she shot back.

The pain of her confession cut him to the quick. "Lauren, honey—"

"Don't try using affection to weasel your way out of this," she said through clenched teeth.

"I'm not having an aff—"

"Save it." She held up a hand, quelling his words, jerked out a tissue from her pocket, and wiped her nose. "Aunt Mia isn't the only reason. This separation has gone way beyond what either of us predicted."

He whole-heartily agreed with that.

"I think…" She sniffed. "We both felt it was something we were doing for Little Jack. But I can't endure this purgatory any longer. It's a prison neither of us deserves."

A prison.

Nugget.

Caged.

Colton's thoughts bounced from one word to another. The last one hit him hard, inserted its cold, boney fingers through his ribs, and clutched his heart so tight he thought it might stop beating.

*She's like a caged bird who's lost its will to fly.*

He could see the shadow of imprisonment in her

glossy, red-rimmed eyes so clearly now. Those bright and beautiful orbs had lost their luster. Once aglow with vitality, they now bore the effigy of a gray, overcast day.

"You want your freedom."

"I want a life, Colton," she whispered and swiped her cheeks. "I'm thirty-four and I feel dead inside. I don't want to feel that way for the rest of my life. The world is passing me by." She gave a fragile smile that damn near ripped his heart in two. "I want a healthy, physical relationship with a man who loves and needs me, a man who wants to touch me."

Wants to touch her? There wasn't a night that went by when his arms didn't ache to hold her. His brain scrambled for something to say. Tell her you're that man. *Tell her you love her and will until your last dying breath. Tell her you need her —want her.*

*Tell her,* his heart demanded.

But his mind knew words wouldn't matter now after all his years of silence. Even if he explained Mia was his sister and not his mistress, he would not stay Lauren's decision. He'd told himself that what happened between them could eventually be resolved and that love would heal their marriage. But that wasn't going to happen.

A powerful wave of inevitability slammed into him. His silence had cost him his marriage. His wife was divorcing him, and the dreaded end he'd feared had come.

Colton turned his back and stepped to the window. He could see the barns and paddocks and the flat earth of the canyon floor as it stretched to the foothills of the Big Belt Mountains. Moonlight reflected off their snowy caps. Above them, stars twinkled against the cobalt backdrop of the wintery night sky.

Two days before he left for deployment, he'd gone for a ride through the prairie and up to the mountains, mentally taking stock of everything he saw. On those long nights in Iraq, he'd thought about those places, about going home safely to Lauren and Little Jack, what the future would hold for the three of them and for the life he envisioned they would have together.

"Little Jack is growing up." She heaved in a broken breath and let it out calmly, as if to ease the burden of a heavy load. "And I want more babies."

The agony of the sniper's bullet tearing through his flesh was never far from Colton's mind. Surviving that shot gave him a tenacious attitude towards life and made him believe that no matter whatever he faced, he'd already been through the worst. But the pain slashing through his heart now was unlike anything he'd ever encountered.

When they'd gotten engaged, they'd planned for four children, two boys and two girls. But his injuries and the separation had stalled those dreams. Now, those babies would never be conceived.

"You'll inherit the Lucky Jack tomorrow, there's no doubt about that. I don't want any of it and I don't want money. Where Little Jack is concerned, things stay the same. Child support until he turns eighteen, summers with you and alternate holidays. Do you agree?"

From the corner of his eye, he watched her remove the slim gold band he'd given her nearly a decade ago from her finger and place it on the desk. "Colton, do you agree?"

"Yeah," he choked out. "I agree."

"I want a clean break before more damage is done. I want to walk away without hard feelings, regrets, or grudges between us."

She already had hard feelings towards him, and his regrets would torment him until the day he died. She wanted babies, for Christ's sake. Babies he wouldn't father.

How could she possibly think he wouldn't be bitter about that?

"I won't fight the divorce." He stopped to clear his throat. "I'll do whatever you want, but I have never been unfaithful to you. Never."

"It doesn't really matter now."

"It does to me."

She stepped to the door and paused to say, "I just want it to be over and I want both of us to be happy."

After she closed the door behind her, he picked up the wedding band. His happiness just walked out the door and there wasn't anything he could do about it.

LATER THAT EVENING, AFTER THE MOURNERS DEPARTED AND Little Jack was in bed, the house fell quiet. Colton settled into the recliner in the living room and nursed a glass of whiskey. The heat of the fire and the burn of the alcohol should have warmed him, but he was cold.

He lifted his right hand and rubbed a thumb over the small band that barely fit over the first bend of his pinky finger. It was all he had left of Lauren.

He could hear her words, dead inside echoing inside his head.

He hadn't known she'd felt that way or that she'd been in such misery. If he had, he would have acted, done something—anything to stop her from hurting.

Since his recovery, Colton thought a lot about what Lauren had gone through because of him. Because she'd loved him enough to stay when he'd been near the brink of breaking.

When he'd married her, he hadn't considered how

lonely she'd be without him, or how hard raising a child by herself would be.

A young wife and mother living in rural Montana on a cattle ranch without her husband. What the hell had he been thinking?

Nothing. Not a damn thing. His younger self had been reckless and selfish. His senseless logic about leaving his wife for deployment had been, "Mom did it. Lauren can too." Sue Ritter had done it, but it cost her a husband, her marriage, and probably a good portion of her heart and sanity.

The young soldier who'd marched off to war, armed with pride and foolish notions of invincibility, hadn't considered that he might not make it home or that his wife might be a widow left to raise their son alone.

Death hadn't crossed Colton's mind until he'd felt the sniper bullet knock him on his ass. Gasping for air and disoriented, he'd raised his head and saw blood oozing down his shoulder and his mangled fingers hanging from his hand.

When he'd returned home, he'd been a mess, so consumed by his wounds and trauma, he'd pushed Lauren aside so he could further worm his way into the guilt he harbored about being the only survivor of his team.

The guilt was still there and probably always would be. But his wife was gone.

When Colton walked from the den, Lauren was nowhere in sight. He'd see her tomorrow at the lawyer's office, but he wouldn't try to talk her out of the divorce. Colton would keep his word and take the loss like a man. He wanted her to be happy and if that happiness was with another man, then so be it. He'd let her go, but he would never stop loving her.

One whiskey turned into two and two into three, and

before long, he'd lost count. He hadn't planned on drowning himself in the stuff, but he needed something to soothe the sting of it all.

His mother poured herself a glass of wine and sat down in the chair next to him. She slipped her shoes off and sighed. "I'm so glad this day is over."

"Me too," he agreed, knowing the days to come would be the worst.

Sue twisted the stem of the wineglass; a telltale sign, she was thinking. "I have something I need to tell you."

Colton fought the urge to groan because he'd lost his dad and Lauren in three short days. He didn't think he could take more bad news. He might stagger his way out the door. But he was too drunk to run, so he held his breath and waited for what he was sure would be more devastating news.

"Remember Ed?"

He'd met Ed a few years ago at one of the Foundation's bachelor auctions. He was McCrea's father-in-law, an ex-Marine, and the only man, besides his dad, who could make Sue Ritter giggle like she was sixteen again.

"I remember."

"Well, as you know, we've been dating for a while and…" She glanced over at him, her eyes pleading for understanding. "It's become a serious relationship."

Thank Jesus. It wasn't something bad. "How serious?"

"I love him, and he loves me."

Colton wasn't a child, and what his mom did was her business. But she wanted his approval.

He forced a smile. "Finally, some good news."

Her pained expression softened.

"So why didn't you tell me sooner?"

She shrugged. "I don't know. I guess I wanted to be sure it was the real thing."

"And you're sure?"

"I am."

His mom was in love, and he was happy for her. She'd met someone to share her life with and, unlike him, wouldn't have to suffer an empty existence. "I like Ed."

Her face lit up. "I thought I might invite him to our Christmas dinner."

"I'll tell Mia we're having a guest. She'll be thrilled." The more the merrier, he hoped. Maybe he could talk his mom and Ed into staying through the end of December.

Company would be nice.

Colton settled into the plush cushioning of the chair. The fire crackled and hissed and filled the house with the smell of hickory.

"Your father loved sitting by the fireplace. Remember that?"

He nodded, recalling his dad and happier times, but also curious. "Did Dad know?"

"About Ed? Oh, yeah." She waved a hand at him. "He knew. I told him all about the trip we're planning to Mexico next year. He was happy for me, mostly."

Mostly. A strange mix of empathy and trepidation washed over Colton. Sympathy because his dad had suffered with the heartbreaking knowledge that the woman he loved had fallen in love with another man. Dread because he'd vowed to let Lauren go, even if it was into the arms of another man. Jonas Ward was her boss and office romances happened every day.

Damn that prick.

"I knew about your father's affair with Mia's mother," Sue broke in to say.

Colton thought as much. His mom had been just as shocked to learn of Mia's existence as his dad had, but she hadn't gone to pieces because he'd had an affair while they were married. "For how long?"

"From the beginning. Neither of us were aware of Mia's conception, of course. The divorce wasn't finalized yet, but we both knew the marriage was over years before the papers were signed and," her face clouded. "He was lonely. It wasn't right, but I forgave him."

Lauren had been ready to tie him to a tree, slather his genitalia in molasses, and let the bears eat him because she'd *thought* he was having an affair. His dad had confessed to his affair, yet his mom hadn't been angry or held a grudge.

But his infidelity had hurt her.

A clearer picture of his parents' divorce began to materialize, and for the first time in his life, Colton realized the sacrifices they'd made to remain friends.

"I would never tell Mia this," she went on. "but Jack Reid told me the affair was only physical. That it wasn't like what we'd had."

"And you believed him?"

Her forehead pleated. "Your father never lied to me and besides, at that stage in our relationship, he had no reason to."

His mom had a point, but he couldn't imagine him and Lauren discussing his relationships with other women. And there was no way he could sit through a discussion about her lovers.

Sue dug an elbow into the arm of the chair and straightened so she could look at him. "I saw you and Lauren go into the den. Do you want to talk about it?"

"There's nothing to talk about," he said, swilling down the last of his liquor. "My wife is divorcing me."

"Oh, son." She sat back in the chair. "She's been so

distant lately. I figured something was up when she announced she and Little Jack were moving out."

He smirked. "I guess she figured living with her ex-mother-in-law would be a conflict of interests."

"Don't be sour," she ordered quietly. "It'll only make things worse."

His sarcasm wouldn't make matters worse. Worse was yet to come. "I told her I wouldn't put up a quarrel, that I'd agree to whatever makes her happy. But I'm not like you or Dad. I can't watch as she falls in love with someone else. I can't. I'll kill me."

For a long time, they sat quietly gazing into the flames, both absorbed in their reflections and the gravity of the day.

"You father once told me he had a plan to get the two of you back together." She grinned, her eyes lifting towards the ceiling as she reminisced.

Colton let his head settle back and the whiskey take hold.

"It was before Mia came to the ranch and right after his first biopsy. Remember that?"

"Yeah." Doctors missed the cancer in that biopsy and as the lung infections and shortness of breath had become worse, his dad had declined more testing.

"He was still groggy from the sedative. He said," she stopped to chuckle, "Sue Lula, those two kids need a second chance and I'm gonna give it to 'em. Like he had the power to do that."

"Sue Lula," Colton repeated. "Where did he get that nickname?"

"I don't know." She chuckled again, her eyes shimmering with pleasant recollections. "Jack Reid was one of a kind."

"He sure was," he admitted. "He always had a plan and a backup plan in case the first one didn't work."

"He was a Marine and a rancher. He had to be resourceful, and your dad was a genius at making things work, even if they were broken beyond what everyone else thought unrepairable."

Broken beyond repair. That was an accurate characterization of his and Lauren's marriage because there was no amount of duct tape, wire, or good old fashion ingenuity that would fix it. And even if by some miracle, there was, Colton feared some of the most significant pieces were lost.

"I wish his plan had worked." He closed his eyes, praying that when he opened them, this would have all been a dreadful dream. "I've lost her, and I have no one to blame but myself."

As he drifted deeper and deeper into the whiskey sleep, he felt the wisp of a brush against his forehead and perceived he must have dreamed the murmuring words, "We'll see, son. Remember. Jack Reid always had a plan."

# CHAPTER FIVE

LAUREN WOKE DREADING THE DAY AHEAD, BUT EMBRACED IT as a new chapter in her new life. Colton had agreed to the divorce. He wouldn't try to stop her. It would be a smooth transition.

With that in mind, she showered and dressed in a comfortable pair of jeans, a long sleeve flannel top and a pair of cowboy boots. Plain, without fancy stitching, worn at the bend and slightly scuffed at the toes.

She packed her bags and set them on the bed. Checkout wasn't until noon, and she estimated the reading of the will wouldn't take more than a couple of hours.

Zipping her coat, she walked down the hall and out the front entrance. Tiny snowflakes dotted the wind, whirling around her whimsically, and added to her fear that the weather might deteriorate before they made it to the airport. Or worse, their flight would be cancelled, and she'd be stuck in Crossfire Canyon until the storm passed.

There was a time in her life when she'd loved snow. But now, it reminded her of how close Colton had come to dying. Shoving her hands into the pocket of her coat, she dipped her head to fight off the wind and shivered as she thought about how he must have felt lying in that snowbank, alone and desperate for warmth.

Cutting across the street, she headed for the rental place to return her keys. Crossfire Canyon was a small town with a population of less than a thousand people. Business owners had trimmed the quaint shops and restaurants with merry Christmas bows, wreaths, and garland. Gretel Gillespie, the proprietor of GG's Curl Coral and Beauty Salon, outdid the other shop owners along Main Street, trimming the front window with lights, tinsel, and plastic icicles.

The flashing bulbs of the casino sign down the street couldn't outshine Gretel's handiwork.

Lauren smiled, thinking of the people she'd considered as family. She'd loved living in Montana and missed the beauty of the mountains, the caring people of Crossfire Canyon. A part of her heart and soul would always be here.

After she returned the keys, she continued down the street.

The Humphry and Dane Law Office was nestled in the middle of a set of historic buildings. Over the years, the buildings had been renovated, then bricked in the seventies, and dreadfully needed another renovation.

Lauren stood in front of the door and took a deep breath, reminding herself that the hard part was over. A few more hours and her failed marriage and Montana would be behind her.

She tugged the door open and walked across the vacant waiting area to the conference room where Sue had instructed her to go. She could hear deep male voices on the other side of the double doors. Her intention was to ease quietly through the door and find a place in the back of the packed room without bringing attention to herself. She twisted the knob and tried clearing the door, but a set of broad shoulders clad in a blue and black checked flannel shirt blocked it. "Pardon me."

"Oh." The cowboy did a side-step and opened the door for her. "Sorry about that."

Lauren didn't recognize the man, but replied with a smile as she searched the room for Little Jack.

"You're Lauren Ritter." He winced and corrected himself. "I mean Mrs. Ritter."

*Not for long.*

He greeted her with his huge right hand. "I'm Ian Moore, the Lucky Jack's forman."

She accepted his handshake. "Call me Lauren. Have you seen my son?"

He raised his head to peer over the crowd. "I think J. D. is in the front row."

*J.D.?*

"Yeah, I see him." Before Lauren could ease to the wall, Ian laid a hand on her shoulder and parted the wave of cowboys with a deep, commanding voice. "Let's make a path for the lady."

"That's unnecessary," she said as he moved her forward.

"Oh, yes, it is," he insisted. "They've saved a seat for you."

Two columns of metal folding chairs had been arranged in rows of four. Colton was sitting on the left side next to the aisle. Her reserved seat was next to him.

*Perfect.*

She and Colton were expected to sit together. Sue was seated to the left of Lauren's vacant seat, and Mia casually occupied the chair at the end of the row.

*How cozy.*

Contempt swathed Lauren. If it weren't for making a spectacle of herself, she would have marched past Colton and properly unseated Aunt Mia. But this wasn't the time or the place for a clash with a rival.

*Rival?*

*Good grief, Lauren. You're not a brawler.*

If the woman wanted Colton, she could have him. Lauren would not fight for a cheating husband. She'd keep her peace, preserve her dignity, and respect Jack Reid's last words to his family. She owed that to her in-laws.

Seated in the second and third rows were some of the same faces she'd seen last night. The empty chairs on the right, she guessed, had been reserved for the men clogging the doorway, the Lucky Jack cowboys.

Colton did a double take when he saw her and Ian coming up the aisle. He stood. A stiff guise took hold of his face as he stepped back so she could get to her seat.

"She had trouble getting through the crowd," Ian explained, without acknowledging his boss's furious scowl. "Nice to meet you, Lauren."

"You too, Ian."

Once she was in her seat, Colton sat down beside her and set his Stetson on his thigh. She noticed he still wore the wedding band she'd placed on his finger.

"Since when are you on a first name basis with my ramrod?" he demanded, his tone hushed but sharp.

Colton wore a plain olive drab flannel shirt and jeans but was, by far, the handsomest man in the room. She'd never had eyes for any other man but him, and that hadn't changed. "I didn't see the need for formality. I won't be Mrs. Ritter for much longer."

His brown eyes cut into her with a haughty stare. "But until that damn divorce is final, you are my wife."

He had the gall to act possessive now when his mistress was sitting two seats down from them?

*The nerve.*

Lauren pointed to Mia, smiled sweetly, and wrinkled her nose. "She's so cute. Like an accessory you take everywhere."

"For the last time. I'm not having an affair." He leaned forward, positioned his elbow on his thigh, and studied down at the floor. "Why can't you give me the benefit of the doubt, Lauren?"

He looked so exhausted, he might tumble out of his seat. Jack Reid's illness and death had taken a toll on him, and she'd made his plight worse by giving him those divorce papers.

A surfeit of culpability swept over Lauren. She was a hundred percent positive their marriage was beyond salvaging. But that didn't give her the right to accuse Colton of something he might not have done.

Why did she suddenly feel guilty?

*Because he might be telling the truth?*

Lauren shifted in her chair. She couldn't start second-guessing everything now, and the last thing she wanted to do was argue.

"I don't know what the big deal is," she said, trying to soothe the tension and prevent the butt chewing she knew the ramrod would get if Colton didn't pipe down by morning. "Ian was just being friendly."

He straightened and hauled in a deep breath. "Oh, I'm sure he was."

She shifted around in her chair, surveying the room for her son. "He said Little Jack was in the front."

Colton pointed to his right, the grim line of his mouth stretching to a slight smile. "He insisted on sitting with Mack and Duce."

Little Jack was seated in the front row between two burly cowboys she knew had been with the ranch since before she and Colton were married. Dressed in new blue jeans, a freshly pressed white button-down shirt, spotless black boots and a cream-colored Stetson, their son appeared much older than ten.

Lauren's heart twisted with the painful realization that in a couple of years Little Jack would be a teenager and after, a man. Her son would join his father at the Lucky Jack Ranch, fall in love, and start a family of his own.

She settled back into the chair, and Colton trained his eyes on the stately walnut desk in front of them. Sue was engaged in a conversation with Aunt Mia, so Lauren had nothing to do but sit quietly and watch at the wall clock.

Sue laughed.

Mia giggled.

Lauren felt nauseous.

She knew her mother-in-law would never ignore an extra-marital relationship or be friendly to her son's mistress, so Lauren could only assume Sue didn't know.

Well, Lauren would not be the one to tell Colton's mother that her son was having an affair. That responsibility rested entirely on his shoulders.

The nausea made Lauren's empty stomach churn like a ship riding out a storm. Her supper last night had been a pack of crackers and a Diet Pepsi from the lodge's vending machines because she'd been too tired to find a proper meal. This morning, she'd been in a rush to get to the law office.

Impatience and hunger gnawed at her. Most of the men from the Lucky Jack had taken their seats, a few leaving behind a trail of cheap aftershave and horses.

The older, more seasoned men, the ones with weathered faces, scruffy beards and tired eyes, had little tolerance for the shenanigans of the younger ranch hands who couldn't seem to sit still. One of the older cowboys raked his dusty Stetson from his head and swatted at the two sitting next to him. They pouted and grumbled something under their breathes but heeded the man's warning.

Lauren kept a check on the time, growing more restless by the minute. By nine-thirty, everyone else was too. Feeling a bit flushed and woozy from stale air and cheap aftershave that lingered, she began fanning her face with her hand.

Colton did a second glance at her. "Are you okay?"

"I'm fine," she assured him and leaned closer to Sue. "I thought this was scheduled for nine."

"It was, but Jack Reid's lawyer, Bill Humphry, is out of town." She pointed to an older woman standing near the front. "Darlene said he won't be back until after Christmas, so his grandson, Marty, will handle everything."

"The airport is over an hour away and our flight leaves in three hours," she reminded her.

"That depends on the weather." Sue nodded to the window. The sporadic flakes of snow that had been falling when she'd come out of the Inn were now as big as golf balls.

Lauren's stomach did another roll. They could not miss that flight. Jonas would fire her on the spot if she wasn't at work on Monday.

Fifteen grueling minutes later, the door to the right opened and out walked a thin man who looked too young to be presiding over anything above a high school debating club.

"Thank God," she whispered under her breath.

One side of the man's grey business jacked was skewed higher than the other, showing he'd probably buttoned it on the run. His burgundy tie hung loose around his neck and the end was thrown over a shoulder.

"May I have everyone's attention?" He laid a stack of papers on the table and progressed to fidgeting with his tie. Failing to have everyone's attention, he tried again. "H–Hello. Please, may I have your attention?"

An unanticipated and ear-piercing whistle broke through the air, quickly quelling the crowd.

"T–thank you. Ah," his smile faltered slightly, "I'm Martin Dane and, as many of you know, my grandfather was Mr. Ritter's attorney. However, due to unforeseen circumstances, he could not be here. I'll be conducting the reading of Mr. Ritter's will."

Colton shot Sue a skeptical glance that communicated his doubts about Martin's competences. She shrugged as if to say, what choice do we have?

Martin planted himself in the chair and, with a few quick scoots, situated himself closer to the table. "Now," he said, unfolding what appeared to be the will. "Let's get started. Shall we?"

Clearing his throat, he began. "I, Jack Reid Ritter, resident in the town of Crossfire Canyon, County of Bardwell, State of Montana, being of sound mind, not acting under duress or undue influence, and fully understanding the nature and extent of all my property and of this disposition thereof, do hereby make, publish, and declare this document to be my Last Will and Testament, and hereby..."
The legal jargon continued as Martin went down the list of bequeaths to Jack Reid's close friends, distant relatives, and the men from the Lucky Jack.

An hour into the reading and a dozen pages later, Martin downed a few sips of water and glanced at Sue. "To my ex-wife, Sue Lula. I wish things had worked out differently for us. I wish, well, I wish we hadn't called it quits so easily."

Sue dried her eyes and tried her best to keep the tears in. But failed, as did Lauren.

"I wish we'd fought harder for our marriage and been more patient and forgiving towards each other. But I am thankful you stayed in my life. You were my wife and my best friend, Sue Lula, and I will always love you."

Lauren took Sue's hand and squeezed it. Colton swiped a hand over his eyes. Jack Reid's earnest declaration had touched them all, and she was sure there wasn't a dry eye in the room. Even Mac and Dude were pulling out their handkerchiefs.

"I could never place a monetary value on what you've given me, but please, accept my gift of two-hundred and fifty thousand dollars."

Sue gasped.

"You've always wanted to travel. Go. See Mexico, my sweet, sweet Sue."

Martin waited for the chatter among the cowboys to dissipate before he continued. "To my grandson, Jack David, I bequeath my arrowhead collection and my coveted Winchester rifle. We made many cherished memories together and I hope you remember every one of them. My only regret as a grandpa is that I won't get to watch you grow up."

That broke Colton. He bent his head forward and covered his eyes with a hand. Though he didn't make a sound, Lauren saw drops of tears dropping to the floor.

Martin cleared his throat again and proceeded. "To my daughter-in-law Lauren, I bequeath my horse, Church, and my favorite lariat."

Lauren smiled through her tears. Jack Reid had left her a horse and a rope as a reminder of their time spent together. They were worth more to her than gold, and it was just like him to know that.

"Don't give up, honey. It's not too late to rope your dream."

That broke Lauren. She slapped a hand over her mouth to muffle the noise, but it was no use. She was sobbing. Only she and Jack Reid knew what that dream was. He'd believed she could do it, but to her, it had been hopeless. Thank God Jack Reid wasn't here to witness her and Colton divorce.

∼

"FINALLY, TO MY SON AND ONLY CHILD, COLTON JACK."

*Only child?*

Colton glanced at his mom. She was also stunned by what Martin had read.

What about Mia? The cabin and land?

"Son, you're a wonderful father and a fine example to Jack David. You're a good man and being your father was the greatest honor of my life."

Colton rested his elbows on his knees, cradled his head with his hands, and waited for the tears he knew were coming.

"I am so proud of you."

Here they come.

"You were one hell of a soldier. Never doubt that. You made sacrifices, some nearly killed you. Others cost you priceless moments with your wife and son and time you can never get back."

Those moments were scored in Colton's heart. Supporting Lauren while she was pregnant, tying her shoelaces, midnight trips to the store to satisfy her cravings, holding her hand as she labored to bring their child into the world. Crying and kissing her face when the baby was born. Little Jack's first steps, his first words, his first day of school...

"A man seldom gets a second chance," Martin continued. "So when you see that chance, by God, you take it."

Second chance? Colton swiped his face and raised his head. He didn't like where this was going.

"Don't make the mistakes I've made. You've worked hard and invested your blood, sweat, and tears in the Lucky Jack Ranch, so it's yours, lock, stock, and brand. On one condition."

*Condition?*

Martin paused, raising his eyebrows as he read the condition silently then, he cleared his throat. "Lauren must move back to the ranch."

Lauren jumped to her feet. "What?"

Shock and speculation rose from the crowd, and Colton swore he heard bets being placed. "Christ, Dad."

"Oh, Jack Reid," Sue groaned. "You didn't."

"He did," Colton said.

"And." Martin held up a finger, indicating there was more. "Live there for a total of three-hundred and sixty-five days. No more. No less. Starting within twenty-four hours from the time this will is read."

"A year?" Lauren blared at Colton. "He wants me to come back to the Lucky Jack and live for a year? That's insane!"

"No." Colton came up from the chair. "That's Jack Reid's idea of a plan."

"Plan?" she asked, eyes glaring and nostrils flaring. "What plan?"

"What happens if she doesn't?" Sue intervened to ask Martin.

His head tipped quickly from side to side as he

mumbled through the remainder of the will. "The ranch and the rest of Mr. Ritter's estate are to be auctioned off."

"Shit," Colton hissed out and raked both hands through hair.

Lauren, still hotter than a firecracker, aimed her forefinger at Colton's nose. "You said you wouldn't fight the divorce!"

"You think I had something to do with this?"

"Didn't you?"

"Hell, no!"

Her tear-filled eyes searched his for the truth. She had to believe that he hadn't had a part in this scheme. Otherwise, she'd never forgive him. They'd never be friends.

Colton opened his mouth, ready to defend his innocence, but before he could get a word in, her arm fell to her side, and her eyes took on a dull glaze.

"Lauren?" he questioned.

Suddenly, her eyes rolled closed, and she fell bonelessly against him.

"Oh, God," Sue exclaimed.

Whispered comments and gasps flew through the crowd. People hurried to the front and formed a circle around them.

"That concludes the reading of the will," Martin rushed to say as he gathered his papers for a quick getaway, but unlike him, the crowd wasn't interested in leaving.

"Don't you go anywhere," Colton ordered Martin. "I'm not done with you."

"Take her into Bill's office," Darlene said, leading the way. "There's a sofa in there."

He lifted Lauren into his arms and cradled her against his chest. God, he'd missed this. Holding her, breathing in the sweet smell of her hair, feeling the softness of her body pressed against his. Dormant parts of him spang to life and yearned for more, but Colton had learned to ignore what his body wanted.

With his mom and sister behind him, he followed Darlene down the hall to the office. He laid her down and brushed her hair away from her face. As it did with any emergency, Colton's basic medical training kicked in.

He felt her pulse and checked her respiration, then he laid a hand against her cheek. It was warm, but she didn't have a fever. Given the green-around-the-gills color she'd had earlier and the shock of his dad's will, he didn't think this was anything serious. If he had, they'd be on their way to the hospital. "She just passed out."

"I can't say that I blame her," Sue said, massaging her temple. "I can't believe Jack Reid did this. I mean, he said he had a plan, but this?"

"There has to be some sort of mistake," he said, motioning Martin to come closer. "Let me see that will." Martin handed it to him. Both Sue and Mia looked over his shoulder and read it with him. "This is the wrong will. It's dated over two years ago, before Dad knew about Mia."

"And your point is?" Martin asked.

# CHAPTER SIX

Young Marty rubbed Colton the wrong way. The greenhorn hadn't offered to investigate, or willing to consider that there might have been a mix-up with the will. "Our dad wouldn't have left his daughter out of his will."

Mia couldn't hide the disappointment in her eyes. "Maybe Dad changed his mind."

"No," he stated adamantly. "Dad had Bill make a new will two weeks ago. Bill came to the house. I was there."

"I don't know what to say. This is the will on file." Martin gestured to the will. "These are the stipulations of your father's Last Will and Testament. The end."

It might very well be, especially if Lauren thought he was in on his dad's ridiculous plan to reunite the two of them.

"Lauren." He palmed her face and brushed a thumb over her cheek. "Wake up, honey."

She groaned, then stirred. Her eyelids fluttered open, and she searched his eyes. "What happened?"

"You passed out."

Her face buckled, and she capped a hand over her forehead. "God, tell me I imagined it all."

"Afraid not." He didn't like the way her face had gone pale again. "When was the last time you ate something, honey?"

She must have concluded he was telling the truth before she passed out, because she hadn't torn into him.

"I have to catch that flight, Colton." She was tearing up again. "If I'm not at work Monday morning, I might lose my job. No job. No house. No car."

Colton would never let that happen. He might not be able to stop Jonas the Bear from firing her, but she'd never be without a home or transportation.

"Don't you have vacation time?" Sue asked, and Darlene handed Lauren a wet paper towel for her face.

Lauren laid it over her eyes. "Not a year's worth. Was Jack Reid on pain meds when he thought of this brilliant plan?"

"No," Martin answered. "And to prove it, he had two doctors sign the will stating that he was of sound mind and body when he made it."

Lauren groaned. "Why would he do something like this? To me? To us?"

*Because a man seldom gets a second chance.*

This was the second chance his dad was talking about. But could this crazy plan save their marriage? Maybe or it could end any chance he and Lauran had at remaining friends after they divorced. It was a high-stake gamble Colton was sure he couldn't lose. He was willing to bet his life and every square inch of the Lucky Jack that a copy of the updated will which included Mia's portion of the ranch was in the safe at home.

He could go back to the ranch, retrieve the will, and she would be on her way. The Lucky Jack would be

Colton's, Little Jack's inheritance would be secured, and the course he and Lauren were on before the reading of the will would continue. The divorce would be finalized in a couple of months, and she'd be gone forever.

Or he could stall. Not for an entire year, but maybe long enough to help Lauren fall back in love with him.

Yeah. That just might work.

But… A dismal thought came to his mind. He hadn't read every detail of the new will, especially the last part about his inheritance of the Lucky Jack. He hadn't seen a need to. Everyone, including Colton, assumed he'd inherit the ranch. No questions asked.

Damn. What if his dad hadn't removed the year-long stipulation?

*Lauren will murder you in your sleep or make you wish she had.* For him, his wife divorcing him was far worse than her smothering him with a pillow. Colton saw his chance and by God, he was going to take it.

"How much vacation time do you have?" he asked, setting a different course that he prayed would eventually circle around and lead them back to the beginning of their marriage. A starting-over point, before his deployment.

"A month, maybe."

A month. He rubbed a hand over his face to hide any evidence of his enthusiasm and let out a long, troublesome sigh. "This is a hell of a mess."

"Agreed," Lauren mumbled.

No one could know. His mom would never go along with the plan and bless her heart. Mia couldn't keep a secret if her life depended on it. And if it all went to hell, he didn't want any blame to be placed on them. "Is it possible you might stay a couple of days?"

Lauren yanked the paper towel from her face. "No."

"I'll call Bill." When the time is right. "I'm sure he'll

have this whole mess straightened out in no time."

"And if he doesn't?" she challenged and sat up. "What if there's no way out of this–this mess? I can't stay at the Lucky Jack for a year, Colton. I'll lose everything I have, but if I don't stay, our son will lose his inheritance."

"We have to try."

Behind those beautiful blue eyes, behind the sadness and painful memories, he knew there was a woman who had once loved him. He had to reach her somehow, some-way, and he could if he just had the time.

"Please, Lauren."

*Come on, honey. Say yes. Give us that chance.*

For a second, he almost believed she was going to. But then she blinked, shoved him to the side, and swung her feet to the floor. "Absolutely not. I couldn't even if I wanted to. It's December. One of the busiest times of the year for our office. I'm in charge of the Christmas carnival and–and Little Jack's in the parade."

"Isn't Belle Coldiron on the Christmas committee?" Sue asked, and Lauren nodded. "I know she'd be happy to help and there are plenty of volunteers to help with the carnival."

"But I don't want to miss the parade, Grandma," Little Jack cut in. "We've worked so hard on our float. I have to be there."

Little Jack was a member of the Junior Ranchers Club and had helped create the design. He'd sent Colton a picture of the crayon rough draft. The boy was proud of their concept: papier mâché cows with reindeer antlers, red boots, and Santa hats. He and the other members had worked on the float since October. Taking part in the parade was the celebration of their hard work and gave him bragging rights, which was crucial for a kid in the fourth grade.

Sue wrapped her arm around the Little Jack's shoulders. "He can stay with me. That way he doesn't miss the parade."

He smiled. "Thanks, Grandma."

Sue would never deliberately cajole Lauren into anything she didn't want to do or be a willing accomplice to his dad's plan. She was honestly trying to help.

"No." Lauren paced back and forth between the desk and the couch. "I have meetings and committees that I work with. Reports to finish, invoices to pay, supplies to order!"

"I have a laptop you can use." Colton tried offering a solution. "Video conferencing would solve the meeting problem."

"What?" Lauren spun around.

"It's great. I use it all the time to talk to my grandma," Mia said. "You can see and hear the other per—"

"I know what a video conference is," Lauren snarled.

Poor Mia dropped her head and gradually backed away like a scolded child.

Colton continued. "Everything else can be taken care of by email until this is resolved, right?"

Lauren folded one arm under her breasts and propped an elbow on it. Her fingers tapped restlessly against her chin. "Jonas would never agree."

The guy had her so afraid of losing her job; she was scared to make a move. "Don't give him a choice."

The tapping stopped. "I beg your pardon."

Colton shrugged. "You're a dedicated employee and after what you just said, it's obvious that you do more than any one person should. I don't think Jonas could run the town without you."

"He's right," Sue agreed. "It won't kill Mayor Ward to give you some time off."

Lauren knew she was defeated. Her arms fell to her sides. Her shoulders wilted, her eyes closed, and she made a fretting sound. "This can't be happening. There must be another way. It's—it's blackmail!"

"No one is forcing you, Mrs. Ritter. You have every right to refuse," Martin explained. Carefully taking the will from Colton's hand, he placed it back in the folder. "But Jack Reid named my grandfather as the executor of his estate because he knew his last wishes would be carried out. My grandfather is legally obligated to place the ranch and Jack Reid's possessions up for auction if you are not at the Lucky Jack by," he checked his watch. "Precisely, ten-fifty-two tomorrow morning."

LAUREN STOOD ON THE SIDEWALK OUTSIDE THE TRAVELERS Inn, hands shaking in a daze of disbelief and confusion. How? How was this happening?

She'd come to Montana to cut the ties to a dead relationship, end her marriage, and start a new life—move forward. But thanks to Jack Reid, she was moving backwards, back to the Lucky Jack with a man who didn't love her.

A man with a mistress.

Lauren wanted to fall to her knees and cry.

"It will all work out, honey." Sue took Lauren's face between her hands and gave her a look of motherly assurance. "You'll see."

She knew her face reflected her depressing feelings, but she was too desperate to pretend. "I hope so."

Colton handed Sue's luggage to Ian. "You're hauling precious cargo. Drive slow and watch for ice."

"I got it," was all Ian said as he loaded their luggage into the back of the crew cab pickup.

Lauren secured the zipper of Little Jack's coat. "I'll be home in a few days. A week at the most. Okay?"

"I'm not a baby, Mom," he said, pushing her hand away.

She raised and straightened his hat with a playful tug. "No, you're not."

Ian opened the passenger door for Sue and helped her into the truck. Holding to Little Jack's shoulder, Colton guided him to the truck and opened the back door. "You be good for Grandma."

"I will, Dad," he said, using the same flat tone he had with Lauren.

Colton bucked him in. "We'll see you at Christmas."

*Christmas?*

He closed the door and waved a goodbye.

"There's no way I'm staying until Christmas, Colton," she said, dumbfounded that he'd made such a remark.

"You're not waving."

Lauren rose to her tiptoes, waved. "Bye, honey!"

As Ian steered the truck into the street and headed towards Billings, Lauren felt a sense of dread come over her. Sue and Little Jack had been a buffer between her and Colton. It would just be the two of them until this mess was straightened out.

When the truck was out of sight, he picked up the only piece of luggage she'd brought with her. An overnight bag containing the dirty clothes she'd had on yesterday and her toiletries. "Are you ready?"

"No," she answered. "I'm not. Not in the least. I'm woefully dressed for a week in Montana. I packed for an overnight trip. I have no clothes, no clean underwear, no jeans, shirts, or shoes, other than the clothes I'm wearing. I came here thinking I was leaving all this behind me, and now, I'm right back where I started."

He looked guilty, so guilty that she almost believed he'd had a part in Jack Reid's dreadful plan. But why would he do something so risky?

*Because* Colton knows you'd never let Little Jack lose his inheritance. But why would he want to keep her at the ranch when he had Aunt Mia? He had nothing to gain and everything to lose.

"I am sorry, Lauren. I did not know Dad had something like this in his will." He glanced up as the streetlight above them flickered on. "It'll be dark soon and the snow is getting heavier. I'd like to be home before the roads get bad."

Reluctantly, she walked to the truck. Once they were inside the cab, he turned the ignition, switched the heater to high, and maneuvered onto Main Street. A few blocks down, the street intersected with the state highway. From there, it would be a thirty-minute drive to the Lucky Jack. Lauren could drive this road in her sleep. She'd taken it hundreds of times while she lived in Crossfire Canyon.

"Don't worry about clothes," he said, out of the blue. "I'll buy you whatever you need."

"I have money. I don't need you to buy me anything, Colton."

"It's the least I can do." He drove towards the ranch with darkness settling around them. Snow pelted the road and cut across the headlights like the truck was shooting through space at warp speed. The only sound was the radio. A low country song was playing. She couldn't make out the words, but the melody sounded sad and made her feel even more alone.

He tried again. "It's really coming down. We might have three feet by morning."

A thick blanket of fluffy snow lay across the road. But Lauren had seen enough Montana snows to know Colton was exaggerating. Higher elevations might see that much, but the worst of the storm would more than likely blow past the canyon.

"Ah, hell, Lauren," he swore softly after miles of silence stretched on. "Remember when we talked to each other? It used to be easy. How did it get so damn hard?"

Hurt and anger exploded inside Lauren. "How dare you ask that."

Colton's big shoulders stiffened. "I didn't mean—"

"Because I tried," she cried, hand to heart. "I tried so hard to talk to you, but you wouldn't. Not one word about what happened over there, about what you were going through, the nightmares—us."

"It was hard for me to talk about those things. Damn hard." She watched his maimed hand tighten into a fist against his thigh. "My head wasn't screwed on right back then."

The bullet had blown away a large part of the lower side of Colton's hand and traveled through his right upper shoulder. Doctors had amputated his pinky finger and reconstructed what was left of his hand. But it had taken months for him to regain the use of it.

"After I left," she pulled in a deep breath, "I kept telling myself that things would work out. That you'd get treatment and that eventually, Little Jack and I would get to come home."

The dimness of the truck cab hid most of his face, but the instrument panel on the dash bathed his impassive expression in pale blue light. "So why didn't you?"

She shrugged his question aside.

His hand twisted nervously around the stirring wheel. "I know you had needs that I wasn't able to meet—"

"It wasn't about sex, Colton," she said, taken aback that he'd thought such a thing.

"Then what was it? Were you too afraid of what I'd do?"

Fear hadn't kept her from the Lucky Jack, but he'd never know how unloved or abandoned he'd made her feel by shutting himself away for years. "No, of course not," she said, raising her head to stare out into the night. "I wasn't afraid. I guess I thought, what's the point?"

At least in Texas, she'd had Sue and her friends. If she'd gone back to the ranch, it would have been just the three of them, and she hadn't wanted to expose Little Jack to that kind of mental isolation. Of course, he would have had Jack Reid, but that wouldn't have prevented their son from witnessing the day in, day out, icy discord fermenting between his parents. And then there was her guilt over abandoning Colton. That would never leave her.

Lights from a passing vehicle prompted Lauren's focus to an old billboard sign that read: Crossfire Cafe. Good food. Good friends.

The restaurant had been one of her favorite places to eat and was true to its advertising tagline. "I had close friends in Crossfire Canyon, shopped in the stores, and ate in the café without you, Colton, and back then, all I wanted was to be with you."

"You're the daughter of a Navy commander," he said, hard tinges stitched his voice. "You knew how military life was before you married me. You knew how deployments were and that we'd be apart for long periods of time."

What she hadn't known was how hard living with her husband would be once he came back from war. A shell. A shadow of the man she'd known.

But Colton had a history of pushing her away that reached back to the beginning of their marriage. "It wasn't just during the deployment, Colton. Even before you left, sometimes it was like I wasn't here."

"No," he argued.

"Okay," she said evenly. "Name one thing we did together after the honeymoon was over, other than have sex."

He stared out the window, silently trying to recall a specific time that would support his contention. He found none.

She allowed a brief silence, then ended it with a sigh. "So, fast-forward eight years. I'm sitting less than a foot away from you, and it's the last place in the world I want to be. In fact, I'd rather be anywhere but here, next to you, so how did it get so hard to talk to someone you thought was your soulmate? You figure it out because after four or five years, I stopped trying, and if you're being honest, so did you."

"No," he was quick to say again. "I've never stopped thinking about us, and there's not a day that goes by that I don't want you here with me."

Her tight-fisted heart unclenched, beckoning those love born flights of fancy notions she'd had when she'd first fallen in love with Colton. God, she wanted to believe that he was sincere and that fate might grant them a new start to their doomed marriage.

She could go home to the Lucky Jack.

But then, she saw that huffy tom turkey sitting in the middle of her kitchen. That wasn't her gobbler. It was Aunt Mia's, and that fact couldn't be argued or denied. "Really?"

"Really," he said, keeping his eyes on the road as he cautiously navigated a snow-covered curve.

"Were you thinking about us — me—when you decided to have an affair?"

# CHAPTER SEVEN

"CHRIST, LAUREN," HE CURSED WITHOUT FIRE. "STOP throwing that in my face. I'm not having an affair."

"Whatever you say."

"Why are you so damn determined to make me the bad guy?"

*Because hating you is easier than loving you,* her heart confessed.

"Like I said before, it doesn't matter." Calling her divorce attorney for help was out of the question, but perhaps he could recommend someone with expertise in estate planning. There had to be a way out of this year-long sentence without losing the ranch. "The divorce will be over soon and who you sleep with won't be any of my business."

She wished cutting emotional ties was that easy. But in her heart, she knew it would take years, maybe even a lifetime, to forget him. "If I heard Martin correctly, Jack Reid said I had to live at the ranch. But he didn't say where."

Lauren was sure she'd won that minor battle, but

judging by the coy smirk on Colton's his face, her victory might be short-lived. "What's that look about?"

"I know where you're going with this."

"Oh, you do, do you?"

"Yeah, so I was thinking about your lodging options," he said innocently. "There's the barn. I'm sure Sire wouldn't mind having you around."

Her eyes rolled. "I'm serious."

"But it gets pretty damn cold in there." He ignored her and continued. "Plus, he's a tomcat, so he's usually gone for days at a time. The bunkhouse is warmer, but smells about the same as the barn. And you'd be sharing that with cowboys."

She stared at him with a deadpan expression. "Are you done?"

His smirk deepened. "For now."

"I was referring to Jack Reid's cabin."

"I knew that was next and there's a problem with that too."

"What's the problem."

"Mia lives there and," he scrunched his nose, "it just doesn't seem right having my wife and my cute accessory living under the same roof."

She wanted to slug him right in the kisser. "You think that's funny?"

He chuckled. "Very."

"You are an asshole, Colton."

"Maybe." His laughter waned. "But assumptions can go both ways, Lauren."

She crossed her arms over her chest. "Meaning?"

"It would be easy for me to assume that you're having an affair with Jonas Ward," he said with an icy undertone.

Her jaw dropped. "How could you assume such a

thing? Jonas is—is…" She stuttered because, in her mind, there were no words that accurately described her boss.

"Athletic, handsome, and recently divorced," he supplied. "I could also assume he's the real reason you showed up at my dad's funeral with divorce papers in your hand."

She was sick to her stomach. "That's not fair."

"Assumptions usually aren't." Colton gauged her expression with a quick glance. "And that awful sensation you have right now in the pit of your stomach, the one that asks: how could he think I'd do that? I felt the same way when you accused me of having an affair and I won't lie. The possibility that you were sleeping with another man crossed my mind."

He had successfully proven his point by turning everything around, so she could experience what it was like at the receiving end of an assumption, and she didn't like it. Nor did she like the fact that he might pin an affair on her based on her own assumptions about him.

"But my heart stepped in. It made me think long and hard about the woman I fell in love with. The woman who vowed to love me and only me until death do we part. I believe you're still that woman and that woman would never have an affair, so I ask you to do the same. Would the man you fell in love with, the man you married, the man who took a vow to be faithful to you, have an affair?"

That was where his point fell short.

"People change, Colton," she said weakly. "When you came back from Iraq, you weren't the man I married. So, to answer your question, no. The Colton I married would never have an affair. But the man sitting beside me in this truck might."

He clamped his jaw tight and didn't respond. He knew he couldn't deny being a different man than the one she married, and he couldn't convince her of his faithfulness based on the man he'd been then. The husband she'd lost fighting insurgents.

Lauren rested her head against the window and watched the road. It had been a long and emotional day and she was tired to her soul. All she wanted was to crawl into bed and sleep until this mess was over. But sleep wouldn't come until she knew Little Jack was safely in the air.

If the storm had reached the airport or there was the slightest danger, the flight back to Texas would be cancelled. The upside to that was Sue and Little Jack would be back at the ranch until the snow cleared. The downside was the uncertainty of human error if the flight wasn't cancelled, and the weather was bad. All sorts of things could go wrong upon take-off.

Colton slowed the truck and made the turn onto the ranch road. Dim lights shone from the bunkhouse windows. Most of the men turned in early, some stayed up to play cards or watch a movie. The barn and utility house were well lit and cast a blue light on the snow-covered ground.

It was tranquil and picturesque and resembled a Christmas card scene. But a sinking sensation hit Lauren in the stomach as the house appeared in the beam of the headlights.

Once the truck was parked, Colton killed the engine and opened his door. He walked around to the front and waited for Lauren to follow him up the steps. After he unlocked the door, he flipped on the foyer light.

It cast a rectangular glow onto the living room floor. Major was lying next to the fireplace. The Shepherd opened his eyes but didn't move from his lion pose.

"The old boy hasn't been the same since Dad died,"

Colton explained, and proceeded up the stairs to the second floor. "The bedrooms haven't changed. I sleep in our master bedroom."

*Our master bedroom.*

"Little Jack has his room. The extra bedroom has my military junk in it. I set a bed in your sewing room when I heard you were coming for the funeral. Mom spruced it up with clean sheets and a quilt."

He reminded her of a tour guide, giving a well-rehearsed speech.

"I'm beat," he said, casually, as if there weren't years of unspoken words or painful memories between them. "You know where everything is. Make yourself at home."

Lauren watched him walk down the hall and disappear into the room they'd once shared, thinking that this house would never be her home again. She hesitated before opening the door to her sewing room.

The small room had been so much more than a place to sew. It had been a sanctuary, a place she went when the loneliness closed in around her.

What changes had Colton made to the room? What had he tossed in the garbage or sold? She was tempted to slip downstairs and sleep on the couch. It would probably be more comfortable than the lumpy rollaway bed she knew Colton had pulled from the attic. Whatever the changes, she'd have to deal with them. This wasn't her house anymore, and her sanctuary was now a guest bedroom.

Backache, here I come.

Lauren twisted the knob and opened the door, ready for what she was about to see. But nothing could have prepared her for what was in the room.

The antique dress form she'd bought at a secondhand store still stood by the window with patterns of the dress she'd been making pinned together. Alphabetized and neatly housed on their shelves, her sacred library of sewing magazines and how-to books hadn't been touched. Even her carefully organized, multi-colored thread rack was exactly as she'd left it. Not a single spool was out of place. Sue's retro sewing machine sat beside the dress form, the needle midway through the last stitch she'd made. It was as if time had stopped when she left.

And Colton hadn't pulled the lumpy rollaway bed from the attic. Instead, he'd assembled a new full-sized one in the middle of the room. The wooden, low-profile bed was fitted with pristine sheets and fluffy pillows. A beautiful quilt with patterns of pale yellow and mint green lay folded near the bottom. A small sachet tied with a yellow ribbon lay on top of one pillow.

She held it to her nose and inhaled the subtly sweet scent of summer wildflowers. Complements of Sue, no doubt.

Her cell phone vibrated. She quickly pulled it from her coat pocket and read Sue's text.

WE'RE AT THE AIRPORT AND THERE'S NO SNOW HERE, SO NO DELAYS. WILL BE HOME IN A FEW HOURS.

The apprehension Lauren had had about the weather and take off floated away and she let herself relax. Little Jack was safe and sound and headed home with his grandma.

She shed her coat, draped it across the back of her sewing chair, and laid her purse in the seat. Lifting her bag onto the bed, she unpacked her small wardrobe and toiletries.

Lauren had fallen in love with the ivory petal-soft silk

gown and robe set in Sue's bridal boutique. She hadn't been a bride in a long time, and rarely gave into indulgence with a high price tag attached. But Sue had let her purchase it at fifty percent off the cost. Shimmering silk with Calais lace decorated the cuffs of the long robe and low neckline of the gown. It was exquisite and the sensation of material sliding over her body made her feel feminine—sexy.

"Exactly what you need," she muttered, reminding herself that there wasn't a man in her life to appreciate the gown or her appearance.

But maybe in a few years there would be, after she got back into the swing of things.

The swing of dating? That sounded menacing.

She'd married Colton a few years out of high school and dated no one seriously until he'd come along. How did a single mother her age go about building a romantic relationship?

She moved to the oval mirror by the door to inspect her reflection.

*Start by ditching the braids.*

She yanked the black band from the bottom of her braid and loosened the strands. Giving her head a shake, she combed a hand through the wavy strands.

The windblown look wasn't sexy on her.

She turned from side to side and told herself she had a decent figure. Sliding her hands under her breasts, she pushed up. Why couldn't she have been endowed with more than a B-cup?

"Oh, lady," she said, wearily. "It's not about how you look."

It was just as well because, standing there with her hair a mess and no makeup; she looked more like a disheveled Highland heifer than a seductress.

Taking her small bag of toiletries, she stepped out into the hall. There were two full bathrooms upstairs and a half bath downstairs. The master bedroom had its own private bath. Her sewing room, Little Jack's room and the room, as Colton had said, with his junk in it, shared a bathroom at the end of the hall.

She grabbed her toothbrush, toothpaste, and facial soap and stepped into the hall to feel for the light switch she knew was just past her sewing room door.

She flipped it up, filling the hallway with dim light and her with a heartbreaking sight. The walls were bare.

The photo booth college she and Colton had taken on their first date, their eleven by sixteen gold-framed wedding picture, Little Jack's first baby picture—the one of him wrapped in the blue quilt Sue had made—the wooden framed photograph of her, Jack Reid, and Church by the paddock and a dozen more were nowhere to be found. The walls were bare and freshly painted, with a light shade of yellow. It was lovely and her favorite color. But all traces of what they'd had together as a family were gone.

How could he discard them like they were nothing? Suddenly, the disappearance of all those happy memories and moments in time merged with the betrayal of Colton's affair, birthing resentment, and heartbreak like she'd never known.

Lauren hurried to the bathroom, closed the door, and leaned against the sink. Why was she shaking? Why was she so damn upset over bare walls? It wasn't as though she'd come to Crossfire Canyon to salvage her marriage.

She'd come to end it.

She splashed water on her face and raked her hands through her hair. This was Colton's house. He could do whatever he wanted with it.

There were two light taps to the door and then Colton's deep voice. "Lauren?"

"What do you want?"

"To talk," he said, softly. "Just for a second, please."

Tightening the belt around her waist, she steadied her racing heart, took a deep breath, then opened the door.

It was the second time tonight she'd been unprepared for what she saw on the other side of a door. But this wasn't neatly organized thread or sewing magazines. It was her soon-to-be-ex-husband standing barefoot and shirtless with nothing on but his belt and jeans.

It had been a long time since she'd seen him without a shirt. Shrapnel wounds from a roadside bomb that had killed three of his closest friends cut across his right pec and down the middle of his stomach. He'd been lucky that day and made it out with only superficial scars.

The wound from the sniper bullet that had clipped his right clavicle bone had left an indentation in the top portion of his shoulder. He'd been self-conscious about his upper body, so much so that after he'd returned home, he'd never gone without a shirt.

He clearly wasn't insecure about his appearance anymore.

Muscular and tall with mussed hair and the shadow of stubble along his right-angled jaw, he could have easily been one of those sexy male models in a cologne advertisement. He was all cowboy, dressed in denim, leather, and a shiny silver buckle that drew her eyes to an awkward focal point.

Disdain and bile bubbled up her throat and converged with self-loathing. He was a cheating low life. She would not allow herself to think about how handsome or sexy he was or what was just below that piece of silver.

Colton had also found a focal point. But unlike her, he

didn't seem the least bit embarrassed about admiring her breasts. His dark eyes swept down her body with an appreciative gaze.

Lauren crossed her arms to shield her breasts from his eyes. "Is something wrong?"

Relaxed and confident, he rested a large hand on the door frame and shifted his hips to accommodate his weight. The position stretched the smooth muscles of his bicep and forearm. "Nope."

"Well, speak then, 'cause your second was up two minutes ago."

He held up an envelope, much like the one she'd handed him yesterday.

She eyed it curiously as she took it. "What's this?"

"Proof that the man beside you in the truck tonight isn't having an affair."

Proof? What evidence could he possibly have to prove that? "Colton, I—"

"You don't want to be here, and I don't want you here against your will. But until we can get this sorted out, we're stuck together, so let's try to make the best of it."

He stepped away from the door, daring another quick look at her body before he turned and strode back to the master bedroom.

# CHAPTER EIGHT

H OURS LATER, L AUREN WAS AWAKE AND LISTENING TO THE wind as it blew against the outside of the old ranch house.

After Colton had left, she'd finished her nightly facial routine, walked out of the bathroom, ignoring his said proof, and crawled into bed. Because in her mind, there was no proof that could clear him of what she'd seen with her own eyes.

But what if he was innocent? That question had left her tossing and turning for a couple of hours. Then her curiosity got the better of her. She threw the covers back and padded to the door.

Earlier, she'd heard him walking around in the master bedroom, but the house was quiet now, and she was sure he was asleep. She opened the door and slipped into the hallway, hoping to retrieve the envelope without being seen. Once she'd read the absurd evidence of his supposed innocence, she could return the envelope to the table, and he'd never be the wiser.

She had the envelope in her hand and was about to walk back to her sewing room when she heard Colton's muffled voice coming from the master bedroom. She couldn't make out the words. Maybe he was on the phone. But at this time of night? Maybe he was talking to Aunt Mia.

Lauren wasn't above ease dropping. After all, he was her husband. She crept to the master bedroom door and leaned in closer.

"No! I can't!" A familiar sense of dread centered in the pit of Lauren's stomach. Colton was having a nightmare.

The noise had brought Major up the stairs. He approached the bedroom door with raised ears.

She gave him a pat on the head. "He's okay."

Major raised his paw to the door and scratched. He was worried about his master. She twisted the knob, eased the door open, and quietly shut it once the dog was inside.

"I'm sorry," Colton groaned, as if he was in agony. "So sorry."

His visions of war were as real now as they'd been the day she left. The therapy he'd undergone hadn't helped with the nightmares or his survivor's guilt.

Lauren stayed by the door until she was sure the nightmare was over, then walked back to the sewing room.

Four and a half hours later, she sat in the middle of her bed, dumbfounded by what she saw. She massaged her temple to ward off a headache and sifted through the contents of the envelope again as she tried comprehending what was in front of her. Birth certificates, DNA results, and letters from Mia's mother to Jack Reid lay scattered on the bed.

Mia was Jack Reid's illegitimate daughter.

She was Colton's half-sister, which explained why she'd been holding onto his arm at the gravesite, why she was living in Jack Reid's cabin and why he'd made the pun about having his wife and his accessory under the same roof.

Why he'd thought the comment was funny was not obvious to Lauren. He knew once he gave her undeniable proof, she'd feel like a total ass.

And she did.

"Aunt Mia," she groaned and fell back on the pillows. Colton had been right about her assumptions. He'd tried to explain when she'd handed him the divorce papers, but she'd jumped to judgements. But the proof he'd given her of his innocence wouldn't keep her from going through with the divorce.

She stacked the papers into a neat pile, shoved them back into the envelope, and was about to return them to the hall table when she discerned the shuffling sound of Colton's boots scuffing softly against the hardwood floor of the master bedroom.

She'd been so preoccupied with what she'd been reading that she hadn't remembered ranch life and the military had made him an early riser.

An extra early riser.

While most people were sleeping snugly in their beds, Colton and the Lucky Jack cowboys were starting their day hours before the sun rose over the Big Belt Mountains.

Lauren heard him exit the master bedroom, walk down the hall, and pause at the bathroom.

"Crap," she whispered. It was too late to return the envelope to the table, and even if she had secretly put it back, the fact remained. She owed Colton an apology.

A huge apology.

He continued past the sewing room and walked down the stairs.

Without clean clothes to change into, she'd have to wear her gown and robe until her dirty ones were washed

and dried. The laundry room was downstairs and just past
the kitchen, which meant she would have to parade past
Colton in her nightgown and robe.

It was near five o'clock. Colton would go out to check
water warmers and feed the cattle, so she'd wait until he
was gone before she went downstairs to do her laundry.

A half an hour passed, and Colton hadn't left. Soon,
the tempting aroma of coffee and cinnamon wafted up the
stairs, making Lauren's empty stomach growl. By six, she
was convinced he was trying to wait her out and by six-
thirty, she was desperate enough to venture down the stairs
for coffee and a cinnamon fix. Gathering her dirty laundry
in one arm, she took the envelope from the bed and
headed towards the kitchen.

She found Colton sitting at the kitchen table with a big,
booted foot propped on his knee, freshly shaven and showered. He was wearing a red and black checked flannel shirt
and dark jeans.

Major lay beside his chair. Considering the dreary
glance he gave her, the animal's poor spirit hadn't lifted.

"Morning." Colton greeted her from behind a
steaming mug of coffee.

They hadn't spoken in eight years and now they were
chumming it up in the kitchen. It was more than strange. It
was eerie, and she wasn't sure how to handle the vibe.
"Good morning."

He looked as tired as he had yesterday, but the dark
circles under his eyes were new.

"Can I do my laundry?"

He eased the cup from his mouth and swallowed. "It's
your house too, Lauren. You don't need my permission to
do anything."

"You're right. We're not officially divorced yet, so technically, it is my house." Why was she rattling on? "But it's your home."

Colton didn't agree or disagree. He just sat there assessing her the same way he had last night, with a raw sort of male appreciation that quickened a long-ago stir of desire. A tiny ember that had the power to reanimate those dead places inside of her.

When his eyes finally made it to her face, he smiled. "So, did you sleep well last night?"

*You know I didn't.* "Not really. How about you?" she asked, just to see if he might mention the nightmare.

"Like a baby," he lied. "But something bizarre happened."

Lauren eagerly waited, thinking that maybe he might tell her about the nightmare. "Oh?"

"Yeah." He took another sip of coffee and swallowed it calmly. "Major was downstairs when we went to bed last night."

*I don't know why I'm surprised. You never told me about the nightmares before. Why would you tell me about them now?* "And?"

"This morning, he was at the foot of my bed."

"Hmmm…that is bizarre." She looked down at the dog with suspicion. "Perhaps Major has learned how to open doors."

Colton winked at her. "Perhaps."

She laid the envelope on the table in front of him. "I guess I owe you an apology."

A rueful grin teased his lips and, despite their fatigue, his eyes sparkled with a hint of mischief. "I guess you do."

She winced. "You're going to make this painful, aren't you?"

"Yes." His grin widened. "I am."

Knowing he had every right to wear that arrogant smile, she choked back her pride and made herself say the words. "Okay," she huffed. "I'm sorry I accused you of having an affair."

He frowned and leaned forward in the chair. "I didn't get that. Could you repeat it, only slower?"

This was the Colton she remembered–funny, teasing and smiling. The man she'd married. Not the man she'd left eight years ago.

Restraining a grin, she pushed her tongue against the inside of her cheek. "I'm sorry."

"For?" he prompted.

"Oh, stop it." She threw one of her dirty socks at him. He quickly deflected it with a hand, sending it bouncing across the kitchen floor.

"Okay." He let out a raspy laugh. "You're forgiven. I think I know why you did it."

Something about the all-knowing way he'd said that raked across Lauren's badly bruised humility. "I did it because I thought you were an only child and because I saw another woman clinging to your arm."

Colton let his boot fall to the floor and pushed his chair back so he could stand. He stared down at her with suspicion. "Are you sure that's why?"

"Why else would I have done it?" she asked, the intoxicating male sent of soap and leather hovering around her.

"Because handing me those divorce papers was easier when you thought I was a cheating SOB."

Handing him divorce papers wouldn't have been easy, even if she'd known the truth. But maybe it was time she admitted to herself that she might have fabricated a mistress to buttress her decision to divorce him. Betrayal could purge the deepest love from the strongest heart and adultery would, without a doubt, sever what was left of their marriage and any hope they had of a life together.

But he wasn't guilty of the crime.

"That had nothing to do with it. I saw what I saw and jumped to conclusions. The end." Tightening her hold on the clothes, she snatched her sock from under the cabinet, hurried across the kitchen and into the laundry room. She opened the washer lid and added load of colored clothes.

Colton took a cup from the cupboard, filled it with coffee, and ambled over to the laundry room. "And now that you know I'm not having an affair, do you still want the divorce?" he asked, offering her the cup.

She accepted the cup and cradled it between her hands. He'd agreed to the divorce. But the question made it sound as though he might be having second thoughts. "I told you there were other reasons, and it's not about what I want. It's about what's best for you, me, and Little Jack."

He leaned a shoulder against the door frame, studying her as he continued to consume the java. "And you've decided, on your own, that a divorce is in everyone's best interests?"

She poured the liquid laundry soap into the dispenser and shoved the tray closed. "I assumed you did too."

Raising a dark eyebrow, he cocked his head sideways, "You assumed wrong, again."

Oh, God. He was having second thoughts. Desperation and irritation kindled inside her. She let the washer door slam shut, grabbed her coffee, and headed back to the kitchen. "Stop hounding me about my assumptions. When there's no communication, it's all a person has to go on."

"I'm not trying to hound you." He followed her to the counter. "And I've tried several times over the years to talk about us and what happened."

*What's there to talk about? I left you when you needed me.*

For Lauren, that was where their talk had to start, but she was as unprepared for that conversation as Colton had been about being caught in the crosshairs of a sniper or his recurring nightmares. He couldn't talk about the buddies he'd lost or the shot that nearly killed him. She couldn't talk about how her husband had made it out of the hell of war alive, but nearly died at home because she'd been too weak to stick it out when their marriage was in trouble.

"A lot happened, Colton," she replied, her voice weak. "Are we going to waste another eight years talking about things we can't change?"

He set his cup on the counter, exhaled heavily, and scrubbed a hand over his eyes. "No," he said. "I'm done wasting time."

"Knock, knock." Mia called from the foyer. "It's me. The mistress."

Heat surged to Lauren's cheeks. "You told her?"

"We're in the kitchen," he answered Mia, then murmured, "I thought it was best after the way you tore into her at the lawyer's office."

Lauren cringed, knowing she had that apology to make as well.

"You're lucky my sister has a forgiving heart. She considered the whole thing hilarious."

Mia rushed into the kitchen carrying a large paper bag in each hand. "I come bearing bags of food."

Colton relieved her of the sacks. "You should have left these in the truck. I would have brought them in."

"They're not heavy." She discarded her blue beanie, swiped a hand through her dark hair, which Lauren noted was the same color as Colton's, and beamed a bright and friendly smile at Lauren. "I hope you like casseroles."

"She loves them," he answered for her and lifted the bags onto the counter.

"Ah, yes," Lauren stumbled to agree. "Yes. I love a good casserole.'

"Mia's casseroles are better than good. They're irresistible," he boasted as he wrapped an arm around his sister's shoulder. "And her pasta dishes are amazing."

"I can't take all the credit. I had an Italian grandmother who insisted I learn to cook so I could find the," Mia hooked her fingers into quotation marks, " 'right man.'"

"Hey," Lauren said, winking. "There isn't a hungry man who can resist casseroles and pasta."

"Hot dog." Mia wiggled an eyebrow at Colton. "Did you hear that? I'm irresistible to hungry men."

He grunted his response.

Mia giggled and whacked him with her beanie. "Oh, stop. There are a lot of good men around and speaking of good men. Have you seen Ian? He promised to return my cookie tin."

"No." Colton chomped out the word. "I've not seen our ramrod. His job is to help me keep this ranch running, not return cookie tins to pretty women."

"Ah," Mia nodded. "So you're saying if I was ugly, it would be okay for him to return my tins?"

Lauren let out a laugh, then tried to hide it with a cough. "I had a tickle in my throat."

"I'll bet," he said, eyeing her with a bogus scowl as he unpacked the casseroles. "No, it wouldn't be okay and some of those men you've labeled as good might be a wolf in sheep's clothing."

Mia put on a pensive frown. "Do all your metaphors involve animals?"

Colton closed his eyes and mumbled something under his breath. It could have been a prayer, but Lauren leaned towards it being a curse. She was instantly fond of Mia and watching the two of them banter like siblings was heartwarming.

"Oh, I almost forgot. I left a plate of cookies and hand

pies in the truck." Cramming the beanie on her head, Mia headed to the foyer. "I'll be right back."

"Well." Lauren blew out a breath of relief and let her shoulders slump. "That went better than I expected."

"Like I said, she's very forgiving." He strolled past her to the rack near the door, thrust an arm into a shearling coat, and picked up a Dunn Resistol.

Lauren had seen the felt hat go through so many stages. It had been a formal hat for their first date, then developed into a go-to-town hat. It digressed into his every day, sweat-and-work hat after the brim surrendered its form.

"Do me a favor," he said, a wavelet of concern on his face as he glanced down at Major, who hadn't moved from his spot next to the table. "Pay him some extra attention today. I'm worrying he might grieve himself to death."

She crouched down to pet the dog's head. "I'll give him a little extra TLC, but I'm sure he'll be fine."

Major lifted his golden eyes to hers and whimpered.

"I hope you're right." Colton's mouth twisted as he apparently considered life without the old dog. "It would kill me to lose him too."

"How old is he now?" she asked, trying to recall the exact year Jack Reid had brought him to the ranch. "Nine? Ten?"

"He's twelve. The laptop is on my desk," he said, placing the Resistol on his head. "I normally eat dinner at Mia's."

"Okay," she said. "I have loads of work to do, so I'll probably just take something from the fridge."

*And I need to call Jonas to deliver the news of my unplanned vacation.*

"She's expecting you too, Lauren."

Of course she was.

He stepped towards the door. "Dinner is at six. I'll be in around five."

"Oh, don't forget to call Bill."

He paused, clamped his jaw, and offered her a curt nod.

A rush of cold air passed through the kitchen as he strode out the door. She went to the window and watched as he paused on the back porch. He shoved his hands into a pair or well-worn leather gloves, his wide shoulders expanding with another deep breath. His face bore the same doomed likeness as it had when she'd presented him with those divorce papers.

# CHAPTER NINE

COLTON BRACED HIMSELF FOR THE BITE OF THE WIND AS HE stepped off the back porch and onto the snow-covered earth. The storm front hadn't deposited over three or four inches, nothing by Montana standards. He embraced the cold as the frigid wind cut through the thick lining of his coat and layers of thermal and flannel. Welling in a deep breath, he quickened his stride.

Nightmares weren't as frequent as they had been when he'd first returned from deployment. But sometimes Ray and the others came to him. The day they'd died was hard-wired into his brain and could never be erased, and so was the night Lauren left. He regarded those nightmares a life sentence that he'd accepted as his cross to bear.

He seldom had pleasant dreams or happy recreations of his everyday existence or his life before he'd enlisted. Living and working without companionship or a family to come home to hadn't given his brain much to work with.

Last night had peculiarly combined a dream and a nightmare he knew was prompted by Lauren's return to the ranch. He'd tossed restlessly, moving in and out of sleep. His mind had taken him on a cruel ride, from making love to her to seeing her face painted in blood. The gash caused by the fall had needed stitches. But the brain, for all its complexity, had a primitive and punishing knack for distorting reality.

Seeing Lauren this morning helped to wipe away the residue left behind by those bloody nightmares. He relished those dreams of making love to her. They'd taken him back to the days when they'd been newlyweds, when the passions of love were all they knew. He'd had those dreams before, but Lauren had been thousands of miles away then, not sleeping across the hall from him.

Clutching those dirty clothes to her breasts, she'd entered the kitchen in that silky gown and robe, looking disheveled and sexy as hell.

His mind was a scrambled mess, and his body hadn't been this overly aroused in years. It expanded to the early morning temptation with the same enthusiasm it had last night when she'd opened the bathroom door. Lauren's absence from his life had done more than make his heart grow fonder. It had given him a giant pain in the crotch.

Jack Reid's most recent will, the one with Mia's portion of the inheritance, was in the safe, just as Colton thought. Mia deserved to know she'd been included in their dad's will. But Colton couldn't reveal that to his sister yet.

His dad hadn't eliminated the requirement of Lauren's stay at the ranch. But he'd lessened her mandated time to a month.

Colton wrestled with whether he should come clean to Lauren and Mia or continue the farce of the will Martin read. He decided on the latter. There was truth in what Lauren said about him not being the man she'd married.

In a lot of ways, he wasn't. Becoming a soldier had changed him. He wasn't the cocky jarhead Lauren fell in love with. He was the older, astute cowboy who'd learned the value of life.

Lauren had changed, too. She wasn't the naïve young woman he'd met in at a football game. She was a mature, confident, and independent woman.

But for all their differences shaped by wisdom and time, they were, at the heart, the same people. The foundation of love and commitment to each other was intact. Once he signed those divorce papers, it wouldn't be. He was sure they could rebuild everything else needed for a happy marriage, so at four this morning, he'd texted Ian to say he'd be late for work.

Colton wasn't fool enough to think that dropping the bombshell of Mia's identity would change Lauren's mind about the divorce. He hadn't expected her to do an about face and fall into his arms, but his questions had made an impact. He'd seen it in her eyes. For a second or two, she'd had second thoughts.

As he set a course for the maintenance garage, wind whipped around him and stirred a spiral of snow around his body. He clamped a hand over the crown of his Resistol, braced his shoulders, and lifted his collar to shield his unprotected face from the fury of the gust.

The pungent odor of manure, hay, and bovine hit his nostrils as he hurried past the steel corrugated barn and to the maintenance garage.

He opened the door and stepped inside. The clanking of wrenches and the rattling sound of air ratchets quickly replaced the mooing and bellowing from the cows outside.

Though winter was officially a few weeks away, Colton and the men spent most of fall preparing for the cold weather that would arrive early next month. They'd changed the old stock tank heaters with new ones, added more space to the calving barn that was just south of the ranch house, and repaired windbreaks.

Colton had never been what people called easygoing. He despised small talk, and he'd never seen much point in shootin' shit over a few beers with other ranchers and cowhands around Crossfire Canyon.

Maybe it was the lone wolf in him, or maybe it was the soldier. Whatever the reason, his impassiveness hadn't helped him win any popularity contests among the men working for him and, mostly, he hadn't cared.

When he'd taken over the ranch, all he'd demanded from the cowboys at the Lucky Jack was respect, and a hard day's work for more than decent pay. But that was before he'd learned the most important part of running a business. The people part, the human and heart component that established long-lasting employee relationships and, if a man was lucky enough, friendships.

Three of the cowhands were experienced in mechanics. Duke Wagner was nearing sixty and had problems with his back. Riding for long periods of time was tough on him. Stan Hastings broke an arm during spring round up a couple of years ago and the injury deteriorated into debilitating arthritis. Bert Turner was the oldest of the cowboys. He'd turned seventy-three on his last birthday. The three never shied away from hard work. They were dependable and possessed more prudence than the entire crew.

Colton considered them one of the Lucky Jack's best assets, so he'd devised a plan. He'd asked the men if they would help around the garage in their spare time. They'd eagerly agreed, and their spare time quickly evolved into full-time mechanics jobs. The men were able to keep their positions and their dignity. Plus, the garage was warm in the winter and cool in the summer. They kept ranch equipment running smoothly, and no one complained about how many breaks they took or how many hours they worked.

This week, the trio was working to complete an equipment maintenance checklist Ian had given them. But George Carlson, a.k.a. Scrap, a young cowhand and new hire, halted their checklist. The men dubbed him Scrap because when he'd hired on at the Lucky Jack, he'd been a mere scrap of a man and overly thin. Colton guessed he was half starved.

Scrap had hit a pothole on his way back from town yesterday and busted one of the truck's axels. Colton had hit a few potholes in his time and knew accidents happened. But Scrap sported a led boot that might get him killed one day.

"I don't want to hear another damn word about how this ain't your job," Duke said, agitation riding hard in his tone. "You bust it. You fix it. Got that?"

"Yeah," Scrap grumbled.

Colton cupped his hands together and tried blowing the chill from them as he walked to where the truck was on the lift.

"How's it going?" he asked, hoping the axle could be repaired without having to order parts.

Duke swiped the back of his hand across his wrinkled brow, leaving a smudge of grease behind. "Slow. We had a hell of a time taking the wheel hub off, and Smith's Automotive doesn't have the axel. I checked. I can order it, but it'll be at least a week before we get it. I'll see if Jinks has one."

That was the usual route Duke took to repair whatever piece of machinery was broken around the ranch. If the automotive store in town didn't have it, Jinks' Junkyard did.

"Where's Ian?" Colton asked.

Duke wiped his hands on an old grease rag, then swung one towards the back door of the garage. "He took a batch of Mia's cookies out to the men earlier. Said after that, he was going to run a few errands, but would be back soon."

Scrap's gaunt face beamed. "I sure love your sister's cookies."

Colton made certain his eyes conveyed everything he wanted to say about Scrap's interest in Mia's cookies.

The young cowhand's enthusiasm evaporated. "Liking her cookies don't break the rule, boss," he mumbled, then gulped.

Colton's expression didn't change. Scrap hadn't meant anything derogatory by the comment and he was right in saying that favoring cookies didn't break any of the Lucky Jack's rules. All the cowhands felt the same way about Mia's cooking. Some even jokingly remarked that horses were complaining about carrying around all the extra weight they'd gained since she'd been preparing their meals.

But Scrap's recklessness irritated Colton. "Carelessness can get a man killed out here and has no place on this ranch." He walked to the back door and gave Scrap another dull glare. "Keep it under the speed limit or the next axel will come out of your last paycheck. Understand?"

Scrap nodded.

Colton stepped outside and heard laughter and muffled words. Four of his men were standing inside the shed next to the paddock, warming themselves by a fire they'd built in a steel barrel. It was a common break spot for the cowboys in the colder months. The metal structure wasn't insulated like the garage but provided a sufficient shelter from the harsh winds.

With their backs to Colton, they weren't aware of his approach.

"Damn, these are good," Rory Gentry said, as he reached into the aluminum container for another of Mia's cookies.

Mitch Post nudged him with an elbow. "I bet they don't taste as good as the gal who made 'em."

Both men chortled.

There went rule number one. White-fiery anger washed over Colton. He eased behind a tractor brought in for repairs yesterday and waited.

Punch Baker, one of the older cowboys, shook his head. "Talk like that'll get you on the boss's shit list."

"Ah, come on, Punch," Rory ribbed. "You know you'd like a sample of that honey jar."

*Careful, Punch.*

Punch held his hands over the flame, then rubbed them together. "First of all, I don't let my affinity for honey override my common sense."

"Affinity," Rory mocked. "Such fancy words."

Mitch laughed. "It's all them books he reads."

"Second," Punch shoved the brim of his Stetson up higher on his forehead. "It's too damn cold to stand in the unemployment line nursing an ass kicking from the boss."

Colton rubbed his knuckles, anticipating when his fist slammed into Rory's and Mitch's mouths. Last winter was hard, the worst one in over forty years, his dad had said. Many neighboring ranches had experienced a high calf mortality rate because they'd been unprepared. The Lucky Jack went mostly unscathed, but ranch work in Crossfire Canyon was scarce. Those who were employed wanted to stay that way.

"Most importantly," Punch said. "The Lucky Jack

women are off limits. Old J.R. would have tied you to his horse and drug you to death for talking disrespectfully about Miss Mia. It goes against the rules and even if it didn't, it's wrong."

*Smart man, Punch.*

"Aw, hell," Rory grumbled. "What the boss don't know won't hurt him."

*Oh, so it's like that.*

Mitch snorted. "Speaking of the Lucky Jack women. Did you see the missus?"

"Holy hell," Rory cursed, and pulled in a lustful breath between his brown teeth. "She's a fine one."

Mitch inserted a dirty forefinger into his mouth and gave it a loud suck. "What I'd give to taste that honey."

If Colton had any mercy towards the cowhands, that comment would have crushed it. He cracked his knuckles as the simmering anger boiled.

"Christ, boys. Have some respect," Punch said, shaking his head as he vacated the shed and started towards the garage.

Rory and Mitch laughed and reached into the tin for another cookie.

Punch walked by the tractor and did a double take when he noticed Colton. The cowhand's expression switched from disgust to dread.

Colton made a gesture with his head, silently telling Punch needed to move along quietly, and he did. But before Colton could make his presence known to Rory and Mitch, Ian appeared from behind the shed.

With a tight jaw and a deadly glare, he slipped his hands from the pocket of his barn coat and jerked Mia's cookie tin from Rory. "Pack your bags and get the hell out of the bunkhouse. I'll have your pay waiting for you at the gate."

"But—" Rory started.

"If you like your teeth, you'll keep your mouth shut and get your ass moving."

Ian had been with Lucky Jack for nearly five years. Jack Reid hired him; said he saw something special in the young cowboy. Colton wasn't as quick to label him as anything but a half-decent ramrod.

But Colton gave credit where it was due. He hadn't a single work-related criticism about the man. During Jack Reid's sickness, Ian had taken on more than his share of ranch work and responsibilities without a single complaint.

Ian had proven himself a loyal employee.

After Rory and Mitch slithered off to the bunkhouse, Ian removed the lid from the bottom and secured it over the top of the tin. Then he withdrew a clean handkerchief from the back pocket of his dirty jeans and wiped the container clean.

Ian had the same gentle consideration for all females. He was a well-mannered man who was courteous, like when he'd escorted Lauren through the crowd of noisy cowboys at the reading of Jack Reid's will.

But it didn't sit well with Colton that his sister and the ramrod might be more than just friends. Mia stocked the bunkhouse kitchen twice a week now instead of once every two weeks. Ian made sure he was there to help her, and Colton had seen Ian's truck driving back from Mia's cabin four times in the last month.

Colton didn't want to pin the stolen bovine embryos on anyone until he had proof. But he had a bad feeling about his ramrod.

The subtle changes in Ian and Mia's friendship began around the same time the first embryo was stolen. That threw up warning signs Colton couldn't ignore and made him question the ramrod's intentions towards Mia. Did Ian

have a genuine interest in her or was his romantic atten-
tions geared towards something more sinister, like helping
him cover his tracks?

# CHAPTER TEN

COLTON HAD YIELDED TO LAUREN'S ARGUMENT, AGREEING any attempt at reconciliation beyond this stage in their marriage was meaningless. He'd finally seen that a parting of ways was what they needed. He also wanted a fresh start.

She should be relieved and ready to go forward. After all, the divorce was her idea. But Lauren felt more broken than before.

Her marriage was over. The finalizing would take a little time, but this was the dissolution she'd been expecting.

Lauren stood at the kitchen window long after Colton disappeared into the mechanic's shop. Ranching was strenuous work. Colton and his men worked long hours and confronted the elements to keep everything functioning smoothly at the ranch. The rumble of tractors and diesel trucks rolling across the frozen ground floated into the house. Cowboys whistled commands to their horses, talked loudly, and laughed heartily as they worked to move cattle closer to the barn.

Through the grimy glass and torn screen, the vista of an elongated mountain range and its snow-capped peaks stretched for miles then tapered off into the clear blue skyline.

Lauren had stood in this spot dozens of times, washing dishes and preparing food. It was her kitchen, her house, and for a few short years, her piece of heaven. She'd missed the spectacular view of rugged summits, rich prairies, and foothill savannas of the ranch.

Whatever time it took for the will to be sorted out would be the last days of her life in Montana. She'd never be able to go home, and her heart ached from that existence.

She wrapped her cold fingers around the hot cup of coffee and angled away from the view. She and Little Jack had their own home now. They'd make memories and share a future full of wonderful opportunities. She'd rebuild her life — a life without Colton.

"I don't know if I'll ever get used to this cold," Mia said, rushing into the kitchen with a shiver.

"I can relate. It took my body months to acclimate to these frigid temps."

Mia placed a box of hand pies and cookies on the counter next to the casseroles, then discarded her coat and beanie. "Texas heat will do that to you. We get snow in Arizona but nothing like this."

"I hear you." Lauren carried her coffee to the kitchen table and sat in the chair Colton occupied earlier, relaxing now that he was gone. "I'm a military brat, so I'm used to a little snow, but Montana has its own kind of cold. It sinks all the way to a person's bones."

Mia shivered again with the thought. "A military brat. That's pretty cool."

Lauren gave her a wiry smile. "Not really. I was born in Nevada and moved to at least six states before I was in junior high. We were transferred to Texas my sophomore year of high school."

Mia joined her at the table with a cup of coffee and the plate of cinnamon buns. "And that's where you met Colton."

"Yeah, in a roundabout way, I guess you could say. We met by accident at a football game. He was the quarter-back and I just happened to be at the game with a friend. We sort of bumped into each other after the game and our relationship evolved from there."

Mia rested her elbow on the table and palmed her chin. "That's so romantic."

At the time, it had been very romantic, but romance alone couldn't hold a marriage together.

Mia continued, staring dreamily into the air as she spoke. "Two strangers falling in love. How often does that happen?"

Lauren didn't want to talk about romance and how she and Colton fell in love. She was too bitter about their failed marriage, so she took a bun from the plate and switched topics. "Mia, I owe you an apology."

"No, you don't."

"I do and I am so sorry for snapping at you in the lawyer's office and for..." She could hardly say it.

"Thinking I was the other woman?" Mia asked, a laugh bubbling in her throat. "I'm not offended and the whole notion is—"

"Hysterical?" Lauren supplied.

"Exactly, and so is the notion that my brother would have an affair." Mia tore into a bun and chewed between words. "He couldn't even if he wanted to. All the man does is work and I'm not exaggerating. When I moved in, the refrigerator had three cans of beer, a jar of pickles, and a pack of lunchmeat that smelled." She pretended to gag. "Like Arizona roadkill in late July."

Mia possessed a pleasant personality, and Lauren was at ease around her. Colton was right about her forgiving heart. The young woman didn't seem bothered by the way Lauren had treated her or by the accusations that had been slung her way.

"My brother's idea of dinner is a processed mystery meat sandwich from Willie's Truck Stop, so I earn my keep by doing the grocery shopping and preparing meals. The cowhands don't seem to mind it."

Lauren knew the place and about her husband's mystery meat preference over actual food. She also knew he would never make Mia earn her keep by cooking and cleaning, but she clearly enjoyed helping. She pointed to the plate of buns. "Let me guess. You made these."

Mia's head bobbed up and down. "They're quite easy to make."

The washing machine dinged, signaling the cycle was complete. Lauren rose and walked to the laundry room. "Maybe for you, but everything I bake comes out of the oven burnt or so hard it can be used as a lethal weapon."

"I'm sure it's not that bad."

"It is. I'm just glad I didn't have access to one of my banana nut muffins when I saw Colton escorting you across the cemetery," Lauren joked. "I could have done some serious damage to that cowboy."

She heard Mia snicker. "You're saying I should do the holiday baking?"

"Yes. We'll all be safer if you do." Lauren wanted to say, ship me a fruitcake because I won't be here for the holidays. But the conversation with her sister-in-law was going well. She would not spoil it.

She placed the clean load in the dryer, set the timer, and pushed the start button, then added another load before she returned to the kitchen. "Thankfully, Colton was also quick to forgive me. Although, I could have done without the arrogant grin."

Mia placed the buns back on the counter and dusted the table clean of crumbs. "That arrogance was the side of Colton I saw first, only he didn't grin much around me then."

Lauren remembered a time when her husband hadn't grinned. But she didn't think his reaction to Mia had anything to do with PTSD. "Learning he had a sister must have been a shock."

"It was," Mia agreed, grimacing. "And I totally went about it the wrong way."

Lauren held her smile, but frowned a little. "Is there a right way to do something like that?"

"Hmmm, no." Mia pretended to think. "I don't think there's a set of rules for introducing yourself as someone's illegitimate sister."

Mia looked to be in her early twenties. That meant Jack Reid's affair with her mother happened while he and Sue were married. Maybe that was the real reason Colton had a hard time accepting Mia and why Lauren hadn't learned of her existence until now. "How long have you been at the Lucky Jack?"

"A little over two years."

The woman had been at the ranch for two years and neither Sue nor Little Jack had mentioned her?

Mia's expression changed to sad. "That isn't long at all when you've missed a whole lifetime, but I'm so thankful I had that time with Dad."

Lauren felt deep sympathy for the young woman. Colton had lost Jack Reid, but he had a lifetime of memories to cherish. Mia had only two short years.

Mia propped an elbow on the table and braced her chin in her palm. "Colton didn't accept me right away. In fact, he hated the ground I walked on."

The friction between brother and sister might explain why no one mentioned Mia to Lauren.

Mia traced the stitching around a leaf in the autumn tablecloth. "I think somewhere in the back of Colton's mind, he knew Dad was dying. I showed up out of nowhere, so he thought I was some sort of con artist here to get what I could and leave. But when I gave him the proof, he couldn't deny that I was his sister."

"How did Jack Reid handle the news that he had a daughter?"

Mia's eyes glistened with tears as she thought about her dad. "He cried, then he hugged me so tight I thought I'd never breathe again."

"Aww." Lauren's face buckled. "That's so sweet."

Mia wiped her eyes and smiled. A soft glow of love and acceptance covered her face. "He never doubted I was his. Not once. He said I looked just like my mother."

They talked for a little while longer. Then Mia stored the casseroles in the freezer, said her goodbyes, and left for home. Lauren finished her laundry, shower, and dressed before she called Jonas. She used her phone to email him about her absence and copied each member of the town council and the chair of each committee she served on, then she made the dreaded call.

She wanted all her bases covered if her cranky boss decided to fire her for not doing her job.

The phone rang a couple of times before he picked up.

"Hello." Jonas answered with the same gruff agitation he did every time she spoke to him.

"Good morning," she tried sounding as chipper as she did at work.

"Lauren," was his greeting.

"I'm sorry, Jonas, but I won't be at work this morning." She heard him sigh.

"As you know, my father-in-law passed away earlier this week and well…" How did she say this? "There've been a few issues with his will that demand I be in Montana longer than I expected."

"How much longer?"

She grimaced. "A week, maybe two, but I have everything I need on the shared cloud account. It'll be just like working from home, which we've done in the past."

His silenced followed.

Finally, she said, "This is important, Jonas, and you know I wouldn't take more time off if I didn't need it."

He let out another long sigh. "I have a list of things I need completed before the end of the workday."

She felt a weight of worry lift from her shoulders. "No problem. I'll watch for your email."

He ended the phone call before she could offer a goodbye or a thank you. The election couldn't come soon enough.

Lauren spent most of the day checking off tasks on the leg-long list Jonas had sent her, and the end was in sight when she heard the backdoor open and close.

Colton was home.

Her empty stomach rumbled, a reminder that she'd worked through lunch. If she'd been at home, she would've taken a hot bath and crashed on the couch with one of those pre-made salads from the grocery store. But she couldn't turn down Mia's invitation to dinner.

When Colton started down the hall toward the den, an odd but familiar sense of excitement raced through her body. It was the sweetest kind of anticipation. It was the same rush of excitement she'd had when he'd come home after his deployment.

His footsteps ended at the doorway. Lauren's body tensed, and she was uncomfortably aware of how dreadful she must look. She'd run a brush through her hair but hadn't bothered to apply makeup.

*Why do you care? You're divorcing the man.* Her brain knew that, but her body held a weak grasp on the verity that a man she was still very much attracted to was about to see her with Highland heifer hair and tired eyes—again.

Colton eased the door open. "It's after five."

"I'm almost finished," she answered, chancing a glance his way. The impression of his Resistol molded his hair, curling the longer portions of it. A smattering of mud was smeared down his right jaw and the scant traces of a five o'clock shadow dusted the lower portion of his face.

He stuffed a hand into the front pocket of his dirty jeans and leaned a shoulder against the door frame. "Hard day?"

"No harder than usual, I guess."

"How did Jonas take the news?"

Pulling her mouth to one side and lifted her brows. "Like I expected."

"But you still have a job," he said, trying to add positivity to the situation.

"Yeah." She huffed. "Along with a ton of work that I'm sure is meant to punish me. Did you call Bill?"

"He didn't answer."

"I called my attorney and asked him to recommend someone who specialized in estate planning."

Colton waited. "And?"

"He recommended Edgar Wallace. He's some well-to-do lawyer in Fort Worth. Edgar was out of the office, but I talked to his assistant. She took some notes and was certain he could find a loophole."

"I don't know," he said, scratching his chin. "Bill's pretty thorough."

"She said he'd do some digging." Lauren put her elbow on the desk and planted her chin in a fist. Her eyes narrowed. "Are you sure that was the correct will?"

Colton's face went stiff. "Why wouldn't it be?"

"It just doesn't make sense. Mia said Jack Reid was ecstatic about learning he had a daughter."

"He was."

"So why did he leave everything to you?"

His mouth turned upside down. "We may never know."

There was an onus of liability in his tone that struck a suspicious chord in her, but she didn't have a legitimate reason for accusing him of lying. "Maybe we'll get lucky."

He cleared his throat. "Maybe."

Lauren moved her fingers over the mouse pad, saved her documents, and closed the laptop.

"So you're still ready to hightail it out of here?"

She closed the laptop. "My bags are packed and ready."

His expression flattened. "Figures."

"Are you trying to make me feel bad? Because if you are, it's not working."

"No, I'm not trying to make you feel bad or argue."

"Who's arguing?" she asked succinctly. "You asked me a question, and I answered it. No one likes being held against their will. I want to go home, get back to work and on with my life."

"Oh, yeah." He seethed. "You're going to find that perfect man and make babies."

Why was he belittling her need for children and a steady relationship? "What's wrong with that?"

"Not a damn thing," he said, smiling with the rancor of a rattler. "Except there are no perfect men."

"I didn't say he had to be perfect." She stood up and slapped the desk with her palms. "You did! And what's wrong with wanting babies?"

His hooded eyes bore into her as he clenched his jaw. Finally, he dropped his gaze to the floor. "There's nothing wrong with wanting babies."

Colton Ritter never surrendered; he never gave up. But he had. The spat ended as quickly as it began. That didn't stop Lauren from suffering the effects of the argument. Her heart pounded so hard against her breastbone that her whole body shook.

"Hell, I want them too," he admitted in a voice painfully low. "If we'd stayed together, we'd have probably been hard at work on baby number four."

"I want two boys and two girls," she'd told him the day they were engaged.

He'd laughed and kissed her soundly. *A pair of each, huh? Yes!*

They'd drawn out plans for extra bedrooms on a napkin from the burger joint where they were eating and picked names for their future babies. David, Ryan, Zoey, and Aurora.

Colton shielded his eyes with a hand for a second or two then wiped them with his thumb. "Jack David is the best of both of us."

"We will never disagree about that," she said, her tone uneven and coarse.

"Yeah. But I always thought at some point in time, the

others would be born." He sighed heavily and raised his eyes to the ceiling. "Ryan, Zoey and... Aurora."

Lauren's fingers tightened around the edge of the desk for support. Colton remembered. He'd spoken the names of their unborn children perfectly and without a pause. God, how that hurt. Pain lacerated her body from the crown of her head to the soles of her feet. Every part of her ached in the most agonizing way. There was no remedy for a broken heart.

And hers was.

The second he'd said those names, her heart jolted from its protected position, fell, hit hard against the rubble of their pasts, and shattered all over again. Because the day she'd given up on their marriage, those precious unconceived babies were carefully wrapped and placed in the center of her impossible dream.

But Colton had carelessly unwrapped them, held them in his hands, and made her relive that misery all over again.

Her pain quickly transformed into anger. "Since our days of making babies together are over, there's no chance that's going to happen."

He straightened, squared his jaw, and gave her an impassive glare.

"What was it you said earlier?" she asked, sporting a baritone voice to mimic his. "You don't want to be here, and I don't want you here against your will. So let's try to make the best of it."

"I vaguely remember saying something like that," he admitted.

"Well." A sardonic laugh burst from her mouth. "I. Don't. Want. To. Be. Here. Period. And you're obviously not trying to make the best of our situation, so until we find a way out of this mess, why don't we make a peace agreement? A ceasefire for what will undoubtedly be the worst Christmas either of us has ever had if Edgar doesn't find that damn loophole. You stay out of my way, and I'll stay out of yours." She returned his glare. "How about that?"

# CHAPTER ELEVEN

COLTON WAS A JACKASS FOR STRIKING OUT AT LAUREN with those verbal low blows about finding the perfect man to have babies with. It wasn't her fault he felt guilty for lying about the will. She hadn't intentionally tried to hurt him by saying she wanted babies.

She deserved children, and she deserved to conceive them with a man she who loved her. He loved her and somewhere deep down, he believed she knew that. But he'd let his emotions spiral out of control during the exchange of words. And it hadn't taken long for his remorse to mix with the memories of what could have been.

Bringing up those babies and saying their names aloud had been a mistake that had hurt them both.

Lauren was angry, and she'd slung that worst Christmas comment at him because he'd hurt her. But there was a distorted and selfish delusion in what she'd said, an element of ignorance, angry or not, that demanded to be weighed in the balance of sacrifice and honor.

So he pushed himself upright, stepped over to the desk,

and picked up a small, framed photo of Lauren holding Little Jack minutes after he was born. With a sweaty face, happy tears, and a beautiful smile, she'd posed for the picture.

Colton had received it in the mail a few weeks later. The picture had been the envy of his squad and a comfort to him when the days were long and the nights were dark.

After he'd come home, he'd put it in a frame to flatten the creases, but it still bore the fold marks from where he'd carried it inside his combat uniform. "My worst Christmas was the one after Little Jack was born."

Colton slid the three remaining fingers of his disfigured hand over the smooth surface of the glass, remembering those homesick moments that still tore at his heart. "I had a new wife and a baby boy I'd never laid eyes on. I was worlds away from everyone I loved and felt so alone. The only thing I wanted was to be home with you and Little Jack. Instead, I spent Christmas night on patrol praying I didn't die before I got to hold you and our baby."

He set the photo on the desk and walked back to the door. Clasping the knob, he said, "So while this may be the worst Christmas you've ever had, it certainly won't be mine."

Twenty minutes later, Colton and Lauren were in the truck and on their way to Mia's for dinner. The cabin sat a few miles from the ranch house. When the weather was good, the trip was quick. But the temperature had been in the teens today. There were frozen spots on the gravel road that were completely covered in ice, so he drove slowly.

Lauren had been quiet and reserved for the first part of the drive, but spoke minutes before they arrived. "I'm sorry for what I said about this being the worst Christmas. It was a selfish and spiteful remark, and I didn't mean it."

"I know you didn't." There was something different about this apology. It was without pride and sincere. Something about the way she was staring down at her hands and the soft tone of her voice gave it more gravity than the one she'd made for accusing him of being an adulterer. "I'm sorry too. Can we just forget it happened?"

"Yes, let's do." The truck cab was warm, but Lauren rubbed her upper arms as though a chill had just run over her. "I'm sure if I am stuck here until Christmas, God forbid, it won't be anything compared to the Briggs family Christmases."

Colton had attended two Christmas celebrations with his in-laws, and that was enough for him to accept that he loathed them. But out of respect for Lauren, he never voiced his opinions of them.

"Mom chain-drinking martinis and Dad pretending there was some sort of national emergency, so he didn't have to spend the day with her."

Thomas and Celia Briggs were complete opposites, rarely spent any time together as a couple, and when they were together, they constantly argued. Colton wasn't sure why they'd stayed together all these years. "Isn't it ironic that my parents divorced but were friends and yours hated each other but haven't divorced?"

"Very ironic."

Lauren hadn't had an easy childhood. She hadn't gone hungry or without material things a child needed. But love and affection had been scarce.

"I haven't been home for Christmas in years." Her voice sounded so hollow. "The last time I was there, Dad badgered me about our separation, said I should go back and make it work."

Colton had never been fond of her dad, and he'd liked

him even less after the commander had become his father-in-law. But for once, he agreed with the man.

"We left before dinner. I wasn't about to take advice on making my marriage work from a man with two mistresses."

"Two?" he asked, astonished that the old, polished brass was tarnished. "Is Cecilia aware he's..?"

"Oh, she knows," she said, abhorrence in her voice. "When she found he was cheating on her, which I learned was years ago, she evened the score. She's very fond of Steve, her yoga instructor. A guy half her age and twice as energetic as my dad."

"They're both having affairs?"

Lauren nodded and the mystery of why she'd been so quick to label him an adulterer was solved. "Little Jack and I spend Christmas with Sue and Ed. He's been more of a grandfather to him than my dad ever was. He never misses Little Jack's football games, takes him fishing, and picks him up after school when I have to work late."

Colton was becoming quite fond of his mom's fellow. "Mom's bringing him to Christmas dinner."

"I don't think I've ever seen your mother so happy," she replied, her mood brightening a bit.

Colton missed having Lauren in his bed. He missed waking up beside her and making love to her. But he missed this more. The simple conversation of two people who loved one another. It was just him and Lauren taking a drive on a snowy night, talking like they hadn't been separated for nearly a decade.

It was wonderful.

The last couple of days had been stressful for Lauren, and he was mostly to blame for that. He hoped that in some small way this would make up for it and allow her to relax, at least for a little while. With Mia there, she was more likely to enjoy the evening.

The gravel road curved and Mia's cabin came into view. The western red cedar log home was nestled in a thicket of ponderosa pines a half a mile or so from Whiskey Creek. His dad had chosen a prime spot to build with a fantastic view of the canyon.

Colton had had lots of good times there. He'd spent a lot of time helping his dad construct it. Before the roof had been built, they'd brought sleeping bags and camped out under the stars.

He'd been in his teens then and with no plans for settling down and starting a family. But he'd promised himself that if he had children, this was the life he'd give them. The mountains, fresh air, and time well spent with their dad.

Colton had other memories that were just as precious. The time before, his mom and dad had divorced when the three of them were a family.

He'd started off on the wrong foot with Little Jack, but he'd done his best to make up for the time he'd lost with his son. Fortunately, Little Jack didn't seem scared by his parents' separation. But Colton wanted him to have good memories of his mom and dad together. He wanted his grandchildren to have those memories as well, and those memories weren't going to be made unless he could make Lauren see that their marriage could work.

"Looks like we're not the only guests," she said.

Colton's eyes homed in on Ian's blue crew cab Chevy sitting next to Mai's truck. "Looks that way," he said, trying not to sound as irritated as he felt.

"I know that tone."

"There is no tone." He eased the truck to a halt in front

of the cabin and shoved it into Park. "I wasn't expecting Ian to be here, that's all."

"Why don't you like the man? Has he done something?"

"I'm not sure, but I think he's interested in more than Mia's cooking skills."

Lauren studied him for a second, then clicked her tongue against her teeth in a reprimanding way. "She's a grown woman, Colton."

"That fact is hard to deny," he grumped as they exited the truck. He walked behind her up the stairs and was about to open the door.

"Wait. Aren't you going to knock?"

Knock? He wasn't going to give Ian Moore a warning. "Nope." Ready for what he thought he might see, he twisted the doorknob and shoved the door open. It swung back and hit the wall with a subtle thump.

Lauren gave him a dull, condemning stare.

"What?" he questioned innocently.

"That was real adult of you," she said, walking inside.

He grinned and followed her. He didn't mind having his level of maturity gauged. It reminded him of the old days when he'd acted before thinking and she'd called him on it.

She removed her coat as she looked around the large open room that served as a living and dining room. "I can't believe Jack Reid surrendered his drab utilitarian polish for a bit of panache."

His dad hadn't hired an architect or interior designers. Like most ranchers, he'd chosen practicality over aesthetics. But Mia had added her own touch to the home by juxtaposing the cabin's rustic timbers with a tasteful selection of modern furnishings. She'd incorporated a variety of colorful southwestern style rugs, handwoven Navajo blankets, and Pueblo pottery.

Colton chuckled as he shed his coat and reached to take hers. "It was more like a parley than a surrender."

"Tomato, tomahto," she muttered under her breath.

While he hung their coats on the iron wildlife coat rack by the door, Lauren shoved her hands into her back pockets, an uncertain frown forming across her brow. "Are you sure she's expecting us?"

"I'm sure."

Low giggles emanated from the kitchen, transforming Lauren's frown into surprise. "I told you we should have knocked."

Anger spiked through him. "We're here!"

The giggles stopped, and a red-faced Mia hurried out of the kitchen. "Sorry. I didn't hear you knock."

She wore a pink off the shoulder sweater, snug blue jeans that emphasized her slender legs and a pair of black heels. Colton thought if she'd been his daughter, he would have thrown a blanket around her and made her change into something less revealing.

But as his wife had pointed out, Mia was a grown woman.

"That's okay," Lauren said. "We're early."

Colton was glad Lauren was here because he couldn't manage affable words right now.

Ian sauntered into the living room, prompting Mia's cheeks to a deeper shade of red. "Evenin'."

"Hi, Ian," Laure offered a friendly greeting while Colton remained staunch faced.

"He came by to bring me an early Christmas present," Mia explained, retrieving a cookie tin from the dining table. The tin was larger than the one she'd used before and adorned with a snowy mountain scene.

Judging by the look of adoration in Mia's eyes, the unique gift had earned the ramrod a few high-scoring points in wooing.

Ian took the tin from Mia and cradled it in one arm then, looped his other arm over her shoulders. "A friend of mine makes these for the holidays. I knew Mia would want one."

Mia lay her head against Ian. "Wasn't that sweet of him?"

Colton's stone response to the question caused Ian to drop his arm.

"Ah, yes," Lauren agreed, her cordial enthusiasm holding strong. "That was very sweet. I hope you're staying for dinner, Ian."

"He is," Mia answered for him.

Colton couldn't silence the disgruntled sound that shot from his mouth.

"Well, the food is almost ready," Mia said, her beaming smile dimming as she hurried back to the kitchen.

Lauren picked up a corkscrew from the small serving table where Mia had wine on ice and gave it to Colton. "Be nice," she mumbled with stiff lips so only he could hear. "And make yourself useful while I help Mia."

He stepped to the table and yanked the wine bottle from where it was chilling in a bucket.

Ian's smug smile had vanished the second Mia was out of earshot. "I know what you're thinking."

Colton shoved the screw into the cork and twisted. "I doubt that," he returned because at this moment, the only thing he was thinking about was where he could bury a body if his gut was right and Ian was using Mia's feelings for him as leverage.

The ramrod raked his Stetson off and ruffled a hand through his blonde hair. "Is this going to be a problem?"

Colton set the bottle back in the bucket of ice and braced his hands on the back of a dining chair. "If this is just dinner, then hell, no." He offered Ian a flat smile and extended a hand towards a chair. "Have a seat."

He liked being direct. It was the best way to avoid confusion and misunderstandings. But he didn't want to upset Mia by barking at her guest, so he killed the smile and continued. "But if this is you trying to use my sister for a shady agenda—"

"A shady agenda?" Ian asked, his face tight with contempt.

"You can join Rory and Mitch in the unemployment line."

"How'd'you know about—" Ian's eyes narrowed. "You were there?"

Colton pecked the top of the table with a finger. "Damn, right, I was. There's nothing that goes on at this ranch that I don't know about. You remember that."

That was a lie, and Ian knew it. The ranch was a huge operation and there was no way Colton could monitor the goings-on or whereabouts of every employee.

"If you're saying I have to choose between my job and being nice to Mia —"

"Nice," Colton sneered.

"Then you can take your job and shove it up your—"

"This smells wonderful," Lauren's voice cut through the heated conversation with a louder than normal tone used to signal she and Mia were about to join Colton and Ian at the table.

Colton clamped his mouth tight as the women walked into the room.

Lauren sat a large bowl of pasta on the table and Mia added a basket of garlic bread. "Is everything okay?"

"No." Ian didn't hide his anger. "Unfortunately, it's not."

Colton waited, expecting the ramrod to cut tail and run.

Mia's smile dimmed. "Oh?"

The muscle in Ian's jaw twitched as he weighed his options. He eyed his boss with the same disdainful glower he'd been greeted with.

Colton waited, his air reminding the cowboy that the choice was his. Leave and keep his job or stay and go hungry this winter.

"Ian," Lauren intervened, her tone pleasant but unusually firm. "Mia has prepared a beautiful meal. I insist you stay for dinner."

*Damn it, Lauren.*

"Well, now." Ian's flinty demeanor spun lax because Lauren's invitation had just made him the victor in this silent scrimmage. "I can't turn down an invitation from the boss's wife. It would be rude."

Mia grinned. "It would."

"See, Mia, everything's fine." Lauren took a seat, unfolded her napkin across her lap and cut a sharp glance Colton's way. "Mia thought she heard the two of you arguing."

Ian wrinkled his brow. "Us? Argue?"

Colton helped himself to the spinach tortellini. "Ridiculous."

Lauren added a small portion of pasta to her plate. "That's what I said. Ridiculous."

Ian pulled out a chair for Mia. "We were just discussing an incident that happened earlier today."

"What kind of incident?" she asked.

He took the chair next to her. "I had to let two of our best cowboys go."

Lauren wiped her mouth and reached for her glass of wine. "Why?"

"They broke the Golden Rule," Colton supplied, seeing a second chance for the win.

They waited for him to explain. When he didn't, Lauren cleared her throat, implying to Colton that her patience was stretching thin. "Are you going to tell us what the Golden Rule is, or do we have to guess?"

He took a slice of bread from the basket. "I think Ian can explain it better."

The ramrod's back stiffened because after he explained the rule, his "nice" relationship with Mia would be over. Mia wouldn't cost Ian his job. "They made some filthy comments about you ladies."

"Oh, well," Lauren said, surprised. "That's certainly not acceptable, but hardly worth their jobs, is it?"

Colton wasn't going to let Ian off the hook. "The women of the Lucky Jack are off limits to the cowboys. Period."

"Off limits?" Mia questioned.

"Not only is filthy talk a firing offence, so is flirting, dating, or fraternizing with any of the Ritter women."

Ian's jaw tightened.

Mia's face lost its ruddy color. "That a horrible rule."

Colton valued the long-standing rule that had kept the Lucky Jack running smoothly for generations and had never had second thoughts about it until now. The distraught cast of his sister's face made him wonder if applying the rule was the right thing to do. If he suspected Ian of the embryo theft, maybe he should confront the man and leave the rule and Mia out of it. But he didn't have proof. If Ian was the guilty party, Colton wanted Mia safely out of the way.

One thing was for sure, Ian's explanation of the

Golden Rule had changed the atmosphere of the room from tense to choking. Mia arranged and rearranged the tortellini on her plate. Lauren had abandoned hers for her glass of white wine, her glare so hot, Colton expected to spontaneously combust at any moment.

He and Ian were the only ones eating.

What was supposed to have been a relaxing dinner with his wife and sister had turned into a showdown between him and his ramrod.

*Well, hell.*

Colton couldn't backtrack because doing so would give Ian the freedom to date his sister. He had a responsibility as a brother to protect Mia. He'd made an oath to his dad to protect and care for his sister. That meant he couldn't stand idly by and do nothing while his ramrod seduced her for his own selfish sake.

But he had to lighten the grim mood around the table. His eyes caught sight of a holly wreath Mia had hung above the fireplace. "I saw Claire Chisum in town yesterday," he said to her. "I stopped by the café for a cup of coffee before I went to Bill's office."

When Mia didn't engage, he nudged Lauren's foot with his boot.

She gave him a cowboy-you're-on-your-own shoulder shrug. He arched his eyebrows, pleading for her help.

After a minute or two, Lauren relented. Letting out a light, but impatient huff, she sat her glass on the table and picked her fork up. "Claire used to have the best Christmas parties. I only attended one, but everyone in town talked about them. They were so elegant with fancy decorations, and a buffet loaded with decadent hors d'oeuvre."

"Funny you should mention that." Colton refilled their glasses. "She invited us to this year's party. I think we should go."

"We?" She spit the word out like a piece of rotten fruit.

It was fitting reaction and one he should have expected. They'd never attended one of Claire's parties together. She'd gone by herself. He'd either been away on deployment or off doing his own thing.

"Yes, we," he replied, not caring if Ian or Mia witnessed their marital problems. "As in you and I. Together. In public."

Lauren eyed him suspiciously. Then tucked her tongue to the side of her cheek and drew her lips in a tight bow of frustration. "Colton, I'm only here for a few days."

*Not if I have anything to do with it.*

"The party is next Friday," Mia said, finally biting the conversational Christmas bait Colton had tossed out.

"That's over a week away," Lauren started. "I'm sure I'll be gone by then."

"I don't know," Ian eased into the conversation with a half grimace. "I've heard disputing a will can be pretty tricky and time-consuming. If that's the case, you may be with us until next Christmas."

Lauren's face paled. "Oh, don't say that."

"I can't say I'd mind it." Ian looked at Mia and winked. "Would you?"

Mia's brown curls swooshed from side to side. "Nope. Not at all."

What was Ian up to? Why was he trying to win Lauren over?

"I'm afraid I'm ill prepared for a party," Lauren said, sipping the wine. "I don't have anything nice to wear and I wouldn't feel right—"

"We'll go shopping." Mia's smile showed promise that Colton's attempt to revitalize the evening had worked. "Just us ladies. It'll be fun. If we what we want in town, we'll drive to Billings."

Lauren hesitated.

"Come on," Colton poked Lauren with a jeer that he'd pay for later. "You know you want to go shopping."

Lauren's crystal blues blazed with disdain. "Oh, okay," she surrendered with a syrupy sweet smile that made Colton brace for impact. "I'll do it, but only if Ian agrees to come to Claire's party with us."

"Yes." Mia's eyes lit up as her bottom jaw jaunted forward, daring Colton to object.

Ian held his glass up for a toast. "To the party."

Glasses clinked and Colton was left at the mercy of his wife's stubbornness.

•

# CHAPTER TWELVE

It was close to seven-thirty when Lauren and Colton arrived back at the ranch house. She knew when she invited Ian to attend Claire's Christmas party with them that Colton would be horn mad, but she hadn't cared. He'd declined Mia's offer for dessert, stating he and his men didn't keep late hours.

Ian hadn't taken the hint. He'd stayed for tiramisu, coffee, and whatever else two consenting adults might do when their every move wasn't being monitored by an over-protective brother.

Though she'd finished the tasks Jonas had given her this morning, copious amounts of work remained in preparation for the coming year. She could busy herself with that.

But Colton's behavior at dinner had left her so irritated it would be difficult to concentrate. He'd ruined everyone's evening and had firmly planted himself between Mia and Ian and their chances at romance. Every woman needed romance and at least one great love in her lifetime.

Colton was Lauren's and her life with him before

deployment had been wonderful. Their courtship, their engagement, their wedding, and the short but precious days they'd had as man and wife were bittersweet, but she cherished those memories.

A divorce wouldn't erase them. She could lock them away and swear they were gone. But they'd always be there, etched into her heart until she took her last breath.

That fact brought a sobering view of the future to Lauren's attention. The separation had kept her and Colton apart for years, but during that time, she'd carried the possibility that one day there would be a promising resolution to their marital woes.

The brokenness she'd experienced this morning lingered at the edge of her mind. But she refused to dwell on such gloomy thoughts. The time for healing the rift in their marriage had come and gone. She and Colton had had their chance for happiness, and they'd blown it.

What if Ian was Mia's one great love? That ludicrous rule could destroy their chances together, and that made Lauren piping hot.

Colton had been stubbornly taciturn on the ride back to the ranch house, and when the Marine didn't want to talk, he didn't. His unwillingness to communicate had been one of their biggest obstacles as a couple and the one thing about the man she wished she could change.

But Lauren could be just as stubborn.

Since the issue wasn't about the two of them, their wrecked marriage, or their upcoming divorce, he might talk if she spurred him with the right words. She'd prodded on the way home, but he hadn't so much as muttered a curse.

She gave it one last shot before they went inside the house and parted ways for the night. "You have no one to blame but yourself for what happened."

"No," he said grittily, closing the front door behind them. "I can blame you. You're the one who invited him to stay for dinner and to Claire's party."

Finally! Words!

"You put me in the middle of that juvenile pissing contest between you and Ian. What did you expect me to do? Help you ruin what could be a beautiful relationship with that bogus rule?"

Colton shed his coat, tossed it onto the stair rail, and headed for the living room. "It's not bogus."

He'd evaded the major topic—Mia and Ian's potential romance—and gone straight to defending his rule.

"You're a tenacious, hard-headed mule of a man, Colton Ritter," she whispered to herself.

Standing in that foyer alone, Lauren knew she had two choices. Follow him into the living room and make a case for Mia and Ian's courtship. Or go upstairs and let Mia handle her brother.

The phrase 'pick your battles' came to mind.

Colton said he was tired of wasting time, but he hadn't returned the divorce papers to her. If she rubbed him the wrong way, figuratively, of course, he might assert that pigheadedness into stalling the divorce.

Could he be that spiteful?

Tired, annoyed, and undecided about what she should do, Lauren let her head fall back and closed her eyes. Just go to bed and leave it alone. It doesn't concern you. You'll be gone in a few days, and none of this will matter to you.

But it would. The injustice of that damn rule would haunt her. She might not change Colton's rule, but she could make a strong defense against it.

Thinking that would, at least, clear her conscience, she slipped out of her coat, flung it over his, and walked into the living room. "You can't just blow this off, Colton. You saw Mia's face."

He'd removed a large decanter of amber-colored liquid from the liquor cabinet Jack Reid kept fully stocked and was finishing his first glass.

"Whiskey?"

Lauren sat down on the hearth and watched as the burn brought a slight quail to his lips. "You know I hate that stuff."

Taking his Stetson by the crown, he lifted it from his head and tossed it onto the back of the couch. "I do, but as you said before, people change."

"If the rule isn't bogus, how come I've never heard of it until now?" Lauren challenged, ignoring his sarcasm.

"Why would you?" His left shoulder jerked up, accentuating the question. "You aren't a cowboy working for the Lucky Jack. You're my wife. Mrs. Colton Ritter."

"The boss's wife," she said, adding to the titles he'd quickly throw at her.

"The one and only. 'Till death do we part." There was an undertone of certainty in his voice, a possessiveness unusual for a man with his mind set on divorce.

Easing away from that thought, she focused on undermining his rule. "None of the cowboys ever made an off-colored remark or did anything out of the way to me while I lived here and you were on deployment."

Colton smiled coldly. "Exactly. But since I wasn't here to enforce the rule, I threatened them with castration instead of unemployment."

Lauren rolled her eyes. "What a bunch of malarkey."

"You think I'm kidding? Ask Mack or Duce or any of the others that were working here before I left."

She arched an eyebrow. "Wouldn't talking to the boss's wife jeopardize their jobs? I'm surprised you didn't fire Ian on the spot for helping me find my seat at Bill's office or when he passed me the bread at dinner this evening."

"Look, the rule was put in the place by my great-great," he waved a hand through the air, "something or other grandfather back when this part of the country was a hell of a lot wilder. I don't know the details of who it was or when it was, but it is a genuine rule. It protected the virtue of the Ritter women against the men who worked here. Not to punish them and I'm sure exceptions were made—"

"Then make one," she cut in.

"No," he answered firmly.

"Why not?" She pointed in the cabin's direction. "Mia obviously has feelings for the man, and Ian seems like he's sincere about—"

"Mia is too young."

Lauren scrunched her face. "Huh?"

"You heard me." Glass in hand, he strode past her towards the kitchen.

"Too young?" she repeated, trailing behind him.

He rinsed the glass and turned it upside down on a paper towel to dry. "Yes. Too young."

"W—hoa—hoa," she laughed. "Cowboy. You are soooo overstepping your boundaries."

He shifted his jaw from side to side. "I don't see it that way."

"Let me help you take those blinders off." She held up a finger. "First. You're not Mia's father, so don't try sounding like it's your way or the highway because I guarantee Mia will choose the highway."

Colton assumed a stone stance with his hip against the sink, his arms crossed over his wide chest, and his lips flattened into a wafer-thin line.

Up went another finger. "Second. It's her choice, not

yours and even if it was yours, in your eyes, no man will ever be good enough for her."

His chest expanded with a deep breath, signaling Lauren had hit him in the heart with that truth.

"Third." She saved best–and what should have been the most obvious point to Colton–for last. "Mia is about the age I was when you took my vir –"

"Ah-da-da-da!" he yelled, bouncing from the counter like his backside had rammed with a hot branding iron.

Lauren tried smothering a smile, but couldn't. "All I'm saying is she's old enough to make her own choices about relationships and the men she has sex with."

"Enough." Running both hands up the back of his head, he blistered, "I don't want to hear anymore. You've proven your point."

Convinced that she'd presented a persuasive case for Mia and Ian, she hoisted a smug smile. "Good."

"And you don't have to remind me how old you were the first time we made love." His dark eyes were sensual and soft. "I was there, remember?"

After their separation, recalling the sweet love they'd made the night they were married pained Lauren so badly that she'd blocked it out along with all the other nights she'd laid in his arms. But it only took a second for her to recall every beautiful, earth-shattering moment of their consummation.

"A woman doesn't forget something like that," she heard herself admit with a fragile voice that exposed how vulnerable his question had made her feel.

"Neither does a man." His lips curled into that crooked smile that had hooked her into their first date. "Those were the best times of my life."

She could say the same, but wouldn't. Not now, when the divorce was nearly set in stone. Digging up those nostalgic times wouldn't help her now. "How did this conversation go from the Golden Rule to the first time we made love?"

Colton bowed his head remorsefully. "I've been thinking about that night a lot."

"Have you signed the papers?" she asked, sensing the conversation was swerving towards a road she didn't want to go down.

He waged a soul-deep search into her eyes. "No, and I'm not going to."

Shock expelled a deflated scoff from her lungs. "You're joking, right?"

"We can't change what happened or get back the time we've lost together as husband and wife, or as a family." He unfolded his arms, leaned back against the counter, and braced his hands against the edge. "But we can start over."

Lauren felt like the tile floor under her feet had just crumbled. "What?"

"You heard me, honey." The gentle timbre of his voice washed over her. "You may be willing to throw in the towel and walk away from our marriage. But I'm not."

"Our marriage?" she questioned incredulously. Because no. This wasn't happening. He couldn't back out on the divorce now. "What marriage? And why now? You said you were done wasting time, Colton. That you would–"

"Do whatever you wanted," he finished patiently.

What she wanted was to rewind the years and be there to stop him from riding out into the middle of a snow-storm. But that was as impossible as roping those dreams she and Jack Reid had talked about. "I want a divorce."

"No." He dropped his hands, pushed away from the counter, and walked over to her. Though their bodies weren't touching, heat from him radiated through the layer of her winter blouse and jeans. "You want a healthy, physical relationship with a man who loves and wants you."

Why was he so calm when, just a few hours ago, he'd been quipping and snarky about the subject? "I can't find that perfect man," she shoved that verb in for spite, "unless you give me a divorce."

Placing a bent finger under her chin, he tipped her head up. "You have that man. He's standing in front of you."

Her heart raced as hurt, and disbelief swarmed around her. He wasn't doing this. Not now when they were so close to ending it all. "No," was her firm rebuttal.

"I'm not perfect, never will be, but I love you, Lauren. I always have. From the moment I first saw you, I knew you were the one for me. I wanted you to be my wife, and that hasn't changed."

There had never been a time during their marriage when Lauren doubted Colton loved her.

Never.

Not once.

But when they'd separated, she'd questioned if he'd ever really loved her at all. He couldn't simply waltz over to her now and announce that he was that man.

Did he understand how damaged her heart was or how carefully she'd bandaged it just so she could come back to the Lucky Jack for Jack Reid's funeral? She wanted to be whole again, not a body of fragmented pieces left behind by a bitter breakup. If they reconstituted their relationship and it didn't work, leaving him again would kill her. She'd be dead inside without a chance of healing herself or of having the heart to love another man.

Colton gently raked his thumb across her lower lip, sending shivers over her body. She couldn't remember the last time he'd touched her. They'd tried making love after he'd come home from the hospital, but after three failed attempts, he'd started sleeping in the spare room. From that point on, he hadn't so much as held her hand.

But here they were, eight years later, standing in the kitchen of their house, discussing intimate moments. How was that possible? How had they gone from not speaking to absurd dialogue about starting over?

Colton eased closer, cupped her face with both hands, and tenderly caressed her cheek with his. "I've ached to touch you," he whispered against her ear. "Hold you." He inhaled a broken breath. "Make love to you."

Those words blew across Lauren's skin, consumed her body and, in one swift swoop, ignited that tiny ember inside her.

When he kissed her, all those rebuttals blazing in her brain caught fire and rose like sparks from a fire. They disappeared into the air and there were no more doubts or fears. The heat of his lips as they moved over hers enveloped Lauren in the sweet familiarity of home. Not a structure made of wood and stone. But that special place where she felt cherished and wanted, in the arms of her husband, a man who had once loved her so completely she'd thought nothing but death could separate them.

Caught in a fog of bliss and whimsy, she succumbed to his coaxing lips. She'd wanted this for so long.

He stroked her neck, her shoulders, and upper arms. Inch by sensual inch, his hands moved lower until he was palming her bottom.

That drew a moan from her lips.

He let go of a low growl and planted her against his hard erection. A wave of anticipation washed over her, twisting the tension in her body to an aching knot.

Lauren wasn't anchored by the past, time, or the consequences of what was happening. She was climbing higher and higher toward pleasure and fulfillment, a climatic plateau where nothing mattered.

But the faint sound of an electric ring penetrated the pleasure haze of her mind.

The phone, her brain identified. The phone was ringing. It rang again and again, then stopped with a long beep. "Mom? It's me. Can I spend the night at Grant's house? His parents said it was okay. Call me back. Bye!"

*Mom.*

*Little Jack.*

Lauren flattened her palms against his chest and pushed, breaking the kiss. "Stop."

"Why?" he asked, nibbling on her bottom lip.

"This isn't right."

He rested his forehead against hers. The centers of his brown eyes were black, heavy with desire and befuddlement. "It feels right to me." He kissed her again. "So damn right."

It did. Every inch of Lauren's body craved him. But her common sense was clawing its way out of the murky depths of carelessness to take control. More kissing would lead to Colton making love to her. That, she was sure of. What she wasn't sure of was why this was happening.

"What are you doing?" she asked, taking a step back. "Do you expect me to believe that you're still in love with me? After everything that's happened between us?"

He reached for her. "Lauren—"

She went back another step to keep him at bay and shook her head as a horrible thought entered her mind. "Are you afraid I'm going to leave before Bill can sort through the stipulations of the will? That you'll lose the Lucky Jack if, by some miracle, Edgar finds a loophole. Is that why you're doing this, to keep me here?

Her question brought his eyes to a sharp focus and his brow to a hard, scowling frown. "Is that what you think?"

Everything he'd said — the wild claim of love, starting over and that kiss — had blindsided her. She was so confused, angry at herself for being so gullible and hurt that this might be his petty attempt at seduction to keep the ranch.

However, she had to consider that the indignation shadowing his face wasn't that of a scheming man. She'd wounded him with those accusing questions, and she felt horrible for belting them out. But the alternative was that this was really happening.

Colton was still in love with her.

Her head spun with mixed emotions. "I don't know what I think. I don't know what I feel or why this is happening."

"Why it's happening?" he scoffed. "Jesus Christ. Do I need a motive to kiss my wife?"

"You do when the future of this ranch depends on whether I stay or go," she cried, as what composure she had caved. "And you have to admit, the timing for us starting over is very convenient."

Colton spun around so his back was to her, rested his hands on his hips, and stared down at the floor for a few seconds before he retaliated. "I'm not the man you married, Lauren, but my scruples haven't changed. I would never coax you into sex just so I can keep this place."

Could she believe that? Could she forget all the time and distance between them, and trust that what he's said was because he really loved her?

"But you are right about one thing. I am afraid," he confessed. "I'm scared to hell and back that you're going to leave me again. But nothing I said or did tonight was meant to deceive you. I love you and I'm willing to do whatever it takes to rebuild our marriage."

But was she? If he sincerely loved her and wanted to make their marriage work, could she labor through the guilt and find the courage to ask him for forgiveness like he had her? A marriage built on a foundation of secret regrets and silence would crumble.

"And the kiss…" He hesitated, his eyes smoldering with the memory of the passion they'd just shared. "Was just a prelude to what I want to do to you."

Another jolt of desire hit Lauren in the stomach.

Colton strode to the doorway leading to the foyer and stopped. "If you come to my bed — our bed," he corrected as he heaved a deep breath and let it out, "it will be because you want to be there."

Seconds later, she heard the front door open and close.

# CHAPTER THIRTEEN

After Lauren was sure Colton was in bed and asleep last night, she'd gone downstairs to the den for the laptop so she could get an early start to her workday without leaving the sewing room this morning.

Her mood wasn't any better when she'd awoken than it had been after that kiss. Groggy and unable to concentrate on work, she'd stared out the window, wishing she could change the past.

A little past noon, Lauren saw Mia's truck roll up to the bunkhouse. Ian came out and climbed into the passenger's side.

"Good for you," she mumbled.

Mia backed the truck out and drove towards the east side of the ranch. There was nothing up there but cow camp. "Ah-ha," she said, smiling. It looked as though Mia and Ian had a secret hideaway.

Lauren turned back to the laptop and began tapping her ink pen against her bottom lip, happy that the Golden Rule hadn't detoured the couple from seeing each other.

She hadn't quite got used to having a sister-in-law, but she and Mia had become friends, and if things didn't work out between herself and Colton, she'd invite Mia for a visit in Texas.

*Whoa.*

The pen dropped.

If things didn't work out? When had she made a conscious decision about trying to make anything between her and Colton work?

Obviously, some part of her had. But it certainly couldn't have been her brain. Her body wasn't in charge, and she wouldn't let her heart deliver the final verdict.

So. There was that mystery. Maybe the three had conspired together against her and her need for a single life.

It was day four of the Lucky Jack hostage situation and Lauren's faith that Colton would or was at least trying to rectify the will stipulation was diminishing, so she took the matter into her own hands.

She made herself a turkey sandwich and took a bottle of water from the refrigerator. Then she called the Humphrey and Dane Law Office. The phone rang twice before the answering machine kicked in, stating the office was closed for lunch and would reopen at one. She called Edgar's office and was informed by his assistant that Mr. Wallace was "looking into it."

She gnawed her dill pickle, staring grimly into space as she thought about the consequences of being stuck at the Lucky Jack for a year. She'd built a life in Texas, a life without Colton and now, thanks to Jack Reid, that life was in jeopardy. The two weeks she'd told Jonas she needed would be up soon, and she was losing hope that she'd be free to leave the ranch before the new year.

There was one day left until the weekend. Normally, Lauren looked forward to having a few days off from work. Since Harry's stroke, she'd been working most Saturdays. If she were home, she would have lazed around the house in sweatpants.

But she wasn't at home. That pumped her full of resentment. She was being blackmailed by a dead man and forced to stay at the Lucky Jack against her will. She was also angry that Colton had taken the liberty of kissing her.

Well, maybe not angry. Yes, at first, she'd been livid. But now, she was more confused than mad. Because she'd run up the stairs away from Colton and the intensity of their kiss, shut herself in the sewing room, and sworn she wouldn't be swayed in her decision to divorce him.

But it would have been easier to stop the sun from rising. There was no way she could block out the way his kiss had affected her. Being in his arms again had felt like heaven. Her heart was begging to concede to the magic of the way his "I love you" had brought everything inside her to life.

Lauren hadn't felt whole in years, but in those few seconds in Colton's arms, she'd been complete and happy.

*We can't change what happened or get back the time we've lost together as husband and wife, or as a family…. But we can start over.*

Could they?

She hadn't entertained the idea of starting over past the first two years of their separation or let anything remotely related enter her mind in the years after because to her, it was an impossible feat. But Colton had made it sound so simple.

Did she want to give their marriage a second chance? Yes, more than anything in the world. If she knew, without a doubt, that they could make it work this time, she would have emailed Jonas her resignation last night and put her house in Texas on the market today.

But love didn't come with assurance. Solid, well-established relationships failed. She and Colton had learned that the hard way, so why was he willing to take that risk again?

The reservations holding her back weren't solely about Colton's lack of communication or trusting him to fulfill his part of the marriage. They were also about her ability to stick it out when things got tough.

That kiss had been such a shock, so much so that's she'd come close to calling Mia for a ride to the airport. But then, she'd come to her senses. Running away from the circumstance wouldn't solve anything. There was only one way out of this. She prayed Bill or Edgar came to her rescue.

Lauren felt emotionally off center and out of sorts. She'd burst into tears when a diaper commercial popped up on the laptop screen as she was scrolling through the internet searching for resources on estate planning.

Her menstrual cycle was punctual. It was never, ever late, except for when she'd gotten pregnant with Little Jack. The menace was approaching, which meant it was likely her pendulum emotions were a symptom of PMS.

"Good ol' premenstrual syndrome," she muttered sarcastically, opened the email Jonas had sent her.

She stared at it.

More work he could do himself and should. Jonas was an asshat who didn't appreciate her. She wasn't asking to be placed on a pedestal and worshiped, but a simple thank you every now and again would have been nice. Jonas never gave praise to anyone, especially her. Lauren's stress level was through the roof, and she knew that if she didn't return to the office soon, he'd be finding a new assistant.

Adhering to a schedule when she wasn't in the office was hard, so Lauren had set an alarm on her phone for a lunch break and quitting time.

It was almost four when she logged off the laptop and rubbed her aching shoulder. Her stomach was growling. She hadn't eaten more than a few bites of her sandwich.

She opened the sewing room door and saw a piece of notepaper attached to it. In Colton's handwriting was written: When you're done with work, meet me in the horse barn.

She yanked the note from the door and nervously flipped the paper with a finger as considered her options. She could discard the note and pretend she hadn't seen it, like she'd intended to do with the envelope containing the evidence of Colton's innocence. Or she could be an adult, go to the barn, have a visit with Church, and be civil to Colton.

And if she couldn't be civil? She'd throw horse turds at him. That instantly brightened her mood. Snickering, she descended the stairs, snagged her coat from the hook and slipped it on as she hurried out the back door.

Reflecting off the patches of snow, the evening sunlight made Lauren squint. She held up a hand to shield her eyes so she could see the way to the barn.

Unlike the house, the barn and paddocks had changed drastically. The old, weathered barn which used to house horses had been built when the ranch was established. It had recently been replaced and two more paddocks constructed.

She opened the door and walked inside. The barn smelled of wood, hay, and horses. The aroma reminded her of happier days when Jack Reid had been alive. She could see him smiling down on her, his expression crafty, the way it always was when he was thinking of a brilliant plan.

Some plan, Jack Reid.

Once her eyes adjusted to the lighting, she walked through the corridor between the stalls, rousting whinnies and nickers from the horses. Colton and Church were standing outside the last stable next to the open double doors leading outside to the paddock.

Colton looked up from cinching the saddle. "I wasn't sure you'd come."

Lauren didn't mention that her motive for coming was that she might hurl horse turds at his head. "Well, I'm here."

"I can see that," he said, smiling in a way that resembled the one she'd imagined Jack Reid had as he'd plotted his plan. That semblance made her suspicious, but again, she didn't have proof that Colton was lying about his involvement.

She moved to the other side of Church. "Hey, boy," she whispered, sliding a hand over the sleek golden coat of his neck. "Did you miss me?"

The horse whinnied in response. Sunlight shone through the open barn door, causing his white mane to glisten. The palomino was a beautiful animal and, in Lauren's opinion, one of the best parts of living at the Lucky Jack.

The horse was hers, and she wanted him. But there was no way she could take him to Texas with her. Jack Reid knew that, but he'd probably thought his scheme to get her and Colton back together would work.

*That isn't going to happen.*

Lauren forced herself to take a deep cleansing breath because suddenly that deep sadness she'd felt before was back. Without warning, her eyes began burning with unshed tears.

*Oh, God. Not* now. Suck it up. Don't you dare break down in front of him.

She wasn't a heartless woman. She still loved Colton, cared about him, and wanted the best for him. Admitting those things to herself wasn't hard. Also, their divorce was the termination of something that had once been a beautiful relationship, so there were plenty of plausible reasons why divorcing him made her want to cry.

And if those weren't enough reasons, she could always fall back on her pal PMS. After all, blaming her urge to sob on hormones was a heck of a lot easier than admitting to herself that her heart was having second thoughts about their divorce. "Were you able to reach Bill?"

"No. Darlene refuses to give me his cell number. She said we can talk to him when he comes back next month."

"Next month?" Lauren squawked. "The other day, you made contacting him sound simple."

"Calm down," he instructed patiently. "It will be simple once I get his number."

She tucked her hands inside her coat pockets and leaned back against the stable wall. Thinking about the situation and lack of cooperation from Darlene was giving her a headache. "God, I hope so."

He grinned in that boyish way that unique to Colton. "Doubting my browbeating skills, are you?"

She rolled her eyes. Browbeating. Really? She wasn't in the mood for his flirting antics. This was a serious matter. If the stipulations of the will weren't resolved, she could lose everything just to save Little Jack's inheritance. "What is it about the Ritter men that makes them think they have the power to control everything?"

"I wish I had that power, but unlike Jack Reid, I don't have the audacity to think I can move heaven and earth to get what I want. If I did, you wouldn't have left me."

There it was. The truth about why their relationship had failed, spoken from Colton's lips. She had left him, and in a few days, she'd leave him again. This time, with divorce papers in her hand.

Lauren turned away to wipe her tears quickly and covertly. "Wow," she said. "This is some barn."

From the corner of her eye, she saw him gather the reins in his hand. "Yeah, it's an improvement over the last one."

During the Foundation fundraising events, Colton had worn a black tux and tie and left his Stetson at home. It had been years since she'd seen him with a horse and dressed in full cowboy attire. He was the real and complete package.

Watching him with Church cut a deep gash through the middle of her chest, releasing the same old feelings of fear and guilt. In her mind, she could see him and Boaz riding into the snowstorm, bound for a cold demise.

She closed her eyes. Under normal circumstances, she could handle whatever her period threw at her. But damn it, pitching dreadful visualizations and cheap oversensitive shots at her when she was already an emotional wreck wasn't fair.

"If you're game," he said, leading the horse through the double barn doors and into the paddock. "I thought we'd throw a few ropes."

Lauren opened her eyes and managed an arid laugh. "I haven't been on a horse in years, and I was horrible at roping then. I can't imagine how awful I'd be at it now."

"Come on," he goaded and nodded towards the black plastic calf head he had speared into a bale of hay. "It's just you, me, and the dummy."

This had been a bad idea and escaping back without making a spectacle would be nearly impossible. She tried thinking of any excuse that would get her out of the paddock and back to the house. "I'm expecting a phone call from Jonas, and I left my cell phone upstairs. If he calls and I don't answer, he won't be happy."

He shot her an annoyed glance. "I thought you were done for the day."

"It's just a phone call, and he's my boss. I don't really have a choice, do I?"

Colton cursed under his breath. "I don't get it, Lauren. Mom told me you aced those business classes and graduated college with honors."

"So?"

"Jonas has you by the arm. If he says jump, you jump. Why don't you quit that damn job and find a new one? You're certainly qualified for a better position."

Quit? Oh, you're good at that, she heard Tom Briggs say, his expression stiff and condemning as he towered above her. *That may be your only talent, girl. Giving up.*

Lauren's grasp on those tears was slipping. "Because I finally understand what my dad meant when he said quitting makes you a failure."

Colton's expression shifted from irritation to disdain. "Briggs is a stubborn hard ass who would rather die than give up, even if he knew it was the right thing to do."

Her hold snapped, and the tears came. "When is giving up ever the right thing to do, Colton?"

His eyes came to a sharp focus when he saw she was crying. "Did Jonas say something to you?"

"No."

He studied her for a few seconds, then tucked his chin

into his chest and shifted his stance to one leg. "We're not talking about you quitting your job, are we?"

Sniffing with a weak smile, she swiped a knuckle under her eyes and shook her head. "No."

Colton looped the reins over the rail and walked to her, his concern obvious. "Then what are we talking about? What's got you rattled to tears?"

This was the conversation she'd been dreading. The place in time where she was forced to admit that her dad was right about her courage and failure as a wife. "I'm to blame."

The creases on his forehead deepened. "For what?"

Her tear-filled gaze fell to the ground. "I should have stayed, not turned tail and run when things got tough."

"When things got tough?" he repeated, incredulously.

"My dad was right," she cried. "I was never cut out to be a soldier's wife."

"Briggs is wrong." He tried tilting her head up, but she wouldn't let him. "Honey, look at me."

"I can't," she said, sobbing.

Colton pulled her to him, wrapped his arms around her, and cradled her against his chest. "You're a strong woman, which is why I told you to leave. I knew you would've stayed by my side no matter how bad the situation became."

Why was he trying to comfort her? She was the bad guy. "You don't know that."

He rubbed her back and kissed her head. "I do know that because I know the woman, I fell in love with. You should have walked away long before that night. A hit to the head can be deadly. An inch lower and…" He stopped to take a deep breath. "I don't want to think about what might have happened."

"All I got was a cut to the forehead." She'd never

blamed him for what happened. She knew he hadn't meant to hurt her. He'd been in so much pain emotionally and physically that he'd lost all sense of reality. "But you," she hiccupped, "almost died because I wasn't here to stop you from trying to kill yourself in that damn snowstorm."

He took hold of her upper arms. Frowning, he asked, "Is that what you think? That I was trying to kill myself?"

"You don't have to pretend with me. Lots of soldiers have suicidal thoughts. It's a part of PTSD. I've read all the literature—"

"I've lived the literature, Lauren. You don't have to explain to me what that hell is like." Addled, he took a few steps back and rested his hands on his hips. "I wasn't trying to kill myself."

Why was he denying what had happened? To ease her guilt? Or couldn't he accept that he'd been so far past reason? "Why else would a man ride into a storm like that?"

He clamped his mouth together. After a few minutes of thought, he lifted a hand towards the palomino. "Do you know why Dad named him Church?"

Why did Colton think the horse relevant to the conversation? "No."

"Because when he was out there on a horse, his soul was at peace. He said he thought clearer and whatever was bothering him disappeared. It was his church. His way of centering his mind and connecting with the land healed him. When I left the house that morning, the storm was miles away. I was sure I could make it back before it hit. Stupid, I know, but I thought if I could just get out there, it would help calm all the noise and chaos in my head. I wasn't trying to kill myself."

Colton strode to the barn door and pointed in the snowbank's direction where McCrea had found him.

"When I saw the storm was getting worse, I headed for cover. There's a slot canyon on the other side of Whiskey Creek, just past Mars Falls. I knew I could find cover there and ride out the storm. We used to camp there in the summers when we were teenagers. That's how McCrea found me. He knew where to look."

# CHAPTER FOURTEEN

Lauren collapsed onto the bales of hay stacked along the hall between the stalls, stunned by the truth Colton had just delivered. "All this time, I thought–we thought…"

He felt responsible for the guilt she'd carried about what went wrong with their marriage and couldn't believe she and others thought his ride into a storm had been his attempt at suicide. He wanted to call everyone he knew and set the record straight. But more importantly, he wanted Lauren to be free of that burden.

Riding out on the cusp of an approaching snowstorm was something he'd always regret. He'd nearly frozen to death and put Boaz's life in jeopardy. He hadn't meant to harm himself or the horse, but consequences weren't prejudice to intentions. They tailed actions, and his could have been deadly.

With a shaky hand, she tucked her hair behind an ear then, rubbed her palms over her knees while sucking in a deep breath.

He sat down beside her. "Even if I had been trying to

kill myself, you wouldn't have been able to stop me. You can't blame yourself for what happened with me—with us. I'm the reason our marriage fell apart, the reason you left, and the reason we haven't talked in eight years."

And if he didn't tell her about the will, he'd be the reason this new relationship failed.

"No," she told him. "Not talking for all those years is on me. I felt so guilty, Colton. For everything,"

That explained why she'd run away crying every time he approached her. "And now that you know the truth?"

Rising from the bale, she ran a hand through her hair. There wasn't a trace of guilt anywhere in her eyes. They were as bright and blue as the sky on a cloudless summer morning. "It's like a weight has been lifted from my shoulders."

That had ultimately been his goal, but he'd wanted her to say they could finally have that talk he'd wanted to have for years. He wasn't going to insist that they do. It was Lauren's choice, and pushing her into having that conversation might cause more harm than good.

"I'm sorry you went through all this trouble." Her eyes softened, as did her expression. "Maybe next time?"

*If there is a next time.* He winked at her. "Just say when."

The kiss they'd shared was stuck in Colton's mind, chipping away at the patience he needed to carry out his plan. There'd been a culmination of disbelieve and longing in Lauren's eyes as he told her he loved her. Her soft body pressed against his, her sweet lips... As she walked back to the house, the swing of her hips and of her gorgeous round bottom caused him to sigh.

Damn, what a beautiful sight.

Aching and frustrated, he reluctantly unsaddled Church, returned the horse to his stable and the roping dummy to the tack room, then went to check on his men before calling it a day.

He joined Scrap and the other cowhands near the winter pasture. They were working on upgrading the holding pens by replacing the old wooden structures with stronger prefabricated metal pens. Ian was supposed to be handling the job and overseeing the men, but he'd mysteriously disappeared.

"You just missed him," Scrap said.

The ramrod's truck was parked in its usual place next to the bunkhouse, so how could he have just missed him? "Did he say where he was going?"

"No," Punch answered, holding a portion of the pen in while Scrap bolted it in place. "Just that he'd be back in a couple of hours.

Well, Colton decided, grinding away his back teeth, he'd be here to greet Ian when he returned.

Today they were moving Sampson, a two-thousand-pound Angus bull, from the last wooden corral to one of the newer pens, so they could complete the corral job.

Ranching wasn't something one could do with little thought or consideration. A man had to be alert and cautions when it came to working with animals, especially ones that weighed a thousand pounds or more and tended to be temperamental.

But as Colton was opening the gate to usher Sampson into the other pen, he heard a vehicle easing down the east trail. He glanced over his shoulder for a split second and saw the top of Mia's truck as it rounded the last curve before the land flattened out. What the hell was she doing on the east trail? There wasn't anything up there but that old cabin at cow camp.

His brain kicked in. His missing ramrod, his baby sister, and a secluded cabin. "That son of a bit—!" The impact of

Sampson ramming the gate knocked the words out of Colton's mouth and catapulted him into the air.

He landed hard and straight in the bovine's path's left front hoof. He shielded his head with his arms and rolled to the edge of the chute. But Sampson's back hoof caught him just under his ribcage.

"Boss," he heard Punch yell before the cowboy's boots hit the dirt near Colton's head. "Boss. You alright?"

The pain to his side wasn't as bad as being shot, but it was enough to make him curse. "Yeah," he choked out. Between the fall and the kick, he was having trouble catching his breath.

He rolled to his knees and rested his head against the ground. He lay hunched over until he was sure he could get up on his own. After five or so minutes, his pride demanded he get to his feet whether his body wanted to.

It protested, but he stood. The spot under his ribs was throbbing and hurt like hell, but he was sure the damage was superficial.

Mac lifted the brim of his greasy Stetson and gave his head a scratch. "Might need an x-ray to make sure your ribs aren't cracked or broken."

"I'm fine," he lied. Holding his midriff, he limped towards home.

Punch followed.

"I don't need a nurse, Punch," he said.

Punch didn't give a response, and Colton knew he wasn't going to shake the cowhand's determination to see him safely home.

A few feet shy of the back porch, he saw Lauren standing at the kitchen sink. Her head was down, and she hadn't seen him yet. Colton didn't want to alarm her, and he knew if she saw him like this, covered in dirt and looking as though he'd been tossed in a bag with a wolverine, she'd panic and do everything she could to nurse him back to health.

His spirit perked, as did other parts of him. He was tempted to take advantage of the situation. But Lauren had been through enough because of him.

There wasn't much chance he could slip by her unless he went around the house and through the front door, but he didn't have the strength for that. He'd be lucky if he made it up the porch steps.

Taking the steps one at a time, he was about to conquer the last one when he heard the back door swing open.

"Oh, God. What happened?"

"Sampson ran him over," Punch supplied. "Caught him in the ribs. He won't let us take him to the hospital."

"Below the ribs and I'm fine." Colton punctuated his assurance with a pat to her cheek as he eased past her and into the house.

"Thank you…" Lauren paused. "I'm sorry, but I don't know your name."

"Punch Baker, ma'am. I'll be at the bunkhouse if he changes his mind."

"I won't," Colton introjected.

Lauren closed the door and came to his side. "You should go to the—"

"No." He cut her off, gripping the newel post for support as they tackled the stairs. "I've had my fill of doctors and hospitals. I'll be fine. I just need a hot shower, a couple of Tylenol, and a bed."

"Then at least let me help you." She took hold of his arm, looped it around her shoulders, and placed her hand in the middle of his lower back. "Ready?"

"Yeah," he managed, through the torrent of desire building in his body. With each step, her body rubbed against his. By the time they made it to the top, he was hurting in places a Tylenol couldn't help. Again, he was tempted to let her nurse him.

She gave his dirty clothes a once over. "What about your clothes?"

"They're dirty, but salvageable."

"I mean," she reached for the top button of his shirt, "do you'll need help take them off?"

Catching her hand, he squinted, one eye closed. "That's not a good idea."

She frowned. "Why not?"

There wasn't a licentious bone in Lauren's beautiful body, and he loved her even more for trying to take care of him. Making love to her would cure all his ills. But he knew she wasn't willing to soothe that ache.

Holding her eyes with his, he purposefully led her focus to the protrusion she'd erected inches below his belt. "Because if you start undressing me, I'm going to need more than a pill to ease my pain."

She jerked her hand away from his and blushed deep pink. "Oh."

He wiggled his eyebrows up and down. "Maybe next time," he baited for her to reply with just say when.

"Funny," she said, giving him a scowl.

He grinned.

"I am sorry, though. I mean about, well, you know."

"No reason to be. This," he pointed to his crotch, "has been a reoccurring problem lately. But I've learned to live with it."

"Okay, then," she said, moving towards the stairs. "I'll just find us something to eat. I'm hungry. Are you hungry? Ah–I mean," the blush on her cheeks deepened to red as she stammered to correct herself. "For food."

Colton chuckled, then winced and held his side. "No. I think I'll turn in after I shower."

"Right. I'll see you tomorrow." She thumbed towards the sewing room. "You know where I am, so if you need anything—I mean, well, you know. Not that, but—"

"Goodnight, Lauren."

"Goodnight."

❧

RED-FACED AND REELING FROM EMBARRASSMENT, LAUREN had extracted her foot from her mouth and gone to the kitchen for an apple and yogurt.

Major had joined her. He lay contently by the chair, sighing periodically as if he were bored.

Scraping the last bite from the cup, she twisted the spoon around and inserted it into her mouth, backwards. Then she licked the spoon clean.

The shade of crimson she'd felt burn her cheeks lingered, as did the image of Colton and his "reoccurring problem".

She bit into the apple and chewed. "Are you hungry? Are you hungry?" She groaned and glanced down at Major. "Can you believe I asked him that question?"

The dog whined.

"I almost undressed the man, for goodness' sakes!"

And then she'd blushed. She sat back in the chair and chewed the apple. "I mean, it's not like I haven't seen it before." She bristled, teetering her head back and forth. "I shouldn't have been all shocked and bothered by my husband's erection."

But she had been and still was. It was weird that she was now referring to Colton as her husband and not her soon-to-be-ex.

The water pipes pinged against the inside wall when he turned the shower on. Lauren worried about him being in the shower alone. What if he passed out and hit his head? Or what if he was wrong and his ribs were broken? Getting stomped on by a bull wasn't something a man could just brush off. But Colton had. She knew he'd continue to do so and there wasn't anything she could do about it. He wouldn't budge unless he wanted to.

"Stubborn man."

A few minutes later, she'd heard the water shut off and the sound of him moving around the master bedroom. Before long, there was nothing but the sound of Major's light snoring filtering through the silence of the old house.

Night was falling over the Lucky Jack. The quiet darkness was nothing new to Lauren, but something about tonight was different.

She was different.

Having carried guilt for Colton's near-death experience for years, she wasn't sure how to feel now that it was gone. Relieved, of course, but also skeptical that what he'd said was the truth. Riding out that morning had been his attempt at calming his mind and, in some small way, healing himself. The incident was nothing more than a mishap and a misunderstanding on her part.

She was tired, but it was too early for bed, so she went to the living room in search of one of those cowboy novels Jack Reid always kept on hand.

He'd moved out of the ranch house years ago but left a complete series of western thrillers on the top shelf of the bookcase just for her. He hadn't told her that, but she knew because every time he'd dropped by, he'd asked about what she was reading. Then she made coffee, and they'd discussed their favorite characters and plots.

It had given Lauren something to look forward to and helped to stimulate her brain when, most days, her only companion had been a child. She missed him so much and wished he were here now.

Mysteries were her favorite to read. Before she knew it, she'd read three-fourths of the novel before realizing it was hours past her normal bedtime.

Once the lights were out and the doors were locked, Lauren climbed the stairs. After she changed into her nightgown, she walked down the hall to the bathroom. She'd left her supplies there the night before. Since she was the only one using the bathroom, moving them back and forth made little sense.

She brushed her teeth and washed her face and was about to apply moisturizing cream when she heard a faint noise. Listening closer, she tried to identify what it was and where it had originated from. The sound came again from the master bedroom. It was the woeful moan of someone in great pain.

Colton.

She rushed from the bathroom and down to the bedroom door. Major met her there. "It's probably just another nightmare," she whispered to the dog as if he might agree.

The moan came again.

Major leaned his head to one side and whined.

But what if it wasn't just a nightmare? What if Sampson had done actual damage? Colton could be bleeding internally.

The dog pawed the door lightly.

It wouldn't hurt to do a quick and quiet in and out just to make sure he was alright, so she twisted the knob, careful not to let the antique piece rattle too much, and went into the room. Major pushed past her and over to the bed. She followed, tiptoeing so she wouldn't disturb the creaking hardwood floorboards.

Light from the quarter moon filtered through the thin curtains, shading the lower half of the empty bed a pale gray. The moan came again, and the bed moved with the extension of Colton's left leg. From the position of his body, it seemed he'd fallen onto the bed.

"No," he moaned, his face covered in sweat and his expression tight with pain. "Lauren, please. God, no."

Chills washed over her. Why was he having a nightmare about her? What had she done to haunt his dreams?

"I'm sorry, honey," he bawled, his hands clenching the sheets. "Blood... so much blood."

Her heart twisted. Colton was reliving her crash into that desk the night she'd left the ranch. Their talk this afternoon must have triggered it.

*You should have walked away long before that night. A hit to the head can be deadly.*

He'd been quick to say she wasn't to blame for what had gone wrong in their marriage. That was true to an extent. She wasn't responsible for the PTSD or the state of Colton's mental well-being when he'd come home from deployment. But she was the reason he was being tormented by this nightmare. She wanted to rid him of the guilt as he had her.

Moving to the side of the bed, she folded a leg under her and eased onto the mattress. The dark hair of his torso glistened wet in the light. Sweat pooled between his pecs and rolled down the valley formed by the hard muscles of his stomach.

Beneath his ribcage was a large purple bruise. The outline resembled a hoof. Sampson's, no doubt, and proof the bull had stomped him hard. The handstitched patchwork wedding quilt she'd made lay low across his bare hips, reminding Lauren that her husband always slept naked.

*If you come to my bed-our bed, it will be because you want to...*

She ignored the echo of his words and the sudden, desire twist of her ovaries. She was here to help him, not reclaim her spot in their bed.

His face contorted, pulling his eyebrows upright in the center of his brow as his mouth flattened with heart wrenching cry. "I didn't mean to…"

She had to do something, but what? She'd learned early on not to wake him from a nightmare. He'd nearly taken her head off with a swing the first and only time she did that. But that night, his mind had been caught up in the terror and the fight-or-flight emotions of a gunfight.

Tonight, the scene playing out in his head was downstairs in the den. She might not wake him, but maybe she could take control of the dream. It was risky. He might hurt her without meaning to. If that happened, he'd never forgive himself. But she'd be careful to watch his movements closely in case she had to dodge his defense.

"Colton," she whispered.

He whimpered, his head rolling from and side to side.

"It's me, Lauren." She eased farther up the bed and propped her weight on one hand. "I'm okay, Colton."

Her words ushered the same response. He could hear her, but couldn't latch hold of her words.

Swallowing back apprehension, she placed a hand on his shoulder. His skin was warm and damp, but not feverish. "It's okay," she whispered with a slight nudge. "You didn't hurt me. There's no blood. It was just a scratch."

"No," he rushed out. "No. Please, come back to me."

What happened next was like a well-orchestrated plan devised to teach Lauren a lesson. Don't sneak into a man's room in the middle of the night, especially if you know he sleeps in the nude.

Colton kicked his leg. His foot hooked the quilt, yanking it midway of his thighs. And there he was. Uncov-

his internal clock had automatically kicked in at four-thirty this morning. When he opened his eyes and found Lauren beside him, he'd thought it all a dream, a vision conjured by his aching heart and carnal need. But hallucinations weren't soft and warm, and they didn't stretch or sigh.

Lauren was real, tangible, a flesh and blood woman that he could reach out and touch and damn if he didn't want to.

Those mornings when they were first married, he'd lain awake watching her sleep just like he was now. In those moments, he thought himself the luckiest man on earth.

She was all he'd ever wanted and still was. He could lose everything but her and Little Jack. They were the missing parts of his soul, the broken pieces of his heart, and the only hope he had of living a full and happy life.

Colton rose to an elbow and propped his head on his hand so he could see her better.

She lay on her back with her head turned towards his chest. The position exposed her throat. The vein at the base of her neck pulsed slowly. A stark contrast to the blood pumping through his body. A rosy glow brushed her cheeks, and her pink mouth was pouty in a sleeping pose.

God, she was beautiful.

One hand was tucked beneath her chin. The other was laid across the slight rise of her lower belly. Clad in that ivory slip of a gown, she tempted him so. The thin silk draped her body, leaving nothing to the imagination.

But Colton didn't have to envisage what was hidden under the silk. He knew, had mapped out, caressed, and kissed every inch of his wife's body. He'd held those firm, full breasts in his hands and lavished her nipples with his tongue.

And he'd done other things, sweet things that made her cry out and beg. His eyes dropped downward past the curve of her hip and lower to the crux of her thighs. He'd been there too. Cradled between her legs, loving her fully, completely, for hours at a time until neither of them had the strength to move.

A sharp and painful jolt of desire hit him. He could have hammered a hole through concrete. Lugging in a tattered breath, Colton conceded to temptation, and laid his hand on Lauren's hip. She wiggled closer.

He fought a groan. His dick was now nestled against that soft, hot thatch of hair he'd fantasized about seconds ago. The feel of him pressing against her body roused a needy whine that expelled as a warm, moist breath against his chest.

Partaking of his temptations had backfired. Taking Lauren would be so easy. He could feel himself sliding into her, and her tight body closing around his hard sheath. The pleasure he could give them both and the release would be phenomenal.

But that was the downside to impulses. When one was satisfied, another one sprang up.

The fracture of their separation had been left unattended and allowed to widen. Healing it had to be done in steps. Going from barely talking to making love without working through their problems would be a mistake.

Colton knew if he went against his word, if he coaxed Lauren into making love, he'd be jeopardizing their future together. He'd risked too much already. Plus, she was vulnerable in so many ways, and he wasn't going to take advantage of that—of her. When they made love, she'd be lucid. She'd make that choice on her own with her heart and her head.

She stirred, arched her back and pushed her pelvis against his, grinding away his doggedness and reasoning with every twist of her hips.

"Easy, honey," he whispered, his voice tight and rattley.

Her lids eased open, but it took a few seconds for her somnolent mind to figure out where she was and who she was with. "Colton?"

He'd suffered through his fair share of morning erections since their separation. Painfully wasteful, they left him in a growling mood and usually set the tone for his day. But he wasn't going to vent his sexual frustrations by the gnashing of teeth. "I'm more than willing to make love to you here and now, if you're sure it's what you want." Brushing a thumb along her jaw, he smiled. "But I don't think it is."

She scurried back, securing space between them, then gulped, her cheeks growing redder by the second. "We were worried about you."

"We?"

"Me and Major."

He looked to the bottom of the bed where the Shepherd lay sleeping. "Did he open the door for you?"

"You had a nightmare."

Those were nothing new, but this one must have been a doozy, or she wouldn't have chanced coming into the bedroom when she knew he slept in the nude.

She was adorable when she was flustered, and he couldn't resist teasing her. "So you thought jumping into bed with me would help to soothe me?"

"I didn't jump into bed with you," she scoffed.

He raised his brows. "Yet here you are."

She rebounded with a hard shove to his chest.

Pain lanced through the underside of his ribcage. "Oww," he chuckled through it and fell back on the bed.

"Oh, I'm sorry," she said, wincing. "I forgot."

He looked down at the large purple discoloration left by Sampson's hoof.

"It looks bad," she said, sitting up in the bed.

"I've had worse," he said, holding up his left hand. "A lot worse."

"That doesn't mean this isn't a serious injury." Shifting her weight to one hand, she leaned closer to gently probe the area around the bruise.

The quilt had gone with him when he'd rolled onto his back, obscuring his morning hard-on from her. She was innocently sidetracked by his injury, and completely unaware of how her touch was escalating his arousal.

"So, I had a nightmare?"

She glanced up at him, her expression staid. "You don't remember?"

"I usually don't," he said, pausing to suck in a breath when her elbow accidentally brushed the quilt. "And when I do, it's only bits and pieces."

She jerked her hand back. "Did I hurt you?"

"Let's just say that a man can only take so much before he explodes." Holding the quilt over his crotch, he scooted up in the bed. "And I'm close to detonation."

Her focus dropped to his hand and a split second later, she understood his metaphor. "Mornings are," she said, wincing as she retreated from the bed.

He raised a questioning eyebrow to tease her further. "Mornings are what…?"

She motioned towards the quilt and cleared her throat. "Hard, that is—it's hard, I mean—"

Colton burst into laughter. "Ouch."

She folded her arms across her breast and punished him with a searing glare. "Serves you right for laughing at me. To think I was worried about you."

"Well." His laughter tapered off into sporadic chuckles as he swung his feet to the floor. "I appreciate you care enough to risk life-threatening embarrassment to make sure I'm okay, but I'm fine."

"Are you, Colton?"

Securing the quilt around his hips, he stood. She was really worried about him when she shouldn't be. He'd taken tougher punches before going into the Marines and there, he'd been in more hand-to-hand combat than he cared to mention. He didn't want to be the reason she worried. "If it makes you feel better, I'll get the bruise checked out."

"It would, but that's not what I'm talking about."

"Then what are you talking about?" he asked, walking to the dresser drawers that housed his underwear.

Lauren's shyness disappeared as she studied him. "How often do you have that nightmare?"

They were back to that. The tangle with Samson had left him exhausted, so he'd fallen asleep as soon as his body hit the bed and he'd slept soundly. When he was that tired, he rarely remembered anything he'd dreamed.

He wasn't keen on sharing war stories with her, but he'd offer her a pacifying conversation. "I told you, I don't remember most of them, so you're going to have to be more specific.

"The one about me hitting my head?"

Guilt punched him hard, so hard that his stomach knotted. He stopped searching the drawer to look away. "Not nearly enough."

"Don't say that," she ordered. "What happened wasn't your fault."

"Was there some other fool running around the house that night?" he shot back. "Was he the one who pushed you into that desk? Made you bleed?"

"You were confused, Colton."

"That doesn't excuse what I did, Lauren."

"Then finish your apology, the one you started the day of Jack Reid's funeral. That was what you were trying to do, wasn't it? Apologize for hurting me?"

He'd been trying to make amends for all his wrong doings when she'd floored him with those papers. "Yeah."

She began tapping her foot. "I'm waiting."

"I'm sorry," he managed.

Lauren flashed him a smile. "I accept your apology. Does that make you feel better?"

Nothing would ever absolve him of that guilt, and he'd never make her understand that. "No."

Her smile melted. "You can't hold on to this."

The talk of nightmares and guilt had taken a perfectly pleasant morning and turned it into a mood disaster. He was done talking about that night. "I have some place to be, so if you don't mind, I'd like to get dressed."

Her mouth contorted into a twisted smirk. "Oh, I see. You're shutting me out, again."

*Oh, Jesus. Here we go.* "No."

"And you think dropping that quilt will make me leave?"

There was a thought. Because, as fascinating as it was, the fact remained. No matter how many times they made love, seeing him naked always made her uncomfortable.

"Well, Cowboy," she cocked her head. "Think again. There's nothing under there that I haven't seen up close and personal."

*We'll see about up-close and personal.* "That's awfully big talk for a woman who can't kiss her husband without blushing."

She raised her brow and assumed a bored mien. "Roast me all you want, but I'm not leaving this room until you let go of that guilt."

A man couldn't simply open his hands and let penance

fly away. Life didn't work that way, and there was nothing Colton could do or say to convince Lauren otherwise. Dropping the quilt wouldn't end the conversation, but it would throw a wrench into her argument for a little while.

He looked her dead in the eyes and let go of the quilt. But it didn't fall to the floor as he'd planned. Instead, the top portion caught on his erection and hung precariously for a second or two, just enough time for him to smile. He shifted his stance and down went the quilt.

Arms crossed, foot tapping, Lauren shoved her chin forward and stared back at him. It was a stalemate, a silent battle of wills that he knew he'd won when her jaw started rolling from side to side.

*One.*

*Two.*

*Thr–*

"Oh, whatever!" she blistered, tossing up her hands as she did an about face and headed for the door. "Have it your way."

If he'd had his way, the morning would have gone very differently. He wouldn't have been standing bare assed in the middle of the room with a full erection and no relief in sight.

～

THERE WAS AN ICY EDGE TO THE MORNING AIR AND A SCANT trace of snow riding the wind as Colton loaded Major into the front seat of his truck and drove towards town.

Patches of the last snowfall lay scattered atop the brown pasturelands of nearby ranches and farms. Come spring, those fertile acreages would erupt with dark green grass thanks, in part, to the runoff from perennial snowfields and glaciers.

The colossal uplift of the Big Belt Mountains loomed across the horizon. Bare above the evergreen tree line, the mountains' jagged crags of blue and gray climbed westward, while their white peaks soared above the skyline and vanished into the clouds. The mountains were a wild and dramatic milieu for the small, quiet town of Crossfire Canyon.

The veterinary clinic was a few miles past the town, which meant Colton had to navigate the morning crowd of ranchers, business owners, customers, teachers, and school children. He kept his speed below the limit and paid extra attention when he passed the elementary school.

The school crossing was just ahead, so he slowed the truck and prepared to stop. Margie Centerfield, a grand-mother of three and a part-time waitress at the Crossfire Café, held her Stop sign up and walked into the middle of the street, halting vehicles and allowing safe passage for the children.

Major had kept the same dreary-eyed and depressed expression for most of the trip, only lifting his head once when the truck bumped roughly across the train tracks at the outskirts of town. But the chatter of the children's voices caused him to raise and observe.

Colton scuffed a hand over the dog's head and scratched his ears. "Maybe that's what you need. A few curtain crawlers," he said, chuckling at the nickname locals used for kids. "They'd keep you on your toes."

Major whined and licked Colton's hand, seemingly in agreement.

He grinned. "Yeah, I'd like that too."

This morning would have been a perfect time for baby making, but… He sighed and reminded himself of those steps.

Before he could give Lauren those babies they both

wanted, they had to overcome obstacles. He had to convince her their marriage wasn't beyond saving. She was fighting him tooth and nail for that damn divorce, and he knew she would buck hard and hot against his refusal to sign those papers. There hadn't been an easy way for him to break the news to her, so he'd just said what was in his heart. That was something he had little practice doing and a problem, as she'd so vehemently pointed out during the ride home that first night.

Colton was committed to fostering open lines of communication between himself and Lauren. But talking wasn't enough. He had to rebuild that husband-and-wife closeness he'd once had with her.

Confiding in others about his feelings had never been one of his strong suits. He knew now that communication was an important part of their relationship and refusing to discuss his guilt for hurting her hadn't exactly helped his push for emotional intimacy or trust.

He had to work on that.

When he and Lauren first met, the proverbial head-over-heels had happened in unison. They'd both been goofy in love from the beginning.

He didn't have a charming bone in his battle-scared body. "So how does a man make a woman fall back in love with him?" he asked Major.

The dog replied with a jaw-breaking yawn that ended as a long, drawn-out sigh, settled back into his lion pose and pretended to sleep.

"Some best friend you are."

Colton had to figure it out quickly because time was against him and sooner or later, it would run out. He could keep Bill at bay for a few weeks, but now another lawyer was involved. An expert in estate planning.

Jesus, he'd really tripped himself into a mess this time.

Edgar was probably digging through the county records at this very moment.

Colton didn't know what he'd do when Lauren learned the truth of Jack Reid's will or how he'd handle lying about its existence. After she'd stormed out of the bedroom, he'd thought about what he'd say to her. But no matter how he told the story, the inexcusable fact was that he'd lied to her.

A car horn beeped behind him.

The children were across, and Margie had lowered her sign to wave him through. He let off the brake, responded with a friendly four-finger wave without lifting his hand from the stirring wheel and continued through town.

It was almost eight-thirty when they reached the clinic. They were early for Major's eight-forty-five appointment. Colton pulled into the nearly full parking lot and found a space at the back of the building.

He led Major inside. The dog's joints didn't move well when the weather was cold, so he'd let the truck warm before heading into town. But the heat hadn't helped. The old dog was moving slowly.

Colton informed the receptionist they were there and noticed a job posting on the bulletin board next to the desk. Val's practice was looking for an office manager.

The job might help him convince Lauren to stay in Crossfire Canyon. Working in veterinarian office wouldn't be like working for the mayor, but then again, maybe it would be. "Jonas the Bear," he scoffed and took a seat in the waiting room.

A short while later, a door behind the receptionist's desk opened and a young blonde woman dressed in blue scrubs stepped out with a clipboard in her hand.

She called Major's name and smiled politely as Colton and the dog walked through the door. "I'm Beth. How are you today?"

"I'm fine, but I'm afraid Major is a little under the weather."

"Ah," she crooned, looked down at the dog. "That's too bad. Maybe we can help him feel better."

Beth placed them in a room and went about giving Major a preliminary exam, checking his weight and temperature, and going over a list of symptoms. Once it was complete, she gave the dog a pet and went to the door. "The doctor will be with you soon."

Thirty-five minutes later, D.V.M. Valery Dutton a.k.a. Dr. Val came into the exam room. "Good morning," she greeted Colton, then turned her attention to Major. "How's our boy doing?"

Val was a retired Army veterinarian and a leg amputee. She'd seen her share of battle and was an excellent triage surgeon. She'd provided front line care at multiple treatment facilities in Afghanistan for Military Working Dogs.

"He's seen better days."

"I was sorry to hear about Jack Reid," she said, sympathetically. "Everyone here was fond of him."

"It's been hard on us all," Colton admitted.

Val looked at her clipboard. "No appetite, lethargic. He's lost weight since his check up in May. How long has he had these symptoms?"

"It started a few days before dad passed away."

Val gently prodded the dog's abdomen. "Any nosebleeds or rapid breathing?"

"Not that I know of."

She examined his eyes and mouth. "No mucus."

"I'm no vet, Val, but I did some research online." He made long strokes down Major's back. "His symptoms can be a sign of hemangiosarcoma."

"True. But animals mourn, Colton, just like we do, and his symptoms can also be attributed to Jack Reid's death."

She picked up her clipboard and tucked it into the crook of her arm. "I want to keep him here overnight."

"Why?"

"We'll do some bloodwork and diagnostic testing just to make sure." She laid a hand on Colton's shoulder. "Let's not worry until we have too, okay?"

His throat tightened. "Yeah."

"Good." She smiled down at Major. "I'll send Beth in to get him."

"Oh, Val," he said, stopping her before she walked into the hall. "Are you still looking for an office manager?"

"Yes, I am. Why? Do you have someone in mind?"

"As a matter of fact, I do."

"Your wife?"

He was surprised. Val's practice had opened two years ago, and she'd been in Afghanistan when he and Lauren were married. "Yeah, but—how'd you know about my wife?"

Val laughed. "This is Crossfire Canyon. You can't poop without the whole town knowing what shade it is."

He laughed. "That's accurate."

"Have her apply but let her know that we're adding an equine wing to the practice next year. If she gets the position, she'll be responsible for both."

"I will and thanks."

"No problem," she said and exited the room.

The vet tech returned a few minutes later, and Colton said his goodbyes. "We'll take good care of him, Mr. Ritter."

Colton felt odd driving away without his canine buddy, but he knew his stay was necessary. He didn't want to think about what Val might find or the decisions he'd have to make if it was cancer.

# CHAPTER SIXTEEN

AFTER LOSING THIS MORNING'S QUILT DROP SHOWDOWN TO Colton, Lauren had showered, dressed, and logged onto the laptop to check her email. He and Major had descended the stairs a little while later. At seven-thirty, Lauren had heard him walk outside and the crank the truck engine to a start.

She'd inched the curtain back and watched from the sewing room window as he helped the old dog into the passenger side of the truck cab, his undertakings careful and patient. After the dog was situated, he went around and climbed in behind the wheel.

When Colton's truck was just a dot on the horizon, Lauren had let the curtain fall into place and set about preparing for her day.

The video conference had gone well and thanks to Belle and the other volunteers, Lauren felt confident this year's Christmas parade would be a success.

She had monthly reports to finish, invoices to process, and high on her boss's priority list was the email she needed to send to the town council regarding next year's budget meeting, scheduled for the first week in January. A meeting which Jonas expected her to attend in person.

But it was hard to concentrate on anything but the last twenty-four hours. After Colton had explained to her he hadn't gone into that storm to hurt himself, things were different between them. Something had shifted, and Lauren wasn't sure where to plant her feet. Before, she was certain. Their marriage was over, but now she wasn't so sure.

Her heart felt different about the possibility of building that new relationship with her husband.

"My husband," she repeated aloud because that word, that title, had a new meaning to her. She couldn't explain it or attempt to understand it, but when she thought about Colton, she felt happy and lightheaded like she had when they'd first married before the honeymoon stage had ended.

Her mood had changed, too. She didn't want to cry or wish for a life she thought she'd never have, because Colton was offering her the chance to make a new life with him. They could have more children and she and Little Jack could come home.

That possibility had opened Lauren's heart and allowed her to lower her defenses. Waking up beside him this morning had been more than awkward, overly embarrassing, and painfully erotic.

Even now, her body was pulsating from the aftershocks of seeing him fully aroused.

Colton wanted her. He'd made that clear when he'd kissed her, but she'd been so shocked by it all that she'd passed it off. However, there was no ignoring his reaction to her this morning.

Hadn't that been one of the reasons she'd initiated the divorce? She wanted a healthy, physical relationship with a man who loved her. A man who needed her. A man who wanted to touch her.

You have that man, he'd said. She hadn't believed him, not at first, but now...

*I'm not perfect. Neither was she.*

*But I love you, Lauren. I always have.*

The Colton she'd woken up with wasn't the man she'd left eight years ago. He wasn't cold or distant and there hadn't been an ounce of confusion in those dark brown eyes as he'd stared down at her this morning.

Only love and desire.

*I'm more than willing to make love to you here and now if you're sure it's what you want.*

Lauren let out a frustrated groan.

She wanted Colton to make love to her. She craved him and there wasn't a worry in her mind that he could physically satisfy her. But she had doubts he could fulfill her in other ways. She wanted to be a part of his life outside the bedroom, and she wanted him to be a part of hers as well.

"Ho. Ho. Ho."

Lauren jumped as Mia's jovial holiday greeting echoed up the stairs. "I'll be there in a sec." She laid her glasses on the makeshift desk and headed to the kitchen, where she knew her sister-in-law would be waiting.

Mia turned from the window, her smile wide and a touch of rosiness on her cream-colored cheeks. She resembled a burst of fresh winter air.

"You look happy." Lauren crossed her arms and leaned against the open door of the kitchen. "What's up?"

Off came Mia's beanie and coat. "Nothing much. I just dropped off supplies at the bunkhouse, and I thought I'd come by to see if you needed anything."

Ah, Lauren thought. The bunkhouse. So that rosy

color on the young woman's cheeks wasn't from the cold. "How's Ian?"

Mia's smile fell. She scooted a chair out and sat down at the table. "Don't tell Colton, please."

Lauren let her arms fall and took a seat across from her. "I'd never rat you out."

"This rule of his is depressing," Mia grumbled, and crossed her arms over her chest like a disgruntled child. "It's almost Christmas. We should be baking cookies and decorating, not moping around with our lips dragging the floor."

Lauren wasn't at the mercy of a rule, but she could relate to unfair predicaments. She'd given Sue an extra key so she could collect Lauren's mail and water her plants while she was in Montana, but their new house was vacant.

That thought was disheartening. It would have been her and Little Jack's first Christmas in their small, two-bedroom brick house. They'd talked about sitting under the Christmas tree in the corner, and she'd bought a pretty wreath at the fall craft fair for the front door.

Because of Jack Reid's illness, Lauren and Little Jack had celebrated Thanksgiving dinner alone in the small dining room. It had been an eye-opening experience for her. Now that they weren't living with Sue, she'd see less and less of a woman who'd become her closest friend.

The house didn't feel like home yet. She'd hoped celebrating Christmas in it would help them settle in. Now all their plans were on hold.

But Lauren refused to be depressed about things she couldn't control. "Well." She shoved her hands into the back pocket of her jeans, slouched her shoulders, and let out a breath between her lips that made her sound like a motorboat. "Like I said. I'm a horrible baker."

A part of Mia's smile came back. "How about a little decorating?"

Lauren had a hunch that nothing Mia did could be classified as little. She didn't share the woman's enthusiasm or feel the need to immerse herself in dusty garland and faded red Christmas bows. But she couldn't turn Mia down. "Sure, but I have to finish a few things first."

"Yay," Mia jumped from her seat and raised both hands into the air as if her favorite team had just scored. "It'll be fun. You'll see."

Mia went about unpacking the Christmas decorations from the upstairs hall closet while Lauren worked to compose the email to the town council.

≈

MIA HAD ADDED TO THE LUCKY JACK COLLECTION OF Santas by buying a new piece each year she celebrated Christmas at the ranch.

"This one is adorable," Lauren said as she unwrapped a baking Santa, complete with a chef's hat and apron, and placed him near the stove.

Mia fitted the table with a bright green tablecloth and matching napkins with festive candy cane rings. "I bought him at a cute little home and garden store in Jackson Hole."

Mia's finances weren't any of her business, but that didn't mean she couldn't be curious. Jack Reid hadn't bequeathed his daughter money in his will and earning your keep wasn't a legal form of currency, so Lauren wondered how Mia could afford to shop at Jackson Hole, pay her bills, or buy groceries without having a source of income.

Lauren unpacked a wooden Santa figurine and four

reindeer. They were vintage pieces passed down from Colton's grandparents.

"I usually set those on the mantel." Mia winced. "Listen to me. It's your house and I've taken over."

"Nonsense," she said, setting them to the side. "I think they'd be a lovely centerpiece for the mantle."

Once they finished the kitchen, they moved to the foyer to further their decorating endeavors on the stairs with new greenery and bright red bows Mia had purchased last year. "Can I ask you something?"

"Shoot."

"When you and Colton separated, why did you move in with Sue? Don't get me wrong," she was quick to say. "I like Sue. She's a sweet and gracious lady and she's been wonderful to me, especially considering I'm a product of her ex-husband's affair. But wasn't it... awkward living with your mother-in-law?"

"No." Lauren secured the last bow in place around the newel post with florist wire. "Neither Sue nor Jack Reid ever interfered with our marriage, and they were neutral in our decision to separate. Besides, it wasn't like I had a lot of places to go."

"Are your parents alive?" Mia asked cautiously.

"Oh, yeah," Lauren scoffed. "But living with them wasn't an option." She'd had a great time decorating and didn't want to ruin it. She didn't offer any details about her alcoholic mother or Commander Briggs and his complete lack of faith in her as a wife and a mother and their attempts to discredit Colton's character. They hardly knew the man and had made no attempt to change that or their condescending attitude.

"I don't know what I would have done if I hadn't had Sue. She set aside her prejudices as a mother and helped me through those first couple of years. I knew I could confide in her about anything, even my jumbled-up feelings towards Colton. She gave me strength when I felt like I couldn't take another step and was always willing to give me advice." Those years seemed like so long ago, and Lauren saw herself as a different person now, stronger and wiser, thanks in part to her mother-in-law's guidance and support.

Mia straightened a bow. "I can see why you chose to live with her."

"I asked her once if she thought it was possible to make yourself stop loving someone." Lauren laughed airily. "She said, 'Sorry, honey. Love doesn't have an off and on switch. Once it's birthed inside of you, it's a part of you and, like a soul, it never dies. It simply transforms from one form to another. That is the only thing you can control. Don't let this separation reshape your feelings for Colton from love to hate.'"

"That's an ingenious answer," Mia said. "I've never thought about love in that context."

Lauren cut Mia a side-glance. "You've never been in love, have you?"

Mia bent her knees so she could get a better view of the underside of the ribbon, gave it a few finishing touches, and sighed. "I think my relationship with Ian may be headed that way, but I don't see how it can if we stay at the ranch. I can't ask him to choose between me and the Lucky Jack. Jobs are scares."

Lauren's heart broke for the couple. "I'm sorry, Mia. I wish there was something more I could do."

Mia stopped straightening the bow and looked at Lauren, concern mounting in her eyes. "You can't say a word about this to Colton. He'd fire Ian on the spot if he found out."

Mia hadn't just stopped by the house for a social call.

She'd come because she needed a friend to confide in. Lauren knew how hard it was to live in the isolation of the Lucky Jack Ranch without the company of other women. "Go on."

Mia bit her bottom lip for a few seconds, then drew in a wobbly breath. "I wasn't really dropping off supplies. Ian and I have a secret spot. We meet there twice a week just so we can talk and, well…" She averted her gaze to the floor. "You know. Anyway, today he asked me to leave Crossfire Canyon with him."

Your way or the highway. That's what Lauren had told Colton would happen if he pushed his sister too hard. Sometimes she hated being right. "What did you say?"

Mia shrugged a weak shoulder. "That I'd think about it. I don't want to leave. I love it here, but…"

Lauren knew that if she told Colton about Mia leaving the ranch so she and Ian could be together, it would not only cause tension between the siblings, but it would also be the tipping point between Colton and his ramrod. "I'll try talking to Colton again."

"Thanks." Mia's smile was thin. "But I doubt you'll sway his decision. He's hard-nosed about matters concerning the ranch."

She and Colton might have been apart for eight years, but she had the utmost confidence in her ability to soften her husband's hard nose. "Don't let that rule get you down. Love is a wonderful thing when it works.

Mia's hands stilled from working on the bow. "And when it doesn't?"

Lauren didn't want to crush the young woman's dreams of falling in love or her faith in what she and Ian might have together. But it wasn't like she could hide the truth. Mia knew about her and Colton's long separation, and she'd witnessed the discord between them at Bill's office.

"It sucks," she said wearily. "Just remember that all relationships have obstacles, Mia, and neither of you is perfect. My advice is, don't rush into anything. Take your time and get to know the man Ian truly is before you commit to anything. Otherwise, you might spend eight years in purgatory wondering why you fell in love with him."

Mia sat on the bottom stair step and tossed the leftover garland into an empty box. "You're all he talks about, you know."

Mia's shift from Ian to Colton caught Lauren off guard. When she'd first arrived at the Lucky Jack, she would have done an about face and rudely walked away from Mia and the conversation. But so much had changed, so she listened.

"For Colton, it's like you never left."

Lauren sat down next to her. "What do you mean?"

"He's always making plans," Mia said, shaking her head as if she didn't understand. "When Lauren comes home, we're going to do this and that. If I didn't know any better, I'd think you were still living here."

That certainly explained the bewildered expression on Colton's face when he'd pulled the divorce papers from the envelope. Lauren thought about how perfectly preserved her sewing room was, the needle in mid-stitch of the dress she'd been making, the magazines, the spools of thread. Maybe that had been Colton's way of dealing with the separation.

"I don't know what happened or why you left." Mia's face softened. "But he really loves you."

Lauren felt that love bursting inside of her. "He insists he still does."

Mia fidgeted with the frayed end of a ribbon. "Dad told me Colton had a hard time adjusting after he came back from deployment."

"That's putting it mildly. The nightmares were horrible. The last night I was here," Lauren shuddered as she remembered, "I found him wandering around outside in the dead of night, yelling for someone named Ray. From what I could tell, he was living out the day he was shot. He came back inside and started going from room to room like he was searching for someone. He finally came to his senses in the den."

"That must have been terrifying for you."

"More so for Colton than me. When he finally realized where he was and that he'd blacked out again, he went ballistic. He was sobbing and yelling, 'No one can help me!' I tried to calm him down, but nothing I said made an impact. Then he accidentally shoved me. I lost my balance and went down." She raised her hair so Mia could see the scar. "My head caught the corner of the desk."

"Oh, God." Mia clamped a hand over her mouth.

"Head wounds bleed a lot and it looked worse than it was. I could have stopped the bleeding and waited until morning to get stitches, but all that blood..." Lauren rubbed her eyes. "He fell to his knees and bawled like a baby. His last words to me were, 'Get out now, before I can't remember hurting you.' So, I left. If Jack Reid hadn't died, I probably wouldn't be here now."

Mia sat quietly, taking it all in while Lauren tried to shrug off the misery of that night. "Do you think he's lying about loving you?"

"No. I know Colton loves me." Lauren looked down at her bare ring finger, missing the gold band for the first time.

"And do you love him?" Mia asked softly.

"Yeah," Lauren answered, feeling that love intensify. "I do."

"So," Mia slapped her palms against her thighs and snapped to her feet. "I guess that's the end of purgatory."

And the end of an imprisonment neither of them deserved.

Mia turned and headed back up the stairs. "There are a few more boxes. Will you help me pack them down?"

"Sure." A few turned out to be six. They were small boxes, mostly decorations for the tree. Lauren thought packing them downstairs would be a total waste, considering Colton's lack of interest in a Christmas tree. But she did anyway.

On the third trip, Mia retrieved a box from the back of the top shelf closet. "These are my favorites." She stepped from the ladder and opened the box. "Turtle doves. They're hand carved from maple wood. Colton said they were old, a family heirloom, like the Santa and reindeers."

Lauren peered into the box. "Oh, I remember these," she said, reaching for the ornaments. "Jack Reid pulled them out of the attic the first Christmas I was here."

He'd helped her decorate the tree and even hung lights on the front porch. He'd done all that and more while Colton had immersed himself in ranch work. Jack Reid had found the time, but her husband hadn't. That was a nagging fact that kept coming back.

"I think that's the last of it," Mia said.

Lauren was about to return the stepstool to the closet when something in the back caught her eyes. She hunched down and pulled out the silver-framed photo of her and Colton on their wedding day.

"I love that picture. You both were both so young and that look on your faces," Mia sighed wistfully. "You two look so in love."

"We were," Lauren whispered and began pulling out all the photos that had once hung in the hallway. "I thought he'd thrown them away."

"Oh, my goodness," Mia whooshed out as she sat the turtle doves on a box by the stairs. "Why would you think that?"

Why did I think you were his mistress? her conscience dropped in to say.

"When I saw they were gone, I guess I just assumed…" Lauren stopped. The implicitness of her thoughts had led her astray more than once over the last few days. She'd assumed so many things about Colton. She'd been so wrong about him in every way possible. He wasn't having an affair. He hadn't been an accomplice to Jack Reid's plan, and he hadn't thrown away the photos of their happy life together.

How had she come to trust her presumptions over the honorable character of the man she loved?

"It's like clockwork, you know," Mia said, using her fingernail to chip away a piece of yellow paint from the photo of Lauren and Jack Reid with Church. "Every year, Colton takes the pictures down so he can paint the hallway. It's always the same color of yellow and it's always on September 18. Dad said he's been doing it since you left."

Lauren hugged the silver-framed photo to her breast and closed her eyes, tears forming in their corners. Had Colton chosen the lovely shade of yellow because it was her favorite color? Or maybe the color correlated with the day he painted the hall, September 18. The day they were wed and the color of roses in her bouquet. The gesture was so touching and such a sweet and heartfelt testimony to their love and marriage.

"This year, there was so much happening, Dad getting sick and, of course, the problem with the will. Colton hasn't had time to rehang them." Mia crouched down next to her and wrapped an arm around her shoulders, her expression reassuring and warm. "Or maybe it's because he's been distracted by the woman in the photos."

Lauren swiped a hand over her cheeks and sniffed through a chuckle. "Maybe."

"Yeah, that's it." Mia reached into the closet and pulled the creation housing the rest of the photos. "So, how about we put them back on the wall where they belong?"

"Yes, let's do that," Lauren answered, getting to her feet.

# CHAPTER SEVENTEEN

AFTER THE PICTURES WERE HUNG AND THE TREE decorations were tucked in a corner of the living room, Mia headed for home.

Around six o'clock, Lauren sorted through the freezer and chose a chicken enchilada casserole to reheat. She'd just placed the casserole in the oven when Colton walked in the back door without Major by his side.

She slid off the oven mitts. "Hey."

"Hey," he returned her greeting with little enthusiasm. It was obvious that something was wrong. Had something happened with Major or was he holding a grudge because of this morning?

Nah. He'd been smiling and... perky when she'd stormed out of the master bedroom. She coughed to keep from laughing at his own juvenile thoughts.

"I haven't seen Major this evening," she said, clasping her hands behind her back.

Colton hung his coat and hat on the rack and sat down on the bench to remove his boots. "He had an early morning appointment with the vet. Doctor Dutton is keeping him overnight to run some tests."

"Does he think it's serious?"

"Doc is a she," he said, tugging his boots off. "And Val told me not to worry until it was time."

Lauren drew her arms up and crossed them around her midriff. Hopefully, the dog was grieving for Jack Reid and his behavior over the last few days wasn't a sign of declining health. "I'm heating a casserole."

"No, thanks." He slowly stood in a way that suggested his back ached, then padded across the kitchen towards the living room.

She knew without looking that he was pouring himself a drink.

"The house looks nice," he said, his face foursquare, making her think that whatever was eating at him must be serious. Something that had the blood vein at his right temple bulging.

Taking the whiskey bottle with him, he walked to the couch and sat down.

"The decorations were your sister's idea." She moved from the counter to the open doorway between the kitchen and living room.

"Was Ian with Mia?" he asked, the vein in his temple enlarged.

"Not unless she had him tucked away in her coat pocket."

Colton wasn't amused.

"She insisted we leave the living room until we bought a tree. I told her you weren't big on tree hunting so we probably wouldn't bother with buying one."

Colton had never gone with her to Dawson's Tree Farm or helped her hang Christmas baubles on fir branches in the past, so she didn't expect he had much to say about their tree inadequacies. But she'd thrown the tree out there in hopes it might give them something to talk about other than Mia and Ian.

But ice clinking against an empty glass was all she heard.

"Wow." She sighed heavily and rolled her eyes. "You really know how to talk a girl's head off. Please, can we just sit here in silence for the rest of the evening?"

His tired eyes reflected remorse, but he offered her a weak smile. "Sorry. I'm not much of a talker when I'm this exhausted. So, you first. What do you want to talk about?

As she watched him refill his glass, a disconcerting thought came to mind. Colton loved his whiskey, always had. But if he was taking medication to help with PTSD, he didn't need to be chugging glasses of the stuff.

"How about your whiskey?"

His brows raised. "What about it?"

She picked up the decanter. "It seems to be a habit and alcohol and meds don't mix well."

"Mmm." After he swallowed, his lips curled into a sexy smile. "I'm not taking any medication and I'll have you know that my whiskey habit didn't start until you came back. That was a compliment. I'm not trying to ruffle your feathers."

"Obviously," she said.

He chuckled softly. "It's true. If you weren't here, I'd be out there right now, working until I was too tired to keep my eyes open. Now I get to come home and have a relaxing drink and a nice, casual conversation with my amazing wife."

She clearly wasn't the one who had his vein popping. "Working that hard can't be good for you."

"It's not," he said, staring up at her with lazy, bloodshot

eyes. "But it was either work or come home to an empty house."

She could sympathize with that. She'd poured herself into taking classes and working long hours to console herself. But she'd clearly gotten the better part of the loneliness deal. She had Little Jack and before they'd moved out, Sue was there every night to keep her company.

After Lauren left the Lucky Jack, she'd sworn she'd never ask him to talk to her about anything ever again. But he looked weighed down with problems.

She returned the decanter to the cabinet.

"I wasn't finished with that."

"I want you sober when we talk."

"It takes more than a couple of whiskies to get me soused, honey."

She closed the cabinet door, walked to the fireplace, and sat down on the hearth. "I know you're worried about Mia, but there's something else bugging you, so do you want to talk about what's got your jaw set in concrete?"

He propped his sock feet on the coffee table. "I'm just tired. That's all."

"There's nothing you want to tell me?" she flipped her palms up. "Nothing you want to get off your chest."

"No."

Lauren wanted to throw up her hands and walk away.

*That is your MO, isn't it? Walk out when the going gets tough?* she could hear her dad ask, his voice callous and cold as it usually was when she'd failed him. A distinct, irrefutable and unchangeable pattern of spinelessness.

She fought the impulse to clap her hands over her ears and scream until the voice was gone. But that wouldn't silence the condemning utterance of Thomas David Briggs.

So she did what she always did when her dad barged

into her mind.

She ignored him.

If she decided to walk away from this conversation, Colton wasn't going to ride off into a snowstorm and try to end himself. His mental status was as excellent, if not better than it'd been when he'd joined the military. He was more levelheaded and patient with everyone and everything.

His body was strong and fit, and his business was booming. Colton didn't need her for anything other than saving his ranch. When she considered everything that had happened between them since her arrival at the Lucky Jack through that narrow perspective, a wretched feeling came over her. She knew Colton was keeping something from her. But she'd made so many false assumptions about him already. She wasn't going to do it again. He'd told her he wasn't a part of Jack Reid's plan and she believed him.

But she wasn't going to walk away from this conversation. "It amazes me how you can stand on a stage in front of hundreds of people and talk to strangers as if you've known them all your life, without a pre-rehearsed speech or teleprompter. But you can't talk to me, your wife."

Watching Colton deliver eloquent words to donors and volunteers of the Promise Point Foundation was poetry in motion. Year after year, dressed in a black tux and tie, he walked up on that stage and told his story.

"I think that's the first time since you've been here that you've actually admitted to being my wife," he said, before lifting the glass to his lips.

Lauren scooted to the floor as the dismal truth of what she'd said washed over her.

She pulled her up knees and folded her hands over them. Resting her chin on the back of her hands, she looked at him. "Only on paper, Colton."

The brightness of his brown eyes dimmed. His gaze dropped, and his upturned lips fell, stamping a haunted mien on his handsome face. She'd struck a nerve without meaning to.

He turned the glass up and drained it dry, then laid his head back and closed his eyes. "Speaking at the Foundation fundraisers, in front of all those people, was hard at first. But I worked through the butterflies, wobbly legs, and dry mouth. I won't say it gets easier because it doesn't."

Colton's speeches began with a narration of his life from a young man who'd volunteered to serve his country to the proud Marine who'd been the sole survivor of his unit. The surgeries, the rehabilitation, and the sacrifices. He addressed the common misconception among servicemen and women that they should just suck it up and go on when the memories of war came flooding in. He advocated the ongoing need for counseling and life-saving intervention for military men and women suffering from Post-Traumatic Stress Disorder.

Each time, he captured the hearts and souls of the crowd, drew tears and a standing ovation when he said, "Thank you and goodnight."

"Then why do you do it?"

"I owe it to the men and women who didn't make it back." And there it was, the cold, marble-like countenance of the battle-hardened Marine Lauren had last seen the night she left the ranch.

A chill swept over her. She'd made herself believe Colton had been the only survivor of that snowstorm. That the tortured soldier he'd been had succumbed to the cold and laid to rest in an icy unmarked grave somewhere in the pasturelands of the Lucky Jack.

But the Marine hadn't died. He'd survived, and Lauren realized for the first time that the two men couldn't be separated. If one perished, the other would too. With that knowledge came the bone-chilling reality that the battle-hardened Marine had been the one Colton feared would hurt her and Little Jack.

Why hadn't she seen that before? Because she'd been so young and naïve back then? Because she'd been hurt when he'd ordered her to leave the ranch? Or was it because after she left him, she'd too been blinded by her own contrition?

"I owe it," Colton started, but then paused for a hard swallow. "To the ones who fought the war in their minds and lost."

Hurt twisted her heart because she'd witnessed that fight and the turning point in the battle when her husband was on the brink of surrender.

This conversation was the closest he'd ever come to talking about what had happened to him over there, so she waited. But he said nothing. Not a word.

"Colton, every year, you travel all over the country giving speeches to support groups and disabled vets. You visit military hospitals and deliver encouraging words to servicemen and women. You raise millions of dollars and help thousands of people just by saying what's in your heart. Yet, you can't say a full sentence to your wife about your deployment. Everything I know about your time in Iraq, I've learned from those damn speeches," she said, as the same old hurt and anger blowing up inside her. "So I can only assume that it's me."

"Assumptions, Lauren," he reminded her while shaking his head no.

She smiled placidly and countered with the same justification she'd used earlier. "Sometimes assumptions are correct, Colton."

"It's not you," he said simply, as if those three words would solve the entire argument.

"Right," she said shortly. "So tonight, you're just tired."

"Yes."

Lauren's temple throbbed. "Is that always going to be your excuse, Colton? You're tired? Because that was your excuse for not talking to me when you came home from the hospital."

He glanced down at the glass in his hand. "It was the way I dealt with things back then. I made excuses, and I pushed people away."

And he didn't think he was doing that now? "Why? Why did you want to push me away? I know you were going through things and that there were issues you couldn't control. You lost friends. You were shot and nearly lost your life. But we never talked about any of that. I was your wife—"

"Still are."

He was annoyingly insistent on pointing that out because he wasn't ready to give up on their marriage. But he couldn't see that there was no marriage unless he communicated with her.

"I wasn't biased, Lauren," he said, softly. "Back then, it didn't matter that you were my wife. I didn't know how to get the words out or how to make sense of what was going on in my head."

"That was then. This is now," she said, taking steps towards conversations they'd never had. "Has anything changed?"

He lifted his gaze to hers. Those coffee-colored eyes were free from doubt, confident and clear of confusion, just like they'd been this morning. "You tell me, honey. Have I changed?"

# CHAPTER EIGHTEEN

THERE WASN'T A DOUBT IN LAUREN'S MIND THAT PARTS OF Colton's personality had changed. He wasn't the tormented soldier who'd roamed the house at night, unaware of his surroundings.

Post-Traumatic Stress Disorder wasn't a disease that could be cured. It was a horrible and sometimes debilitating psychiatric disorder that had to be managed. Apart from the nightmares, Colton seemed to have adapted. Thanks to counseling and prescription medication, he seemed at peace with the war demons and PTSD, or at least had them under control. But that battle-hardened Marine would always be there.

"In some ways, yes. You have changed, but in other ways." She paused, thinking those demons were probably in a well-guarded prison in the deepest part of his mind and she had to consider the implications if she demanded he talk about them. "You're the same old Colton."

"Would you rather I change all of me?" His expression suggested he was teasing her like he had been this morning. "Or just the parts you don't like."

"There's only one part of you I'd like to change."

"Oh, do tell," he smirked from behind the upturned glass.

"It's the part we just talked about. Your tight-lipped, jaw-grinding reaction when I try talking about something deeper than the weather. You said you wanted to start over, that you wanted to give our marriage a second chance. How can you expect me to say yes to that when you won't confide in me?"

"That's it? That's the one thing you don't like about me. I'm not a deep talker?"

She wasn't sure if he was trying to deflect her serious question or if he was toying with her.

He wiggled his eyebrows suggestively. "No body alterations or extensions?"

The Colton she married had never been this audacious with discussing intimate topics. This Colton was more relaxed, patient, and confident in everything he did, and it was so sexy.

"Cut that out. You know I never had any complaints about your body." Lauren felt that dreadful heat spreading up her neck. She was tired of blushing and knew she could be bold and confident about her own sexuality. "And from what I saw this morning, your quilt hanger has gotten better with age."

A spray of whisky shot from of his mouth.

She beamed in her victory. "Didn't expect that, did you?"

He swallowed what was left of the drink. "No," he said, grinning as he wiped his mouth. "I thought those little noises you used to make when we made love were a sign of satisfaction, but a man never really knows, so feel free to elaborate."

She scrunched her lips together. "Are there words that accurately describe how wonderful an orgasm feels?"

This time, he laughed, loud and hard. It was a lovely sound that warmed her heart and one she hadn't known she'd missed until now. It was strange how she'd forgotten the sound of his laughter. "It's been years since I heard you laugh that way."

"Ah-ha, well." His laughter trickled to a stop, allowing him to clear his throat. "If you promise to stay around, I promise, I'll do it more often."

Lauren felt compelled to make that promise. Her body was set on go, but her head hadn't been persuaded. "You know I can't promise that."

"What if?" He squinted one eye as he thought. "I promise to talk more? Then would you agree?"

"Oh, Colton," she whispered. "It's not just about talking.

The intimacy we once had has to be rebuilt. Lines of communication have to be constructed, 'cause Lord knows, those never existed, and even if I could make that leap from a divorce to giving our marriage another shot, eight years of separation can't be mended with a single stitch of conversation. I need proof that you're serious about those things."

"I am serious, but I don't want to mend our marriage or our relationship. I want a fresh start based on who we are now. We've both changed so much, Lauren. We're adults. Mature adults, not a couple of kids who thought they knew what the real world was like."

God, they had been that. Neither of them was prepared for marriage or parenthood.

"Let's get to know each other." His face showed excitement at what might happen if she agreed. "Let's make something new. Something stronger and better than what we had before."

"Make something new?" she repeated. "An all-is-forgiven, we-don't-have-a-past kind of new?"

He nodded. "Yes."

"That sounds too good to be true."

"It's not, honey," he assured her.

"But what if we commit to making that something new and fail? What if we can't do it?" *What if I can't do it?* Did she have the bones about her to stand with him when things got tough, or would she buckle and run like she had before? "What if we weren't meant to be together? What happens then?"

Shadows of disappointment haunted his face as he searched her eyes. "Do you honestly believe we weren't meant to be together?"

She dropped her head, not wanting to admit what she'd thought for years. "Surely you have reservations about doing this."

"I don't."

"No questions at all?"

He thought for a moment. "My questions are, what if we were meant to be together, but we didn't try because we were too afraid? What if we go through with the divorce and regret it for the rest of our lives? We'll never know what could have been."

Lauren had come back to the Lucky Jack to attend Jack Reid's funeral and the reading of his will. But she'd contacted a divorce lawyer months ago. She'd come under the pretense of her father-in-law's death to deliver, in person, the final severing blow legally to their marriage.

She could do that here and now. All she had to do was say no to Colton. If she stubbornly stuck to her plan to divorce him, he wouldn't push her to reconsider.

After the stipulations of the will were straightened out, she'd catch a flight to Texas, go back to a job she'd grown to loathe, a home that didn't feel like home and continue her life as a single woman.

A single woman in search of a man who loved and wanted her. A father to those children she yearned for. But what if Colton was as he'd said that man? That father?

*Then divorcing him will be the biggest and most excruciating mistake of your life.* This time, the voice inside Lauren's head was her own, not an echo of Thomas Briggs's. This was her chance to take back what had been stolen and her only chance at lassoing her dream.

That thought birthed one word. "Okay."

"Yeah?"

"Yeah," she whispered.

COLTON HAD STARTED THE MORNING AT HIS USUAL FOUR-thirty, dressed, and gone to work. He came back to the house a little after nine to grab the coffee thermos he'd left on the counter. He wasn't usually forgetful of his morning mud. But he and Lauren had crossed a milestone last night.

He'd been on cloud nine ever since. They'd both sat there, staring at one another in shocked silence. Then they'd eaten casserole and said goodnight without kissing.

Today was a new day, the first day of a different beginning with his wife. Every nerve in Colton's body was teaming with excitement and fear. He was no stranger to either emotion or feeling them intertwining in his stomach.

This was the best kind of elation.

He hadn't dilly dallied through his morning chores.

He'd gone headfirst into his daily routine because he wanted to spend the evening with Lauren.

He hurried up the back steps, opened the door and located his forgotten thermos on the counter. As he went to retrieve it, the sound of keystrokes caught his ears.

Lauren was hard at work.

Jonas was compliant about her working remotely, but that wouldn't last much longer. Colton had to face the strong possibility that going along with Jack Reid's Second Chance Plan might cost Lauren her job. So he could add that to the guilt piled high on his shoulders about deceiving her.

*You're really racking up points.*

Lauren would be more inclined to stay in Crossfire Canyon if she had a job. But she wouldn't make the move to Montana for that reason alone. Making that something new with Lauren would take time, and he couldn't blurt out that Val had an opening for an office manager. He needed to come up with a plan so he could subtly approach the subject.

The house phone rang. Not wanting to disturb Lauren from her work, he hurried to the table in the foyer and picked it up before it clicked to the answering machine. "Ritter residence."

"Colton. It's Val."

"Oh," he said, then tried swallowing the large lump that had suddenly formed in his throat. "Hi, Val."

"I have great news. Major doesn't have hemangiosarcoma." He heard the rustling of paper and knew she was looking over the dog's chart. "His test results are normal. He's the healthiest patient I've seen in a while, especially for a dog his age."

The anxiety banding Colton's chest melted as he allowed himself a breath of relief. "That is great news."

Lauren, hearing the call, had exited the den and was now standing in the foyer. He answered her questioning expression with a thumbs-up, causing her shoulders to relax.

She mouthed, "Thank God."

"Whatever is ailing him," Val said, "is beyond my area of expertise."

"Meaning?"

The paper rustling stopped, and she sighed. "My guess is, Major misses Jack Reid, and my professional advice is, give him time to adjust."

"What if he doesn't?" Colton swiped his Stetson off and rested his back against the wall. "Dogs can grieve themselves to death."

"They can," she said. The tone of loss ebbing from her voice was all too familiar to Colton. It was the same tone he'd had when he talked to his therapist about his last mission and the men who'd died. "I lost a Service Dog after his handler was killed in an explosion. The dog simply refused to live and there was nothing anyone could do about it."

"Is that what you're telling me, Val? That Major might give up?"

"That's a possibility, Colton," she answered honestly. "Not a certainty. Pay attention to his behavior. Keep a close eye on his whereabouts and don't let him go off on his own. Dogs isolate themselves to prepare for death and, if anything changes, don't hesitate to call me. Okay?"

"Yeah," he said, swiping a hand over his face. "I'll be by to pick him up soon."

Colton returned the phone to its base.

"What did the vet say?" Lauren asked, moving farther into the foyer.

"That it's hard to gage the will to live." Be it animal

or man, the will to live hinged on the strength of the tether which held him to this world. When Colton had been shot, Lauren's love and his determination to see his son were the strongholds that kept him from giving up. "Major is physically fine, but he might give up now that Dad's gone."

"There isn't much we can do to prevent that, Colton," she said softly.

"I know."

"Do you want me to go with you to pick him up?"

A couple of days ago, Lauren wouldn't have volunteered to take a ride into town with him or would have tried lending him emotional support.

At this very moment, they were constructing those nonexistent lines of communication. But there were other areas of their relationship that needed attention. Areas he wasn't ready to work on. "No, if you take off work again, Jonas might give you a longer To-Do List."

"I'm used to it," she said, trying to buffer her boss's nasty attitude.

Her hair was twisted into a sloppy bun and skewered it place by a pencil, and a pair of thin, gold framed reading glasses sat across the bridge of her cute nose.

After they were married and settled into the house, Lauren had devoured every novel in his dad's western book collection and Colton's detective novels. Then she'd started taking weekly trips to the public library for more books. His wife was a well-read and intelligent woman, who had a studious side that was drop-dead gorgeous.

"I'm not." He reached to draw her closer. She came willingly and didn't back away when their bodies touched. Heat rushed to his groin, engorging him with adrenaline and lust.

Head spinning, blood pumping, he found his voice.

"I'm excited about being newlyweds again, and we can't work on that if you're occupied all night."

Her cheeks pinked again. "I–ah," she cleared her throat as she bashfully glanced down, "can tell you're eager to get started."

She was his wife. They'd made love more times than Colton could count, but in so many ways, they were strangers. The comfortable husband and wife familiarity they'd once enjoyed was no longer there. But neither of them denied that the attraction certainly remained, so he didn't think he needed to make excuses for his body's rowdy uprising.

"Yes, ma'am. I am especially excited about the rebuilding intimacy part, too. But first things first. You were right."

"I was right?" she asked, with a wide-eyed, owlish expression of fake surprise. "Mark this day on the calendar as My Wife Was Right Day."

He winked at her playfulness. "Remind me to do that later."

"Oh, I will," she said, tipping her chin up. "Now, tell me what I'm right about."

He brushed aside the loose strands of hair that had escaped the confinements of the pencil and stroked her cheek with a thumb. "A man should confide in his wife. I've been too quiet for too long, Lauren, and it almost cost me everything I love."

Her eyes softened as she stared up at him.

"From here on, I promise to work on building those lines of communication by sharing with you everything that's in this head of mine."

She laid her head on his chest and hugged him tight. "You don't know what that means to me."

He hadn't, but he did now, and he'd pledged to make

his wrongs right. He kissed the crown of her head. "How about we rent a movie and curl up on the couch with a bowl of popcorn tonight?"

She raised her head, hooked her upper teeth over her bottom lip, then smiled. "That sounds nice."

Spending the evening with Lauren sounded better than nice. It was a dream come true for Colton and a joy he thought he might never have again.

He leaned down and brushed his lips over hers. "I'll be back soon."

Dazed from his affection, she ran the tip of her tongue over her bottom lip. "Be careful. The roads could be slick."

Colton winked, stepped to the door, and went outside. After spending most of his adult life in Montana, he could traverse icy roads in his sleep. But he'd be cautious about navigating his way back into Lauren's heart.

He intended to get a jump on rebuilding those husband-and-wife intimacies she'd brought to his attention last night. But he didn't want to do anything that might help reinforce her notion that he was trying to seduce her into staying at the ranch.

In three days, the stipulations of his dad's will would be met, and the ranch would be his. But Colton wasn't ready to say goodbye. He never would be. He couldn't bear to see her board a plane and fly out of his life.

But he was determined to remain optimistic about his chances of convincing her that the Lucky Jack was where she belonged.

Colton started the truck, backed out of the drive, and set out towards town. He wasn't looking forward to hauling boxes of lights down from the attic or untying a gazillion wire knots. But they were all due for some Christmas cheer.

In town, Katie, the owner of the Crossfire Gift Barn,

had dressed Cookie, the gigantic oak-carved moose sitting in front of the shop, in a Santa hat and strung colorful lights around his antlers.

The poor creature looked as if it had been clotheslined by a Christmas tree, but tourists and townsfolk loved the giant mascot. So much so that Crossfire Canyon had adopted a Cookie Night Light Celebration, which officially kicked off the holiday season.

Everyone but Colton was in a countdown to Christmas. It occurred to him as he passed the Barn that Christmas was only a few short weeks away. He hadn't a single gift for anyone. Most could be purchased locally. Katie had a wide selection of products ranging from Montana stamped clothing to gourmet candy. He'd stop by there after he picked up Major, and what he couldn't find in town, he'd order online.

Little Jack was too old for toys, and he had more electronic gadgets than Colton was comfortable with. Mia would love something for the kitchen. He didn't have a clue what his mom wanted. He'd call Ed for advice on that one.

And Lauren.

What was he gifting his wife with this year?

# CHAPTER NINETEEN

BLUE SKIES WERE SLOWLY RELENTING TO THE TWILIGHT BY the time Colton maneuvered the truck onto the ranch drive. Behind the house, the sinking sun cast beautiful tinges of pink and purple across the snow-topped mountains. Fir trees lining the fence were dusted with snow and sparkled iridescently against the dying light.

Braking the truck to a crawl, he watched the sliver of sunlight slip below the vanishing point. He'd seen thousands of sunsets in different parts of the world during his stint in the military. None were as beautiful as the ones at the Lucky Jack.

He guided the truck up the drive and parked in front of the house. He winced when he stepped out. The bruise on his side was almost gone and only hurt when he moved a certain way.

He snagged the four bags containing the gifts he bought in town. Since Ed was McCrea's father-in-law, it had been easy to get his number, and Ed had been happy to offer suggestions on gifts for Sue.

The only person left on his list was Lauren. Since she

liked to read, he'd considered an e-reader, but after checking with Sue, he learned she had one. A man could never fail with perfume, he'd thought. But after sniffing a dozen or more test bottles, they'd all smelled alike.

And nothing smelled as good as Lauren's natural scent, sweet like a flower in bloom.

Katie had suggested a cozy knit blanket for cold winter nights or fleece house slippers, but those seemed too impersonal to him.

Colton wanted Lauren's gift to be special, something that would symbolize the start of a new marriage. With that in mind, he'd stepped to the glass display case housing the jewelry. In the middle of the case was a beautiful silver band with a half-carat diamond. But he'd thought maybe buying her a ring at such an early stage in their relationship might be too presumptuous.

Lauren might think so. He'd passed on the ring, thinking if things went as planned, he'd let her pick out her own ring.

On his way to the counter, he noticed a card game titled, Talk to Me: Conversation Starters for Couples. The description on the back of the box hooked his interest. Each card had a thought-provoking question aimed at fostering trust and intimacy. He'd purchased the card game and had Katie bag them separately. Maybe they could alternate movie night with game night.

With the cards in his pocket and the packages in hand, he walked around the truck to the passenger side and opened the door for Major. The old dog had slowly made his way through the shops, but he'd loved the attention from shop owners and townsfolk.

Major hopped from the truck with his tail wagging and proceeded up the porch behind Colton. Once the door was open, Major took a path to the fireplace and eased down.

When Colton heard the door to the sewing room open, he clapped a hand over to the newel post and looked up.

Lauren stepped to the railing and smiled down at him. "I was starting to worry."

"No need for that," he said, taking two steps at a time until he was at the top. "We did a little Christmas shopping while we were in town."

Sliding her hand across the railing, she inched closer, while wiggling her eyebrows. "Whatcha get me?"

Caught off guard by her unexpected question, Colton sat the bags down, raked his work hat off and tried thinking of something he could say other than the hurtful truth. But keeping his dad's will a secret from Lauren had done enough damage to his insides. "Honestly, honey. Nothing."

Her frolicsome smile fell. "Oh."

"It's not that I didn't want to, it's just," he dropped his eyes to his hat. "I haven't bought you a Christmas present in a while and I–"

"Colton, I understand," she said, laying a hand on his arm. "I'm in the same situation. I have no idea what to buy for you."

He expelled his relief with a smile and tried to stop handling his hat like a fidgety kid.

"It's like you said," clasping her hands around the opening of his jacket, she smiled up at him. "We're different people now. It's only natural that we don't know what the other one wants for Christmas."

Colton knew what he wanted. Lauren, for Christmas and every day for the rest of his life, this close and smiling up at him with affection and understanding in her eyes.

She slid her palms up his chest and inched closer. "Why don't we wait a little while before we buy gifts for each other?"

"Yeah," he said.

"Good." She wiggled those lovely brows of hers again and rubbed her hands together while raking her teeth over her bottom lip. "Now, let's see what's in those bags."

The woman had no idea what that frisky lip-biting did to him. Walking stiffly, he followed her to the sewing room, moved to the bottom of the bed to hide his lower half, then hoisted the bags onto the bed. She dug in, examining each gift with delight. He couldn't do anything but smile, nod, and suffer.

After Lauren inspected the gifts, she repackaged them into the bags. "Would you like me to wrap them?"

"That would be great. That is, if you're sure it's no trouble."

"No trouble at all." She set the bags next to the sewing machine, crossed her arms, and began rubbing her arms as she stared out the window. "I enjoy doing it. If I were home, the tree would be up and decorated and there would be gifts under it. This was going to be our first Christmas in our new home, and I wanted everything to be perfect. I was going to buy a tree as soon as I got back to Texas, but I'm sure by the time this is over, the lot will be empty."

Colton's guilt was quick to flash a picture of his wife standing in an empty lot with only the twig of a tree to choose from.

She glanced at him with the saddest smile he'd ever seen. "It's just not Christmas without a tree."

The echo of Lauren's words fisted him in the heart. But it was just a damn tree. An overpriced nuisance that shed needles on the floor, so why did he feel like he'd denied Lauren a Christmas essential?

Because he had, not intentionally, of course. He'd never deny her anything she needed or desired. Yet there wasn't a tree cluttering up their living room.

Last night, she'd hinted. *I told her you weren't big on tree* hunting, so we probably wouldn't bother with buying one. And he'd let it fly right past his big ears.

Sure, Lauren could have gone to Dawson's Tree Farm and bought a tree without him, but he'd pledged to make something new, something completely different from their previous marriage.

It hit him then that he'd never chosen to be a part of their family tree buying or decorating experience, something Lauren deemed crucial for Christmas. When they were married, she'd done all those holiday practices and so many other things without him.

"I'm sorry, Lauren."

"It's not your fault," she said, not taking her gaze from the window.

But it was. In his mind, the Lucky Jack was Lauren's home. He'd failed to see that she had expectations about Christmas in their new home. He'd single handedly crushed those anticipations by making her believe she had to stay.

There were things that had been out of his control after he'd been discharged from the Marines, the PTSD, the pain and emotions that came after losing most of his hand.

But before that, when they were first married, he'd had so many opportunities to be a good husband. *I had close friends in Crossfire Canyon, shopped in the stores, and ate in the café without you, Colton, and back then, all I wanted was to be with you.*

A sharp stab of remorse knifed within him.

Those were precious chances he'd never get back. His only option was to make new opportunities. He'd be the husband Lauren deserved, the man who wouldn't ignore his wife's longing or anything, even if it was something he thought was as insignificant as a Christmas tree. He'd be that man for as long as Lauren would have him, and he'd start by getting her the best balsam fir Dawson's had to offer.

With new determination brewing inside him, he tossed his hat onto the bed and walked over to where she was. Then he slid his hands around her waist and kissed her just below the ear. "I missed lunch."

"So did I."

"What say you and me have a night out on the town?"

She giggled and twisted around. "A night on the town? I don't know if you've noticed, but Crossfire Canyon isn't exactly Sin City."

"Will you settle for a burger and a beer?"

"Make it a steak and you've got yourself a deal, Cowboy."

"Steak it is." Taking her by the hand, he led her to the door and down the stairs. "Get your coat.'

"But what about curling up on the couch with a movie and popcorn?"

He gave her a quick kiss on the lips and winked. "I have something better in mind."

AFTER THEY ATE DINNER AT THE ONLY STEAK HOUSE IN Crossfire Canyon, Colton drove them out of town toward the mountains.

"More snow," Lauren said, watching sporadic flakes hit the windshield and melt into a trickled of ice.

He flipped the wiper speed up a notch. "Less than an inch is all that's expected."

He'd been tight-lipped when she'd asked where they were going, labeling their destination a Christmas surprise.

Three miles from town, he made a turn onto a road Lauren knew well.

When they passed the Dawson's Tree Farm sign, she couldn't believe her eyes. "You're taking me to buy a tree."

"Yes, I am." He drove into the parking lot, stopped the truck, and shifted it into Park. Then he opened his door and said, "Like you said, it's not Christmas without a tree, and I'm determined to make this the best one either of us has ever had."

Lauren felt like a kid again, teeming with hope and possibilities for more than simply finding the perfect tree. Colton's something better had transformed into something magical. Her husband had voluntarily driven her to Dawson's to buy a tree. It was a Christmas miracle and one of the best surprises she'd ever received.

And though it might be considered trivial to some, Lauren knew it was a small breakthrough in their relationship. He'd said he was committed to making something new, and this was proof that he was trying. As Colton came around to her side, a splash of giddiness washed over her.

He opened her door and waited for her to step out. When she did, he closed the door and laced her glove-clad fingers with his bare ones.

The snowfall had become heavier and dusted the treetops of the Christmas trees. Large yellow light bulbs crisscrossed over the lot, illuminating the trees with an amber glow. The smell of balsam and freshly fallen snow whirled around them.

It was a beautiful winter wonderland. When she'd visited, the lot was crowded with shoppers discussing which tree was the best, but tonight it was quiet. Tranquil and soothing to her soul. It was as though they'd stepped out of the real world and into a Christmas movie.

Lauren was spellbound by Colton's simple gesture of

commitment. She tilted her head against his arm as they made their way up the walk leading to the gate. There was a dim light inside the cottage-style store adjacent to the lot. "When I bought trees here, closing time was at eight."

"I called Pepper and asked if she'd make an exception."

"And I said, yes." A pretty, red-haired woman walked from the shadows. She unlatched the picket gate and swung it open. "Because in the twenty years since my parents started this business, Colton Ritter has never set a boot on this farm."

He grinned widely. "How can you be sure of that?"

She crossed her arms and squinted. "Are you questioning Bev's integrity?"

He chuckled and leaned over to give the woman a kiss on the cheek. "Never. How is your mom?"

"As feisty as ever," Pepper said, smiling warmly at Lauren as she held out her hand. "We've never been formally introduced. I'm Pepper Dawson."

Lauren accepted Pepper's handshake greeting. "Lauren Ritter. Thank you for staying late."

"My pleasure," she told her. "The store is open. Go on inside and get what you need. I'll be back in a little while to check you out and lock up."

Pepper hurried to the other side of the lot and into the house.

"A friend of yours?" Lauren asked.

"A distant cousin, if I'm not mistaken." A bell jingled over the door as Colton pushed it open. Inside, fresh garland with mauve bows and silver bells hung from the ceiling and white Christmas lights twinkled in the windows.

"I suppose that's plausible, considering Aunt Mia," she kidded.

"It's a small town and we Ritters enjoy procreating," he returned with a devilish grin."

Lauren didn't reply. Their last discussion about babies had ended horribly. She didn't want a repeat.

In the summer, Dawson's farm offered a variety of herbs and vegetable plants and hand-dipped ice cream. The store kept a year-round supply of homemade jams and jellies and fruit pies. During the Christmas holiday, there was an assortment of cordials, bonbons, and cookies in abundant supply.

Though they'd just eaten, the scent of cinnamon and freshly baked bread caused Lauren's mouth to water. She ran her finger along the candy shelf. "A woman could lose her figure in a place like this."

He frowned. "Women worry too much about their size."

"Says the man who can eat what he wants and not gain a pound," she said dryly.

"That's not true. I've put on weight over the years."

Lauren wanted to know specifically where that weight was because all she saw was a tight body with firm muscles.

"And there's nothing wrong with your figure," he assured her as he examined a large wreath. "Never has been. Never will be. You could gain a hundred pounds and still be beautiful to me."

Though she'd never felt like her body needed to be a certain weight, there were things about her appearance that she was self-conscious about: the beginning stages of cellulite on her thighs, the extra skin on her lower belly from the pregnancy and those insistent crow's feet at the corner of her eyes. But Colton's acceptance of her body, no matter how heavy or thin or blemished, touched her deeply.

"You know," she thought back over the years. "That's the first time you've ever called me beautiful."

He looked at her then, his head retracted a fraction. "That can't be right. You must be mistaken."

He hadn't used the word beautiful, but he had used other words to compliment her. Cute, fetching, good-looking and striking were just a few she remembered. "No," she teased. "My vanity would have remembered."

He turned away from her and placed the wreath back on the hanger. "Well, I'm an idiot for not telling you sooner that you are a stunningly beautiful woman."

That tweaked her ego, so much so that she might have given him a kiss as gratitude, but something about the slope of his shoulders made her think she'd been wrong to tease him about his shortfall.

"I can't deny it," he said tersely as he held up another wreath for her viewing. "Mia has the dominant Christmas decorating gene. What do you think about this one for the front door?"

The mere fact Colton was holding a Christmas wreath was astonishing, but to think he wanted to hang one in any part of the house was mind blowing. "It's lovely and perfect for the front door."

"Good." He laid it on the counter, stepped to the candy shelf, and began handing her boxes. "Let's take one of each kind."

"Colton, that's eight boxes of candy," she said, confounded by his sudden need for confections.

"What we don't eat," he started another stack in his hand. "We can send home with Mom and Ed."

With Mom and Ed? He'd failed to mention the possibility that she and Little Jack might also return home. But she wasn't going to give a contradiction.

Not now when everything was so perfect.

She wasn't going to destroy the night with something that wasn't set in stone. However, the contrast between her state of mind when she'd been told the future of the ranch was in her hands and this very moment gave her pause.

That first night, she'd been dig-your-heels-in, positive that she wasn't staying until Christmas. She'd loathed the thought of being stuck in a house with Colton for more than a couple of days and convinced that the issues with the will would be sorted out without delay.

But Colton was making plans to celebrate Christmas with her and Little Jack. Lauren was growing fond of the idea. Her heart desired that special Christmas he'd spoken of. The snuggling on the couch, the tree trimming, and the gifts they had yet to buy for each other.

He reached for a pack of sugar cookies, then withdrew his hand. "I cower in fear of what my sister might do if I bring in a stranger's cookies."

She giggled. "Pretend you never saw them."

He added the boxes to the counter. "Good advice."

Lauren moved to the window. The flakes they'd encountered on the way to the farm had transformed into a steady snowfall. "I thought you said less than an inch."

"The amount will vary in places." He adjusted his hat lower on his brow to shield against the snowfall as they stepped outside. "We may have more at home."

She crammed her hands into the pocket of her coat and shivered. "I guess we better find a tree and get back."

"You're the expert on Christmas trees, so." He waved a hand towards the lot. "After you."

Huddled inside her coat, Lauren examined the first tree. "Uh-huh." Then the second one. "Nope." After she'd passed over a dozen trees, she heard him sigh and fought to keep from laughing. He was being so patient and sweet and completely committed to their tree hunting expedition. But she was having so much fun. "This one."

From the corner of her eye, she saw his head pop up from its tired tilt. "Great," he said, taking hold of the tree. "I'll load it up."

"Hold on," she said, frowning, and pointed to the lower left side. "It has a bare spot right there."

"Can't we turn the bare spot toward the wall?"

She ignored his question and moved to the next tree. "This one looks promising, don't you think?"

He swiped a hand over his mouth. "Yeah, real promising."

She waited, timing her decision to achieve the full effect. "Okay, load it up."

Poor Colton. She almost felt sorry for him and was ready to give up the antics until she heard him say, "Thank you, Jesus" under his breath as he turned towards the truck with the tree in his hands.

"Wait," she shouted.

He stopped and set the tree down on its trunk.

"Is that a broken limb?"

Without a word, he pivoted, returned the tree to its spot, and waited. "We're running out of trees."

"I know. You can sit in the truck until I find one."

"No." He sighed. "I came here to pick out a Christmas tree with my wife and that's what I'm going to do."

Lauren's heart melted. If the man was this dedicated to finding something as insignificant as a Christmas tree, how dedicated would he be to their marriage?

She pointed to the first one she'd picked out. "This one will do."

He eyed the tree then, frowned when he switched his focus to her. "Are you sure?"

"Positive."

His eyebrows lifted, then fell. "This tree it is."

They walked to the storefront. Colton leaned the tree against the fence and opened the door for her. Inside, he dusted the snow from his hands and asked, "Is there anything else you want?"

It was a legitimate question, since they were standing in front of a store filled with goodies. But Lauren's mind went from goodies to the perks of being alone with her husband in a dimly lit room. Taking his jacket by the front, she moved closer and gazed up at him. "Just this."

If she'd stunned him by initiating the kiss, he didn't show it, and he didn't hesitate to give her what she wanted. Slowly, sensually, he moved his lips against hers, teasing her with his tongue. When she pulled away, they were both breathless.

"What was that for?"

"Do I need a reason to kiss my husband?"

Dark with desire, his eyes shifted to her mouth. "No," he whispered, and kissed her again.

From behind them, Lauren heard someone clear their throat—loudly.

Colton turned his head and grinned. "You have horrible timing, Pepper."

"I can see that." Pepper held out two steaming Styrofoam cups. "I thought you two might like some hot chocolate to warm you up. But clearly, you don't."

Embarrassed, Lauren tried smiling as she took a cup. "Thanks."

# CHAPTER TWENTY

It was Saturday and with Claire's party happening in less than a week, Lauren was nervous about finding something appropriate to wear.

Shortly after noon, Mia arrived. She insisted they skip shopping in Crossfire Canyon and drive straight to Billings. Lauren didn't mind, but by the time they arrived, she was starved.

A plain burger and fries from a fast-food restaurant would have been okay with her, but Mia would have none of that. She suggested they have lunch at a new bar and grill that was receiving rave reviews on social media for its clever spin on traditional food and gourmet burgers. Mia was hunting for new recipe ideas. She spent most of their meal trying to identify the ingredients of the smoked bacon gnocchi she'd ordered.

After lunch, they'd taken a short walk down the street to a small dress shop. It hadn't taken Mia long to pick out a dress for herself. She'd chosen a black, above the knee sequined faux wrap that was close fitting at the top with a daring v-cut neckline, a flaring bottom, and puffy cuffed sleeves.

Lauren was positive Ian would love it. Colton, on the other hand, would have to fire the entire Lucky Jack crew if the men got a look at Mia in that dress.

"Oh, I love this one." Mia lifted the velour party dress by the hanger and held it up.

Lauren ran a hand over the velvety knit fabric. The knee-length, hunter green colored dress had ruching on the front with long flowing sleeves. "It's beautiful, but I don't know."

"Are you kidding me? It's perfect for you. Now." Mia shoved the dress into Lauren's hands, took her by the shoulders and spun her around towards the dressing room. "Try it on."

Lauren hurried to the dressing room, closed and locked the door, then checked the price tag. She cringed when she saw the three digits in front of the period but knew she had to buy the dress. She'd practically invited herself to the Christmas party and there was no way out of it.

She undressed down to her underwear, unzipped the back of the dress and removed it from the hanger. The material felt soft and luxurious sliding over Lauren's skin, and the garment was a snug tailored fit that was made for her body. The elegant deep drape cape swooped low and hung just above the curve of her lower back. She managed to get the zipper halfway up, just enough to be decent if there were customers about when she opened the door.

"Perfect," she whispered, and smiled at her reflection in the mirror.

When she stepped out of the dressing room, Mia's eyes popped wide. "Wow. That's it."

She swirled around. "You think so?"

"I know so." Mia twisted her mouth and pecked her

chin with a finger as she thought. "Now all you need are a pair of heels."

Lauren chose a pair of three-inch, silver toe pumps embellished with a simple strand of rhinestones embedded in the ankle strap.

"Fantastic," Mia decided.

They paid for their items and hit the next location on Mia's itinerary, the Tandy Orange Boutique. The women's clothing store combined classic western fashion with chic modern trends at affordable prices.

Lauren picked out two pairs of jeans, a sweater and three tops that she could mix-match together for a fresh look each day of the week and a discounted coat to wear with her party dress.

The trip had put a dent in Lauren's savings, but she'd enjoyed herself. She and Mia had gotten to know each other, and, in a way, they'd bonded. If only Mia had found Jack Reid sooner, maybe Lauren wouldn't have felt so lonely and detached from living at the ranch while Colton was on deployment. But as they say, that was neither here nor there. The past was the past.

She hoisted her treasure trove onto the counter and dug into her purse for her wallet. As the cashier tallied up her bill, her thoughts drifted back to last night's romance in the tree lot, their kiss and the atmosphere between them as they drove home.

It had been comfortable, but tense. They were relaxed in each other's company, but edgy about what they both wanted. Yet neither of them was willing to make the first move towards physical intimacy beyond kissing.

They'd decorated the tree together, another first in their relationship. Colton had enjoyed it as much as she had. After the lights were strung and the ornaments were hung, they'd gone back to their original plan of snuggling on the couch with a bowl of popcorn. They'd watched an old Jimmy Stewart Christmas movie. Lauren had fallen asleep midway through as Clarence Odbody was trying to dry out Tom Sawyer.

Colton had woken her with a gentle shake. She'd said goodnight and gone to bed. She'd heard him climb the stairs and close the door to their master bedroom around one o'clock.

Lauren knew that if their relationship progressed, eventually, she'd be in their bed again. Consummating their newfound love for each other. It was silly for her to wonder what making love to this Colton would be like. Years had passed, and as he'd said, they were different people.

"Ma'am?"

Her head jerked up when she heard the lady behind the counter. "Yes?"

"Will that be all?"

"Oh, yes." She smiled. "That will be all."

Lauren paid for her things, and she and Mia were on their way home within the hour. She had Mia stop at the car rental in Crossfire Canyon so she could have something to drive. She didn't want to ask Colton to borrow one of the ranch trucks. Thankfully, the Jeep she'd returned on Tuesday was available.

It was close to five o'clock when she arrived home. Colton's truck wasn't in the drive, and she was a little disappointed that he wasn't home yet.

Lauren wasn't much of a cook, but she could bake a mean chicken when she wanted to. She'd found one in the freezer this morning before she'd left with Mia and set in the sink to thaw, thinking she and Colton could enjoy the semblance of a home-cooked dinner before their card game. She'd never played cards and was surprised he'd suggested the game. The old Colton hadn't been big on playing or games.

After carrying her purchases upstairs, she hurried to the kitchen to get the chicken started. She gave the meat a good rubbing with olive oil, melted butter, and lemon juice, then added minced garlic, salt and pepper. Had she known chicken was so easily prepared, she would have made it years ago.

She went to the pantry Mia kept stocked and found the box of instant potatoes and a can of green beans. Bread. Colton always ate bread at every meal. Opening the refrigerator, she searched for something resembling bread. Fortunately, there was a can of pop open dinner rolls.

Marvelous.

Until this point, Lauren was proud of how nice the food appeared and that she'd managed to pull together an entire meal without setting off the fire alarm. But the dinner rolls, packaged in their tightly compressed paper tubing, were her Achilles' heel. She hated those ticking time bombs. If she couldn't muster the nerve to free those dinner rolls, all her cooking endeavors were for naught, and what was a meal without bread?

Determined not to let the meal go unfinished, she carefully removed the can of rolls from the refrigerator and gently placed them on the counter. Wiping her suddenly sweaty palms on the apron she'd found in the laundry room, she read the directions from a distance.

It seemed simple enough, but, "One wrong move and kablooey," she mumbled and mimicked an explosion with her hands.

But she would not be intimidated by dough. If she could work for Jonas Ward and handle his crabbiness, she could open a can of dinner rolls. Following what she'd read, she tediously peeled back the paper wrapping and gripped the lower part of the can in her hand. Cocking her arm back, she closed her eyes and gave it a hard whack against the edge of the counter.

The can burst and the dinner rolls were freed. Lauren breathed a sigh of relief.

"That—" Colton's voice caused her to jump and spin around. He was standing with a shoulder planted against the back door and a huge grin on his face. "Was the most awkward thing I've seen in a while."

"Damn it, Colton," she said, embarrassed as she began unpacking the rolls and placing them on the baking sheet. "You scared me."

"Sorry."

She tracked the soft thud of his boots across the kitchen. He propped an arm on the counter and gripped his wrist with his hand. With amusement in his eyes, he examined her from head to toe. "You hate to cook, so why are you duking it out with a can of biscuits?"

"They're dinner rolls." He'd caught her off guard doing something she felt inept at. She knew her face was as red as Santa's suit and there was no hiding it. "I don't hate cooking. It's just I have had little practice at it."

"We could have gone out."

"I enjoy being in my kitchen again," she answered honestly.

His grin relaxed and his eyes became mellow, almost rheumy. "It smells delicious, and you handled those dinner rolls like a pro."

There wasn't a high level of skill in what she'd done, or anything elaborate about the food she'd prepared, but his words made her feel accomplished and adequate. His complement, over-inflated for her sake, she was sure, sent a little thrill of satisfaction through her. "Thank you."

Leaning over, he kissed her cheek, then walked toward the laundry room to wash his hands.

With her heart fluttering and her throat tight from his stimulating show of affection, she opened the oven door and placed the baking sheet on the rack. "Dinner will be ready soon."

∾

HEARING LAUREN RECLAIM HER KITCHEN DID SOMETHING to Colton. It hit him straight in the heart and made him feel warm inside. "Good. I'm starved."

It wasn't that he was glad she was in the kitchen. Because she'd never been a good cook, or even a capable cook, for that matter. Most of the food she'd prepared when they were first married had either been burned beyond recognition or as tasteless as hardtack.

But his wife was happy about being in her kitchen, which was in their house. She'd gone from asking him if she could do her laundry to preparing meals.

The kitchen didn't have a smoke aroma, so maybe the odds she'd mastered at least one dish were in Colton's favor. But it didn't matter how the food tasted or if he had to funnel ashes into his mouth. He was eating whatever she'd cooked and, by God, he'd smile while choking down every bite.

"How'd the shopping go?" he asked.

"Great." Grabbing a large mixing bowl from the cabinet above the stove, she added instant mashed potatoes and hot water, then started mixing. "We had lunch in Billings and visited a few shops. I got a sweet deal on a couple of outfits."

"I'm glad you had a good time."

After opening the can of green beans, she dumped the

contents into a bowl and set them in the microwave for a quick heat.

So far, so good. It was hard to mess up dehydrated potato flakes and canned veggies. Whatever was in the oven, dinner rolls included, would be the true test of Lauren's newfound cooking skills.

She set two plates on the table and went back to the china cabinet for silverware. "Little Jack called earlier."

"And?" he said, discarding the paper towel he'd used to dry his hands on in the trash.

"He wants to Facetime us during the Christmas parade."

Colton reached above her and retrieved two glasses from the top shelf. "He's sure is proud of that float. He's been talking about it for months."

"I've been meaning to ask you." She turned to him, one hand on the back of the chair and the other fisted on her hip. "Since when are we calling him J.D.?"

Oh, boy. Little Jack hadn't confided in his mother about his romantic interest, so Colton was going to have to deliver the news. "I suspect the name change has some-thing to do with Aubrey, Stan and Carlene Smith's daughter."

Her mouth dropped open, and her brows buckled, suggesting her heart was melting. "Little Jack has a girlfriend?"

Colton felt her parental pain. He'd known about Aubrey since last summer and had since adjusted to the fact that their son had a girlfriend. He'd been as stunned as Lauren was now. But happy that he hadn't missed this important part of his son's life.

He scooted a chair back and sat down. "Aubrey is a cute nine-year-old with a gap between her front teeth and freckles."

"Why haven't I heard about Aubrey?"

"It's a guy thing."

Lauren's posture withered.

"Cheer up." He took her hand and gave it a reassuring shake. "Our son has a girlfriend. It's not the end of the world."

"I know," she said, her mouth a wavy line of dissatisfaction. "It's just he's growing up so fast and I wanted him to have siblings that were close to his age. You know?"

He'd thought about Little Jack's lack of siblings over the years. Being an only child could be lonely at times. They both knew that. Colton was more than ready to remedy that by going straight to work on the baby making. But he knew Lauren wasn't. Conceiving a child together would come soon enough, not when they were only days into their new relationship.

"I do, but you can't stop him from growing up and you sure as hell can't stop nature." He wrapped an arm around her waist and pulled her onto his lap. Maybe not the best idea, since the thought of making babies with Lauren had given Colton an instant erection. The feel of her soft, round bottom covering his hardness was the sweetest form of torture.

She quickly shifted from his lap to his thigh, speculation gleaming in her eyes. "What are you up to?"

*About nine painful inches.*

He concocted an innocent smile, dug into his front pocket, and held up the card game he'd purchased at the Barn. "Cards." It was a completely unbelievable justification for the budge in his pants.

She wasn't fooled by his deck excuse, but she snickered anyway. "What are we playing? Strip poker?"

"I'd never—"

"Because if we are," she interjected with a sultry gaze

as she ran a finger down the front of his shirt, "I've never played."

"No?" he questioned, loving every second of this game.

"No." She made a pouty lip and paused, her finger on the top of his belt buckle. "I'd probably lose every hand."

Colton would have gladly forfeited just for the sake of letting her win at a game she'd never played, and hell, yes. He wanted to play strip poker with his wife or partake in any other fun activity that would get them out of their clothes. But he reminded himself that what they were doing now—teasing, flirting, and laughing—was an important part of rebuilding their husband-and-wife intimacy. While he was anticipating making love to her again, he knew emotional closeness had to come first.

"Would you look at that," he said, as he studied the cards and pretended to be surprised. "It is strip poker."

That sent her into more giggles. "Uh-uh. It's too late to change the game!"

Colton tossed the deck onto the table, sending cards across the top and onto the floor. "You should reconsider."

"Oh, yeah," her face was almost glowing. It was the happiest he'd seen in years. "Why is that?"

He scooped her into his arms and rose to his feet. She let out a scream and looped her arms around his neck.

"I'm an excellent teacher," he said, an underlying meaning in his deep tone.

The centers of her blue eyes expanded, as did his dick, and a nearly inaudible sound of longing escaped her mouth. They could agree to starting over with a clean slate, but they couldn't wipe out the moments of making slow, sweet love when she'd been vulnerable and painfully bashful about sex. The moments when he'd extracted every ounce of his patience, calming her fears and teaching her to love physically.

"You," she whispered, sliding a hand along his jaw, "are a wonderful teacher, Colton Ritter."

She lowered her lips to his, and the game was over. It was the second time Lauren had kissed him, the second time he'd held back and waited for her to make the first move.

The hunger in her kiss implied she was closer to the baby-making point of their relationship than he'd thought. He slid his arm from under her legs and wrapped it around her waist without breaking the kiss.

Body to body, the tension in his body grew. She deepened the kiss, explored his mouth with her tongue, and aroused him like she had when they first made love. Her jeans fit snug around her hips and contoured to her curves as though they were tailor made to make him ache.

It had been years since he'd touched his wife's body and he intended to make up for lost time. His hands moved over her form, slowly mapping her back, her waist, hips, and bottom. Lauren had filled out over the years and bloomed lovelier curves with pregnancy and age. Built with a waist-to-hip ratio that reinforced his therapist assurance that his sexual dysfunction problems were only temporary, she was a pleasure to explore.

He wanted her, here, now, on the table, on the floor… The craving to be one with her again drove him. He reached behind her and slid his hands around the back of her thighs, then lifted her and wrapped her legs around his hips. Holding her bottom, he pushed into her, denim against denim. Hot, hard, wet, and, if he had it his way, wild as hell.

He planted her bottom on the table, and with the swipe of his hand, cleared the top. The crashing of glass echoed through the house. He didn't care about broken dishes. He needed her and he was going to have her. What better way to christen their new relationship than by making love at the dining table?

He kissed his way down her neck and began unbuttoning her top. He was at her cleavage, intent on tasting those beautiful breasts, when the ear-splitting screech of the smoke detector went off.

He jerked upright to see a thick cloud of smoke hovering over the kitchen

"The dinner rolls!" Lauren jumped to her feet and shot across the kitchen to the stove. She opened the oven and was met by a plume of smoke.

# CHAPTER TWENTY-ONE

COLTON OPENED THE BACK DOOR TO ALLOW THE SMOKE TO escape, then grabbed a dishrag and started fanning the smoke detector.

Lauren shoved her hand into a mitten and reached into the oven for the dinner rolls. "My pretty rolls." She faked a cry. "They're ruined."

The detector's screeching stopped, compelling him to stick a finger in his ear canal and jiggle it. "Nah, I'm sure they're edible," he said, staring down at the blackened bread.

When she picked up a roll, Colton could have sworn he heard it crutch. Examining it the way he had the deck of cards, she held it out to him. "You first."

He gulped at the prospect of biting into the charred roll, but didn't hesitate to accept it. Never show fear was his motto. Eating her cooking might be the single most important test of their relationship, and he wasn't going to let a burned dinner roll *become a stumbling block.*

*Oh, well. Where's the funnel?*

As he opened his mouth and started to bite down, her

hand clamped around his. "Don't you dare put that in your mouth."

He held in a blow of relief. She wasn't going to make him eat the roll.

*Thank you, Jesus.*

"Why not?" He pretended to dust away the blackened crust. "It's just a little brown around the edges."

"It's disgusting." She took the roll and gave him a quick kiss on the cheek. "But it was sweet of you to offer your tastebuds as a sacrifice to save my feelings."

He hooked an arm around her waist and kissed her roughly. "Does that mean we can finish what we started on the table if I eat the uncharred portion of the meal?"

She laughed. "No."

Lauren tossed the dinner rolls into the trash while Colton cleaned up the glass they'd broken before the smoke alarm interrupted their kiss.

They ate while asking questions from the card game. Neither talked about how close they'd come to making love on the dining table. The meal was surprisingly good, and the questions were entertaining.

She skewed a couple of green beans on her fork and picked a card from the top of the deck. "Which is more important, to be smart or to be kind?"

"You have more peace if you're generous and considerate, so kindness." He took a card, read the question on the card to himself, and chuckled.

She groaned. "Oh, no. What's the question?"

He dramatically prepared for the question by clearing his throat. "What's my best quality?"

"Wow," she muttered. "That's a hard one."

He tossed the card down. "I wouldn't think it's that difficult to identify at least one."

"It's not," she said. "You have so many it's hard to name the best one."

"Yeah?" he questioned, smiling from her complements.

"Yeah. You're a mature, self-confident man who makes me laugh, and that's just off the top of my head."

"I can live with that," he said, winking. "Your turn."

She picked up a card from the top of the deck and read the question aloud. "What's your dream vacation?"

He was at a loss for that one. "What's a vacation?"

She giggled and rolled her eyes.

Colton took his turn. "What's something you've always wondered about me, but never asked?"

"Too serious. Pick another one." Lauren reached for a new card.

He capped his hand over the deck and scooted it out of her reach before she could take one. "That's not how the game is played." Some questions had required thought, but were lighthearted and meant for an entertaining game. What question could cause her to want to pick another card?

Her eyes pleaded with him. "Colton…"

"Ask and don't make something up," he said, pecking the cards with his forefinger. "If we're going to make this marriage work, we have to be open with each other, right?"

"Right," she agreed with an exhale. "But I know there are some things you can't talk about. I'm not going to push you. You can tell me when you're ready."

Colton suddenly felt like he was standing in front of a firing squad without the mercy of a blindfold, and he'd put himself there by not letting Lauren pick another card. But it was too late to turn back now. "How am I going to know if I'm ready to talk about the question if you don't ask it?"

She lay her fork down and let her shoulders slump. "But we're having such a good time."

He took her hand in his and smiled lovingly at her. "Marriage can't be all fun and games now, can it?"

"No."

He let her hand go and sat back in the dining chair. "Let's do this."

Lauren resumed her straight posture, then cleared her throat. "Okay, here goes, but…" She held up a hand. "Remember, there's no pressure to answer."

"I know."

A few intense seconds followed while she worked up the courage to ask, but then it came. "Who's Ray?"

His body went stiff, and her blue eyes filled with compassion.

"Oh, God," she groaned. "I knew it was a bad idea."

"N–No," he choked out. "I'm just surprised to hear the name. How did you know about Ray?"

"That's what woke me that night. You were yelling his name."

Colton pushed the chair back and propped his hands on the tops of his thighs.

"Let me pick another card," she insisted.

"No." He stood and walked over to the kitchen sink. "You need to understand."

"What do I need to understand?"

"That there are some things that a person never gets over. Things that can't be fixed, healed, or forgiven. Areas where the only thing a person can do is function. I function in unforgiveness. Not for the sniper who pulled the trigger, but for me." He tapped a fist against his chest. "Me, Lauren. There are certain things I can't forgive myself for. Like pushing you into that desk and…" He didn't want to say the words. "Causing the death of a good man."

Bracing his hands on the counter, he gazed into the darkness of the cold Montana night. "First Lieutenant Ray

Barnett was our platoon leader and my best friend while I was on deployment. We met during basic training. He was older than most of the soldiers in our unit and a helluva lot wiser. He'd been a police officer in a small town somewhere in Oklahoma."

This was the first time Colton had talked about Ray. No one knew the story, not even his therapist. He'd recounted the ambush to his commanding officer, but no one knew the tragedy of it all or the fate of perfect timing.

"The man was a born leader. He didn't downplay the dangers of living and working in a combat zone, and he always re-enforced the seriousness of being alert and on guard. Ray always kept his cool. He never got excited about anything. Firefights, bombs." Colton shook his head, still unable to understand his friend. "He'd duck and cover when he had to and fight like hell with the rest of us. But when it was over, no matter how bad the fight was or how close he'd come to dying, he'd dust himself off, get bandaged up, and go back out there with steady hands."

Colton gripped the edge of the counter and concentrated on a bright star hanging over the highest peak. "He used to say patrol in Iraq was like being a beat cop. Same route, day after day. No big deal. He said that so much I think I started to believe he was right. But he wasn't. Over there, when you went on patrol, you were risking your life. Stepping on an IUD, being buried by an artillery shell, or my personal favorite, shot by a sniper. There was always a chance that when you went out, you weren't coming back. That day, I was the only one who came back."

Concentrating on that star wasn't going to help him get through this story. He needed another focal point, so he let go of the counter, turned himself around and locked eyes on the one thing that had helped him make it home.

Lauren. She kept her eyes trained on him, giving him the strength he needed to say what needed to be said.

"Our unit was patrolling with Iraqi police. We'd walked the route dozens of times, with Ray leading the way. It was just another ordinary day on patrol. I was behind Ray. Crenshaw, Taylor, and the others were behind me. I remember something wasn't right with my armor vest. It'd been bugging me all morning. I still don't know what it was. Probably a rock or a piece of sand. Hell, over there, it could've been anything." He stopped to swallow and find his voice as he relieved the last moments of Ray's life.

"Ray stopped to help me dig it out." He put his maimed hand on his right shoulder. "Just another day on patrol, he said. No big deal. Those were the last words he said to me. Then I heard the shot. For a split second, there was no sound, no movement, just complete silence and Ray's face frozen in front of me. I'll never forget the way he looked. Never. I'd never seen fear in his eyes until that moment."

Lauren covered her mouth and cried silently.

"The next thing I knew, I was on the ground and all hell was breaking loose."

"I'm sorry," she whispered.

"The bullet pierced a seam in the back of Ray's armor vest, continued through my hand, and out my shoulder."

Hands trembling, tears flowing, Lauren closed her eyes. He hadn't wanted to tell her the details, but now she knew. She knew everything.

"We were taken down by the same bullet. When I reached over, I must have stepped out of the line of fire so that the bullet clipped me. Snipers rarely miss their target, so whatever was in my armor vest saved my life. But it cost Ray his."

"No," she sniffed. "The sniper had Ray in his crosshairs. What happened was out of your control, Colton."

~

As Lauren had silently predicted, the question on her card had ended their fun evening. Colton had helped her clean the table and wash the dishes. But he'd excused himself around nine for bed.

She suspected the conversation might trigger a nightmare, so she'd stayed up late just to be sure. But there were no sounds coming from the master bedroom, no crying or begging.

She hoped that by offering him her forgiveness, he might forgive himself for accidentally hurting her. But she knew that no matter what anyone did or said, he'd never forgive himself for Ray's death.

The next morning, Colton was no worse for wear, or so he pretended. When Lauren came downstairs for breakfast, she found him standing in front of the kitchen sink, staring out the window like he had last night.

She poured herself a cup of coffee and joined him at the sink. But a cattle ranch didn't stop running because it was Sunday. The men took alternating days off work, so that the animals were taken care of. Today wasn't any different from any other day of the week. The view was the same. Bovines, equines, and cowboys were doing their part to keep the Lucky Jack running prosperously. "Whatcha lookin' at?"

"I'm thinking more than looking."

His voice was much deeper in the mornings and the tone of it vibrated sensitive parts of her body. "Whatcha thinkin' about?"

He glanced around and offered her a smile. "Remember the other night when you asked me what was wrong, and I said I was tired?"

She pulled out a chair and sat at the table. "Yeah."

"Well, I, that is." He stopped and let out a quick huff. "This is harder than I'd thought it'd be."

"I knew you were lying to me," she said tersely and sat her mug down. "God, Colton, I hate being lied too."

A frown yanked the corner of his mouth. "I wasn't lying."

"Then what were you doing?"

As he considered her question, his eyes darted back and forth, sweeping her face, searching for a way out. "I skirted around the truth."

"That's your answer?" she asked, irritated he gave her such a ludicrous explanation. "You skirted," she made a snake-like motion with her hand. "Around the truth. Uh-uh. No. Riding the rim of honesty is the same as lying, Colton."

"Lauren." He bowed his head and pinched the bridge of his nose with a finger and thumb. "Listen to what I have to say before you condemn me."

"Hmph." She folded her arms across her breasts and waited.

He took a chair, spun it around, and sat astride it. "What I'm about to tell you is strictly between us."

She could keep a secret. He knew that, but he wanted it to be clear no one could be privy to what he was about to tell her. "Should I cross my heart?"

He rested his forearms on the back and gave her a wiry grin. "That's not necessary."

"I'm waiting on pins and needles. What is it?"

"The Lucky Jack has been the victim of cattle rustling."

She paused in mid-sip to swallow. "A thief?"

"I'm afraid so."

She could hardly believe that in this day and age, people were stealing cattle. "It that a thing nowadays?"

"It is, but our thief isn't cutting fences and hauling cattle away in trailers. Six of our embryos have disappeared in the last two months."

"Embryos," she whispered, in awe as she remembered one article she'd read on the Lucky Jack. "So, it's high-tech, modern-day cattle rustling."

"And it's costing us a fortune."

Losing money would put someone in a bad mood. Those embryos had to be worth thousands of dollars. That certainly helped her understand why he'd been in a bad mood. A hefty theft was cause for concern, but the thief might be dangerous, especially if they were cornered. "Any ideas on who it might be?"

"There are only two keys to the facility where the embryos are stored," he said grimly. "Mine and Mia's."

Lauren recalled something Mia had said. *I think somewhere in the back of Colton's mind, he knew dad was dying. I showed up out of nowhere, so he thought I was some sort of con artist here to get what I could and leave.* Mia seemed so sure that the rocky start she and Colton had had in the begging was behind them. Had she been wrong? Did he suspect Mia? "You don't think Mi—"

"No," he blurted. "Mia would never steal from me, and besides, she has no reason to. She gained a hefty trust fund from her grandparents when she turned twenty."

Ah-ha. That explained her financial resources.

"Then who—?" The answer hit Lauren before she finished asking the question. "Oh, no. Ian?"

"The two of them have gotten really close lately," he said, his eyes reflecting the worry he felt for his sister. "You saw how taken she was by him the other night at dinner. I think she may already be in love with the man."

A chill ran over Lauren. She wasn't going to betray Mia by telling Colton about her and Ian's secret spot, but he already suspected she was in love with Ian. "She is. She all but told me so."

His posture stiffened and his lips thinned. "I thought as much."

"And the Golden Rule." Lauren winced regrettably. "It was a way for you to keep them apart, wasn't it? And I shot it down it, didn't I?

"As you said." He pushed his palms into his closed eyes. "She's a grown woman. And you did not know what was going on."

Nevertheless, Lauren felt like a fool. She'd been rooting for Ian and now there was a chance he might be using Mia to steal from Colton.

"I don't think it would have done any good, anyway."

He let his head fall to one side and shifted his jaw sideways. "The day Sampson plowed into me; I saw Mia's truck coming down the east trail. We both know what's up there."

So Colton knew about their secret spot at cow camp. Lauren was undecided about revealing the rest of what she knew. If Ian wasn't the thief, then telling Colton they were planning on leaving the ranch would be a bad idea. But if she didn't tell him, Mia might be headed down a hard road, especially if Ian knew about her trust fund. "Is there a chance we could be wrong?"

He gave her a doubtful side glance.

"Not cow camp," she replied dryly. "The embryos."

"I don't think so. I've changed the locks twice, so whoever's stealing them has to have access to Mia's keys. The sheriff's office has been looking into Ian's background and finances. He owns an LLC no one knew about."

"That proves nothing."

"No, but the LLC buys and sells cattle. That's pretty damn fishy and a hell of a motive." Colton swung a leg over the chair and rose. "But I can't figure out how he's transporting them. The embryos have to maintain a certain temperature, or they lose viability."

"How's Ian getting in if you and Mia are the only ones with keys? She may be naïve, but she's not stupid."

"It would be easy for Ian to distract her and take her keys," Colton continued to theorize. "But the embryos weren't stolen at the same time. There have been different incidences. Two more were stolen sometime last night. He wouldn't take a chance on taking her keys each time, which means he'd need a key of his own."

"He could have taken the keys once, had a copy made and returned them without her ever knowing they were gone," Lauren added her part to the theory. "What have I done?"

He patted her thigh. "Nothing, honey. I should have told you sooner, but I wanted proof that Ian was the thief before I started throwing mud at the man."

Her empty stomach rumbled. "Do you have proof?"

"Maybe," he said, raking a hand through his hair. "There are only two places in Crossfire Canyon where a person can have a key duplicated. George Jacob's Hardware on Main Street and Luke Barlow's ranch supply store out on Hellcat Road. George and Hannah had their first grandchild a couple of days ago, so they're in Sheridan and won't be back until next week."

"That leaves Luke's store," she said, going to the refrigerator.

"Yeah, so after I left Val's office, I drove to the store.

Luke wasn't there, but the kid he had working for him said he'd made a half dozen keys in the past couple of weeks. I asked if any of them were from the Lucky Jack. He said he didn't know. All sales receipts are kept in Luke's office. I'm going back tomorrow so I can talk to Luke directly."

She took out the bacon and the pack of canned biscuits Mia had bought. "There's also the possibility that Ian didn't have the key made in Crossfire Canyon."

"True," he said.

"I'm hungry," she explained and as she handed him the biscuits. "We can figure out what to do next while we're eating."

"Ah," he said, peeling the paper from the can. "So, I bake and you fry, is that it?"

She shot him a smile.

"Chicken." He chuckled.

# CHAPTER TWENTY-TWO

AFTER THEY ATE BREAKFAST, LAUREN TOOK COLTON UP ON his offer to practice her roping skills. It was Sunday, and she had the whole day to do whatever she wanted, so she'd purposefully left her cell phone upstairs.

She didn't want any distractions from Jonas. If Little Jack needed her, he knew to call Colton's cell.

"How much do you remember?" Colton asked, taking Jack Reid's lariat from her hand.

"That I was horrible at it."

"Dad taught you, so you can't be that bad." He took her by the arm and lined her up with the roping dummy. "But we'll do a quick refresher course."

"Okay."

"The tip of the rope is?"

She thought for a second, recalling what Jack Reid had taught her. "At the bottom of the loop."

"Right. It determines direction."

"So the tip should face the dummy. Got it."

"Where's the eye of the rope?"

"There." She pointed to where the rope slid through the smaller loop.

"Right again." He winked at her. "See, it's all coming back to you."

She clamped her front teeth over her bottom lip and smiled, a giddy sort of excitement running over her. "I'm surprised I remembered all of this."

"Last, what's the spoke?"

"The spoke. The spoke." She knew the word, but it had been so long since Jack Reid schooled her on the basics of roping. *You know this.* Lauren closed her eyes tight. "Oh, I know. It's, ah–the space. No, that's not it." She snapped her fingers a couple of time. "It's the distance between the eye and your hand."

"Three in a row." With a proud smile, he handed her the lariat and stepped behind her. "I'd say you're ready to rope."

With her back against his chest, Lauren positioned the lariat in her hands and waited for Colton's instruction. He clasped his hand over hers, and like a puppeteer, began going through the motions.

"Remember to use your wrist and your shoulder, not your whole arm. You won't get a good swing if you don't."

She started swinging the way he instructed.

"That's it," he praised. "Keep your palm positioned towards the back of the swing and bring it in front of you when you swing forward.

She started swinging, slowly at first, but then faster and faster.

He stepped back to give her room. "Bring your palm face up. That's it."

As the rope crossed over her head, her heart raced. She'd forgotten how much she loved this.

"Swing your loop," he said. "And remember, you're not

on a horse, so step forward when you throw. That'll give the rope momentum."

She swung and swung, then took a step and hurled the rope at her target. It sailed through the air and miraculously landed around the dummy calf's head. "I did it," she said, jumping for joy.

Grinning from ear to ear, he started rolling the rope up for anther go. Lauren threw until she thought her arm might fall off. She'd had a wonderful time and couldn't wait to try roping from the saddle. She grimaced at the image of her trying to mount a horse after all these years.

Colton had taken a spot near the fence. The wind was chilly, but the sun cast a warmth that made thermals and a long-sleeved shirt bearable. He had one on. He'd shed his jacket before he did the roping recap. With his arms spread along the top rail, he leaned back and hooked his boot heel over the bottom rail. The dark brown Cambridge shirt he wore fit him well and accentuated his chest muscles. He'd been in that I'm-sexy-and-I-know-it pose for the last half-hour, and it was no coincidence that her lucky streak had ended at the exact moment she'd noticed him.

Lauren swung, threw, and missed.

"Getting tired?" he asked, smiling as he hooked his thumbs through his belt loops.

*Of throwing ropes. Yes. Of looking at you. Never.*

Her husband was the sexiest man on earth.

That hit her like a bolt of lightning.

Her husband.

The cowboy resting against that fence was hers.

She didn't have to win him, fight for him, or worry that he might not marry her.

Colton Ritter was hers and hers alone.

Hers to hold. Hers to kiss and hers to do whatever she

wanted to with. All she had to do was go to his bed—their bed.

She wedged a hand against her hip, cocked her leg out, and looked at him. "You're very distracting, you know."

Chuckling, he pushed upright and strolled over to where she stood. "Am I?"

Looking at him, she nodded. "And if there weren't so many cowboys watching us, I might just kiss you."

His eyes darkened. "Don't let them stop you."

Reaching up, she hooked her hand behind his head and pulled him closer. It was the most passionate kiss they'd shared so far. Maybe it was because they were outside in the open for all to see. Or maybe it was because, only seconds ago, Lauren had imagined herself making love to Colton.

Yeah, she sighed as she ended the kiss. That was definitely it. Wet and wild took on a new meaning for her.

"Tell me, honey." He licked his bottom lip as if he was savoring the taste of her. "Are you any closer to lassoing that dream now?"

The question blindsided Lauren. Colton wasn't asking her about her ambitions or goals in life. He'd specifically referenced "roping that dream", a single wish she'd shared with her father-in-law about his son; the yearnings of a young woman who feared losing the man she loved.

She knew Jack Reid wouldn't have betrayed her confidence. That meant Colton had based his question on that brief bequest in Jack Reid's will.

Her husband was a smart man. He could have figured out what that dream was on his own. But she didn't think he had. The question was too ambiguous for a straight-to-the-point man such as Colton, which meant he only had a vague notion and had asked, thinking she might fill in the blanks for him.

She didn't have the slightest idea of how to do that because considering everything that had happened between them since the reading of the will, that dream seemed puerile compared to what was happening between them now.

Thanks to Jack Reid, the dream she'd given up on had reshaped itself into something far greater than what she could have imagined. And it lay just beyond the horizon of their second chance.

So, yes, she was closer to lassoing her dream, but the spin was still in motion and if she threw too soon, she might miss.

Lauren took a step back and then another and another until she had ample space to throw the rope. "Maybe."

His left brow hitched upward, while a cogitating expression took hold of his handsome features.

*So, he hasn't figured it out.*

She adjusted her hold on the rope, then started swinging. After four or five, she took that step he'd instructed her to take for momentum and hurled it at him. It sailed through the air and landed perfectly around Colton's wide shoulders.

He calmly took stock of his predicament, glanced at the rope, and then back to her. "You have great aim."

"Thank you. I love roping my target."

The rope wasn't cinched tight, and Lauren wasn't strong enough to hold Colton if he wanted out of the lariat, which he clearly didn't. Taking hold of the rope that had him bound, he began reeling her in, one hand at a time.

Lauren didn't let go. She gripped the rope with both hands, telling him she wouldn't simply give up on that dream. It was hers.

When there was less than a foot between them, he

paused and, without warning, gave the rope a little jerk. She tumbled into him, laughing. He smiled down at her, wrapped his arm around her waist, and dipped her back to kiss her soundly. "Your target loves being roped."

She found it pleasingly ironic that she'd roped Colton with Jack Reid's lariat, the mastermind behind their second chance.

~

Colton raised Lauren from the dip and wrapped his other arm around her, holding her snuggly against him. What he'd aimed to be a quick kiss had evolved into something far more sensual.

"We're drawing," Lauren whispered between kisses, "a crowd.

He opened his eyes and threw a glance toward the Lucky Jack cowhands who had gathered at the fence like wide-eyed spectators at a championship rodeo.

He tucked his hand under the base of her head and gave her that sound kiss on the lips just for show. "They might as well get used to seeing the boss kiss his wife."

She gazed up at him. "Why's that?"

"Because I intend to make it a habit."

Her smile was sexy. "Yeah?"

"Oh, yeah," he said, dipping his voice low.

Colton thought back to the day in Bill's office when he'd begged Lauren to stay, and when he'd looked into her eyes and knew in his heart that the woman who had once loved him was still there. He hadn't seen that woman since he'd deployed, but she was slowly and cautiously beginning to reemerge. Each day there was a little more of her and a little less of the woman who'd left him.

That woman was so vivid right now, her face bright

and happy. She smiled up at him with those big, blue, crystal-clear eyes that were free, radiant, and filled with love.

It was a reunion of sorts.

Colton had never shed a joyful tear in his life. But there was a first time for everything. As a single tear spilled from the corner of his eye, compassion swept over Lauren's features, and he knew she understood. No words were needed.

She snuggled her head against his chest, wrapped her arms around his waist, and held him tight. They were communicating intimately with their hearts. His world finally seemed right again. He felt whole and amazingly happier than he had when he'd made her his bride, and he wasn't so lax as to share this moment with his crew. It was a tender milestone that wasn't up for display. "I think it's time we went inside, don't you? Maybe have lunch and wrap those presents I bought."

"Mmm mmhm, uh-huh." She planted a kiss in the middle of his chest. Her warm breath penetrated the cloth of his flannel shirt. "I'm hungry."

He was too, but not for food. When Lauren raised her head, her eyes conveyed the same, but satisfying that hunger would involve a mutual commitment. After all that had happened between them—the separation, the painful memories, and the bitterness of a dying relationship— making love would be the consummation of a new commitment.

Colton wasn't conceited enough to think he was the totality of that dream Lauren wanted to rope. But he knew he was an integral part of it. Composed of different things that dream would, if roped, create a whole. Pieces of a life she'd secretly longed for since they had married.

That fact gutted him. Because it wasn't him getting

shot or the PTSD that had caused their separation and nearly ended their marriage.

It was him. He was the one to blame for all those lost years, for those unconceived babies, and for her unhappiness.

Over the next few days, the desire for more than cuddling and kisses intensified. Colton worked less, so he could spend more time at home with her, and Lauren refused to make herself available for her job after hours. Her workday ended promptly at four and her lunch breaks were spent with him.

It was a courtship, exciting and new, much like the one they'd had when they first met. But there was also the comfort of being husband and wife, of being two halves that made a whole.

Lauren and Mia had rehung the pictures in the upstairs hall. They'd decorated the house for Christmas. Lauren had persuaded Colton to wrap lights around the evergreens in front of the house. The tree they'd purchased from Dawson's was trimmed and presents were stacked neatly beneath it.

His wife had her tree.

In the evenings, he made a fire, and they sat together on the couch to watch television. They watched Little Jack in the Christmas parade together; they reheated casseroles together, made breakfast together, and ate in town—together.

They'd played the card game so much he doubted there was a single secret between them, but his sore conscience was quick to remind him of the will he'd locked away in the safe.

Things were going well between him and Lauren, but the clock was ticking. Time was against him, but he'd rather be tied to a rattler than confess his lie to her. Colton

hadn't had a good night's sleep since she'd roped him.
Night after night, he lay awake, considering his options.

He could deed Mia her rightful portion of the ranch.
That part he could manage with little effort. But if he did,
his sister would spend the rest of her life thinking their dad
had left her out of his will.

Mia's inheritance wasn't about material things—the land
and cabin. It was about being included in Jack Reid's
legacy. She deserved to be, and there was no way he could
rob her of that. He wouldn't intentionally break Mia's
heart or dishonor his dad to cover his lie.

Their skirted conversation was never far from Colton's
mind, and neither was all the times he'd ridden the rim of
honesty to protect his lie.

His first phone call to the Humphry and Dane Law
Office had been at lunchtime when he knew Darlene
wouldn't answer and he hadn't left a message.

*Skirted.*

After that, he called and used the direct number to
Bill's empty office, bypassing Darlene. He hadn't lied. Bill
hadn't answered.

*Skirted.*

And he hadn't lied about Darlene, refusing to give him
Bill's cell phone number. She'd told him that right before
he left the office the day the will had been read.

*Skirted.*

Colton let out a long sigh and closed his eyes. "Strike
three. You're out."

But he knew he'd be out long before any of those lies
came to light. The second Lauren found out about the new
will, she'd be gone.

Their new relationship. *Over.*

Their marriage. Down the toilet.

Trust. *Out the window.*

Intimacy. *Not a chance in hell.*

Lauren in his arms. Warm evenings by the fire and reheated casseroles. Lonely, cold nights and sandwiches from Willie's Truck Stop.

If he waited too long to confess his contribution of deceit and willingness to aid his dad's plan, he'd have to formulate more lies. He wasn't willing to go that far to save his marriage, but if he didn't, he might not have a marriage.

Thursday evening, the day before Claire Chisum's party, Lauren and Mia went to town, claiming they needed accessories to go with their dresses.

Colton had taken the time to assess the contents of the safe. Last night, whilst staring up at the ceiling, he'd remembered Bill had left his business card with Colton the last time he'd visited Jack Reid because he knew his friend was nearing the end.

But Colton hadn't seen it when he'd read the will after he'd brought Lauren back to the Lucky Jack. There was a chance it had slipped to the bottom of the safe or, he feared, was somewhere in the den.

He reached in for the will, then the thousand dollars in cash for emergencies. A passport his dad never used. The registration papers showing the Lucky Jack's cattle brand Jack Reid had refiled ten years ago and last, his parents' marriage certificate. Colton pulled it out and unfolded it. Bill's business card, tucked halfway in the first fold, had his personal cell phone number scribbled in blue. The number that could make or break their future.

It was nearing dark when the women arrived home. Colton stopped his restless pacing in the living room and decided.

He'd call Bill.

He had to. There was no way around it. No skirting on this one.

No siree.

He just didn't know when to call or how he'd explain what had happened. Marty read the wrong will. No problem. Young Martin could get himself out of hot water on his own.

Colton had his fate to worry about.

He'd come clean and confess to Lauren that he'd lied about his dad's will so he could manipulate her into rebuilding their marriage.

He'd rather swallow fencing nails.

Walking out of the house and down the front porch steps, as Lauren and Mia were getting out of the jeep, he asked, "Need help with the bags?"

"No." Mia held up the three small bags in her hand. "We didn't splurge."

"We accessorized with restraint," Lauren said as she greeted him with a quick kiss.

Colton held out his arm, and she took it. They strode up the walk together and Mia disappeared inside the house. He covered Lauren's hand with his. "You don't have to settle for cheap, you know."

Chuckling softly, she handed him her two bags and brushed her hair away from her eyes. "I didn't settle. I chose fake diamonds and costume jewelry will hardly break me."

When they reached the steps, he waited for Lauren to go first. "I would have bought whatever you needed for the party.

Her steps stalled on the second step. She turned around, took his chin in her hand, and bent to give him another kiss. A sweeter version of the one she'd just given him. "Thank you. But there's no need to spend a lot of money on something I'll only wear once."

"If you stay, you can wear them to next year's Christmas party or buy new ones. We can cuddle on the couch, and you can burn dinner rolls in your kitchen. Mia can teach you how to cook or we'll dine out every night. I don't care. You can find a job here. Val has a job opening for an office manager. If you don't want to do that, help me manage the ranch. Or don't work at all. I don't care. Little Jack can go to school here. We can go to his school events together and I can be a full-time dad. We can be a family again and later, when you're ready, we can have more children."

Lights from the evergreens shone in her eyes, making them sparkle and shine with a passion he was yet to explore. "Are you trying to bribe me with babies?"

"No. I love you, Lauren. I don't tell you that nearly enough, and I want you to know I'd do anything to keep you and Little Jack with here with me."

A faint smile hinted at her lips as she ran a hand up his jaw. "I love you too, Colton."

Her admission should have been enough to ease the weight of their impending goodbye. But it only made it worse because she hadn't told him what he needed to hear.

# CHAPTER TWENTY-THREE

LAUREN WANTED TO HER ENSEMBLE TO BE ELEGANT FOR tonight's party, and she wanted to reinforce Colton's stunningly beautiful compliment of her.

She dressed nice for Foundation events, but never to impress. It was a simple-dress-no-jewelry event for her. But tonight, was different. She wanted to impress and dazzle him.

"Okay," Mia said, handing Lauren a hand mirror. "See how this looks to you."

It had been Mia's idea to get ready at her house and Lauren was game. She didn't want Colton to see her until she was perfect. It was a silly idea, she thought, as she examined the back of her hair through the reflection in the hand mirror. But a person was prone to inane notions when they were in love.

Mia had expertly styled Lauren's hair into a French twist and adorned it with a simple jeweled comb. "Oh, Mia," she gasped. "I love it."

"Good. Now, let's do your makeup."

Colton had seen her in a dress before, and she wore

makeup occasionally. But this was the first time they'd gone out as a couple since they dated.

Jeez. Had it been that long?

Sadly, it had.

The last two weeks had been a whirlwind of emotions. Everything between her and Colton was moving so rapidly that her head was spinning. Their relationship exceeded her marital expectations, and she couldn't quite believe what was happening.

He'd taken her to Dawson's for a tree and helped her decorate it.

Colton Ritter had tried to pick out a wreath for their front door. He had, without any prodding from her, strung lights on the evergreens, for goodness sakes, and never in a million years would she have thought he would have volunteered to attend Claire Chism's Christmas party with her.

The most important part of it all was that he was talking to her, confiding in her as a wife and friend about deep and meaningful things. For the first time in their relationship, they were working to build emotional intimacy.

This second chance was indeed something new.

When she'd first arrived at the Lucky Jack, she'd been overwhelmed with terrible memories, guilt and acrimony. But things were different. She was different. The memories of the early years of their marriage were there, but she didn't dwell on them as she had before. They were behind her. The guilt was gone and so was the animosity she'd had towards their separation.

They were falling in love all over again, and it was beyond magical. He'd poured out his heart to her last night right there on the front porch steps. The sincerity in his eyes as he told her loved her and his heartfelt plea for her to stay had moved her deeply. She'd wanted to throw her arms around him and tell him she'd stay.

But she'd hesitated.

A decision such as that required thought and a weighing of pros and cons. So many wonderful reasons existed to stay. She and Colton were in love and their marriage was reviving. They'd be no more lonely nights for her or Colton or summer trips for Little Jack to visit his dad. They'd be a family again. Their son could grow up on the ranch, and she and Colton could have more children.

Lauren had been joking when she'd asked Colton if he was bribing her with babies, but she yearned for them. Like their marriage, the possibility of her and Colton creating that miracle together again had seemed impossible. But they were planning for them. Each time he mentioned babies, she relived that wonderful feeling of expectancy. The beautiful, soul-consuming love they'd made when their son was conceived. The exact day she'd found out she was pregnant and the moment that precious life was birthed from her body.

But she was a rational woman who wouldn't irrationally make a crucial decision based on a maternal urge.

Living at the Lucky Jack would be a permanent move. If she stayed, she'd be giving up her job, her home, and the stability she'd worked so hard for.

"You're gorgeous," Mia said, breaking Lauren's internal battle.

Lauren didn't recognize the woman in the mirror. Mia had used a cool shade of blue to bring out the color of her eyes, added a little glitter around the edges, and applied a deep plum lipstick to her lips.

"You don't like it," Mia said, disappointed.

"No. No. It's just," she turned her head from side to side. "I can't believe it's me."

"Oh, it's you." Mia patted her on the shoulder. "Now get dressed."

Colton planned to pick her up at seven, and he was right on time. Much to her surprise, he knocked before opening the front door. She took one last look at herself in the mirror. The cubic zirconium earrings and bracelet were small, but she suddenly felt flashy, not elegant.

"Lauren?" he called out from the living room. "Are you ready?"

"I'm coming." She picked up the small black sequenced clutch she'd bought to go with her dress and hurried out of the bathroom.

~

COLTON STOOD IN THE LIVING ROOM, HIS FOCUS ON THE cookie tin Ian had given Mia. Stone-faced and tapping the lid with his forefinger, he looked deep in thought. Shoving his hand into the pocket of his slacks, he exhaled and shook his head.

What was it with him and that cookie tin?

Lauren would ask later.

She didn't want to spend the evening discussing Ian or stolen bovine embryos.

He wore black slacks with a matching Stetson and boots, along with a charcoal gray dress jacket with black yokes and a white button-up dress shirt. Seeing him clean-shaven and stylishly dress in western wear was new to her. Her husband was a fine-looking cowboy.

"I just have to get my coat," she said nervously.

His head came up. His eyes widened and his jaw dropped open.

Oh, God. Was the dress too ostentatious? Was her makeup too bright?

"It's too much, isn't it?" She winced and turned her knees inward. "I knew it."

"N–no," he protested, and cleared his throat. "It's just…" His dark gaze roamed over her with that slow, sensual appraisal. The one that made her feel sexy and wanted. "You are exquisite."

Her smile was jerky, but a thrill raced up her spine. "Oh."

"Uh–" Rubbing a hand over his jaw, he quickly scanned the room. "Your coat?"

She pointed. "It's on the couch."

After collecting the coat, he met her at the door and held it while she slipped it on. "Thank you."

"You're welcome."

"Where's yours? You'll freeze without one."

"Don't worry." He placed a hand on her lower back. "It's in the truck. Where leaving, Mia."

"Okay," she yelled from the bedroom. "Ian should be here soon. I'll see you there."

The temperature had dropped significantly since the sun had set, and a wind blew from the north. It made for a chilly evening, but Lauren was excited.

Colton helped her into the truck cab and closed the door. She buckled her seat belt and waited for him to put the truck in drive. He didn't.

"Shouldn't we be going?"

"I know you've not decided anything yet, and…" His shoulders shifted as if he had a bur under his jacket. "Of course, there's the whole will thing."

Why was he suddenly jittery?

"But when you're free to leave… That is," he cleared his throat again and gave the back of his neck a rub. "I'm not saying anything right."

She chuckled. "Just say what's on your mind, Colton."

"What's on my mind?" he repeated, looked out the windshield, and swallowed hard. After he choked down whatever it was tying his tongue, he reached into his jacket pocket and pulled out her wedding band. "I'd be honored if you'd wear this tonight."

Her heart swelled with love.

*Tonight. Tomorrow and beyond.* Lauren held her hand out, her eyes misty. He slid it on her ring finger and kissed her knuckles.

"I was going to buy a new one. You know, a new start. New ring." He started the engine and shifted the truck into Drive. "But I thought it might be too presumptuous. If you decide to stay, you can pick out the one you want."

Lauren didn't want a new ring. She wanted this one. The first ring he'd placed on her finger and trading it for a new one seemed wrong. It represented the vows she'd taken. She couldn't just discard it.

Curling her hand into a ball, she held it to her heart. "I think I'll keep this one, if you don't mind."

"No," he said, reaching over to pat her knee. "I don't mind, honey."

He couldn't reach Bill and even if he did, there was no guarantee her situation would change. It seemed like Edgar had fallen off the face of the earth, so everything was still in limbo. By the terms of the will, she had months to decide about staying. But Jonas was getting harder and harder to deal with. He was pressing for an answer about when she'd return to the office.

She hadn't given Colton an answer last night because she hadn't had one to give. But she wanted this marriage to work, that much she knew. It wouldn't be easy. Nothing worth having was. She had to decide within in the next couple of days.

The Chisum's were the most affluent family in the Canyon. They operated a large cattle ranch that spread for miles along the edge of the county. Chisum House was seated a couple hundred feet from the edge of the canyon with a long, inclining drive that circled around to the front of the house.

Guests had parked along the shoulder of the drive, and Colton found a spot behind the last vehicle. After helping her out, they walked up the flagstone walk and through the hand-carved mahogany doors. A young woman dressed in a pristine white blouse and black skirt took their coats.

While the exterior of the log castle reflected the rustic Montana landscape, the interior was nothing short of luxurious. The home was laid out in the same sprawling manner as the land itself.

The foyer was as wide as the living room at the Lucky Jack. The great room, with its two-story timber-framed cathedral ceiling, could easily accommodate a fourth of the partygoers, which were rumored to be in the hundreds. The floors were a fitting combination of hardwood and stone with contrasting light and dark shades.

The grand staircase, crafted from wrought iron and timber, was a perfect representation of the Chisum family. Dominating and strong, alluring, and bold.

A towering Christmas tree with gold and blue decorations sat beside the staircase. A talented pianist played classic holiday music on the baby grand piano by the creek rock fireplace.

Large chandeliers with richly finished scroll arms and amber glass hung over the living room and dining area. Matching pendant lights hung in corners and halls, illuminating the house.

"It's as big as I remember," Lauren whispered.

Colton hitched his dark eyebrow high. "Too rich for my blood."

She snickered. "Jack Reid said the same thing."

Claire's Christmas parties were a large-scale cocktail party, the kind corporations threw, but with an open house ambiance. Lauren anxiously fidgeted with the sequins on her clutch. It had been so long since she had socialized.

Colton noticed. "Why are you so nervous? You love meeting new people."

"I do, but attending ugly sweater parties at Little Jack's school isn't the same as a Claire Chisum cocktail party. It's been ages since I've mixed and mingled."

"It's like riding a bike or," he leaned closer so he could whisper in her ear, "having sex. Once you learn how to do it, you never forget."

His teasing made her chuckle, but his innuendo made her body burn hot. "Yeah, well. It's been a long time since I did it. I'm afraid I might be a little rusty."

"At riding a bike?" he asked, moving closer so that his front was touching her back.

She gently elbowed him in the ribs. "You are wicked."

"No." Colton's voice pitched deeper. "I'm a man who hasn't made love to his wife in nearly a decade."

Lauren could feel his arousal nudging at her backside and she couldn't help but tease him by shifting her hips. When she heard him exhale a low growl, she did it again.

"And you damn well better believe I remember how to do it," he said, snagging two glasses of champagne as the waiter walked by.

She flushed, not from embarrassment but from the memory of his expertise. She wanted to remind him she too had been celibate for almost a decade. She was tempted to shove him into a dark corner and kiss her way down that sexy chest. But she refrained. Because this time, when she started kissing Colton, she wasn't going to stop.

"It's Lauren, isn't it?" Claire came out of the crowd to greet her.

"Uh, yes," she returned, surprised the woman had remembered her name.

"I'm happy you made it." Holding her champagne glass in one hand, she used the other one to touch Colton's arm. "I was so sorry to hear that Jack Reid had passed. He was such a sweet man, and quite a character. He never failed to make me laugh. I looked forward to seeing him every year."

"I appreciate that, Claire," Colton said. "Dad enjoyed attending."

Claire was dressed in a black velvet dress with silver high heels. Her copper-colored hair was braided and fashioned into an elegant bun at the base of her neck. Fine diamonds and silver adorned her ears, neck and ring finger.

"You're a sculptor?" Lauren asked.

"Yes, well." she scrunched her face. "I try to be."

"This is lovely," Lauren said, moving to a horse.

"The entire house is littered with those damn things," John Chisum interrupted with a slight slur.

Claire's soft features stiffened, and her eyes dropped to her glass. "Opinions vary."

John snorted and gulped down more liquor.

Lauren had never been fond of Claire's husband. He and his father, Sam, had the same icy stare, and neither of them was as kind nor as friendly as Claire. She was the only reason the lower- and middle-class people were invited to the Christmas party. "They certainly do. I've admired this one since I walked through the door."

Claire's smile was fragile. "That's nice of you to say."

"You know, Claire." Colton stepped around Lauren and shoved a hand into the pocket of his slacks. Closing one eye, he studied the sculpture as if he were a collector of fine art. "Lauren and I have been talking about redecorating our house."

Our house. That sounded strange, but so good. She knew what Colton was doing, and she admired him for it. "Yes," she agreed, helping his ruse. "We have."

"I think this piece would look fantastic in our den, don't you, honey?"

Lauren looped her arm through his and paused for a second look at the sculpture. "You're right. It would."

"That is," Colton sipped his drink, "if it's for sale, of course."

Claire's expression brightened. "Oh, it is."

John snorted and walked away.

"Perfect. I'll write you a check before we leave," Colton said, wrapping an arm around Lauren.

"That was nice of you," she said, when Claire excused herself and walked away.

Colton's expression changed to contempt as he watched John empty his glass. "I can't stomach that sorry bastard."

"I think many people feel that way."

He reached inside his jacket pocket for his cell phone so he could check the time. "It's been nearly an hour since we left Mia's."

"I'm sure they'll be here soon." She whirled around in an attempted to catch the waiter before he got by her but failed. "I can't handle alcohol on an empty stomach. Catch the next waiter that comes by."

He eyed a tray of escargot with disgust. "Are you sure? Some of this stuff reminds me of survival training. Who eats these things?"

She giggled. Money, he had. Class and refinement, not so much. Colton would always be her rough-around-the-edges, no-nonsense cowboy, and she wouldn't have him any other way. "Grab anything that hasn't slithered or crawled."

Predictably, the hors d'oeuvres were delicious and extravagant. There were trays of marinated shrimp, caviar and Creme Fraiche tartlets, foie gras, stuffed mushrooms, warm spiced olives, and a few others Lauren wasn't brave enough to try.

Mia and Ian walked in shortly after nine. She was flushed, and he had a skip in his step. Holding hands, they waved and headed for the bar.

Colton rolled his eyes closed and switched his empty glass for a full one. He and Lauren knew what had kept the couple from arriving on time, but she wasn't going to let it spoil their evening. "Come on." She took his hand and led him into the crowd. "Let's mingle. It'll take your mind off them."

He introduced Lauren to Valery and her husband, Henry, who was also a veterinarian. While he and Colton talked about cattle prices, Lauren and Valery started their own conversation. Val Dutton was a plain-spoken, down-to-earth woman whom Lauren felt comfortable talking too. When she mentioned she might be interested in applying for the office manager's position, Valery asked about the duties she performed at her current job.

The two couples talked for over an hour before Lauren noticed the crowd had dwindled to a couple of guests. Colton paid Claire for the statue and escorted Lauren to the truck.

# CHAPTER TWENTY-FOUR

It had been a night to remember, and it wasn't over. That sweet little hip shift Lauren had made right before Claire walked up told him Colton so.

She kicked off her pumps at the front door. He helped her out of her coat and then shrugged out of his. She set the horse sculpture on the table next to the door, then stepped back to admire it. "I feel sorry for Claire."

He sat at the bottom of the stairs and removed his socks and boots. "Yeah, John Chisum is a snobby dick."

She giggled.

He looked up. "What?"

"Nothing." Another giggle hit her.

She'd stopped at her third glass of champagne. Unlike him, she was a tenderfoot at consuming alcohol. "I think you shouldn't have that third glass."

"It's not the champagne. It's just—" more giggles "—I saw it in my mind."

He raked his Stetson off and reached up to hang it on the rack. "Saw what?"

She assumed a stiff face, turned her nose up in the air

and started marching across the foyer. A couple of seconds later, the giggles returned. "Get it? A snobby penis."

Penis?

Any other night, seeing his wife tipsy would have been funny. But he wasn't making love to her while she was intoxicated. He propped an elbow on his knee and scrubbed his eyes, thinking the hard-on he had wouldn't be leaving anytime soon. "Jesus, honey. Are you drunk?"

She looked insulted. "No."

"Uh-huh," he mocked.

"If I were drunk, could I do this?" She closed her eyes, tilted her head back, and brought the tip of her index finger to her nose.

"Walk a straight line," he insisted.

"Oh, come on," she said, rolling her eyes as she went back to admiring the sculpture. "Just because I said the word penis, doesn't mean I'm drunk."

He grinned. She clearly wasn't, or she wouldn't have connected the word to his suspicion.

"I'm glad you bought the sculpture. It's beautiful. Claire is so talented. She direly needed a confidence boost and the look on John Chisum's face was priceless."

He admired her from his vantage point at the stairs. Slim shoulders, slim waist, round hips, and shapely calves. Calves Colton hadn't seen or touched in years. Seeing her made him regret every night he'd lain in bed alone.

When she'd walked into the living room at Mia's, wearing that velvety green dress, his heart felt just like it had the first time they met. He hadn't believed in love at first sight until that moment.

Colton strolled over to her and slipped his hands around her waist. The feel of her firm, round ass as it pushed against him made him groan. He heard her breath catch and groaned again when shifted her hips. "So, what are we going to do with it?"

"It?" she questioned; her voice silky smooth. "Oh. You mean the sculpture."

"Now who's being wicked?" This was a side of his wife he'd never seen before, and it was driving him wild.

"Not me," she declared modestly. "The sculpture goes in the den, of course. It can be my Christmas present."

"I was thinking." He slid his hand up to cup her breasts. "About giving you something more… personal."

She exhaled slowly and shifted her hips again. "How personal?"

He gripped her hips, bent his knees and pushed up. "Very personal."

The slow, thrusting motion caused her to moan. Lauren had never flirted with him or tried teasing him with her body. Who knew she had such skills?

His hands shook, and his heart beat so fast, his words had a jitter to them.

She turned and faced him. Caressing the outside of his thighs, she slowly moved inward towards his crotch. "But I can put a bow on the sculpture."

A bow?

Was she suggesting…?

She was.

Hot damn, this was fun.

"Honey." He took her hand and cupped it snuggly against his hard dick. "You can put a bow on my gift, too. You can do anything you want to with it."

A sensual laugh was accompanied by a gentle squeeze. "Anything?"

Her unexpected move caused him to suck in a sharp breath and let it out with a hiss.

"I'll take that as a yes."

The movements of her soft body slinking against him were torture. He wanted to push her against the wall and take her. Hard and fast, then slow and easy, until she was yelling his name.

But this was Lauren, his wife. A woman he hadn't made love to in years. He didn't want tonight to be dirty or quick. He wanted to enjoy her, savor her, and love her.

Colton pulled the comb from her hair and let her blond locks fall. Those silky strands smelled of honey and flowers, but Lauren's skin had its own unique scent. He'd never smelled anything like it. It was indescribable and invigorating.

Kissing her neck just below her ear, he trailed kisses downward until he reached the line of her dress. "Your skin." He hooked a finger in the velvety material and eased it from her shoulder. "It's so soft and you smell..." He inhaled deep and exhaled slowly. "Incredible. Why does it drive me crazy?"

"Reproductive—ah—" Her fingers plowed through his hair. "Hormones."

Reproductive.

The word hit him hard, knocking him back to his senses. He wanted those babies, but not like this. When there were uncertainties and secrets between them.

"Honey," he whispered. "I don't have any protection."

"Neither do I," she said, fumbling with the buttons of his shirt.

"What if—" He sucked in a breath when her lips touched his skin. "We make a baby tonight?"

"I don't care if Bill sorts out the stipulations of the will, and I don't care if Edgar finds a loophole. I want to be here with you and Little Jack and," she stared up at him, her beautiful eyes full of desire and love, "if we make baby tonight, I'll be the happiest woman in the world."

A part of him wanted to shout for joy, but the other part of him was terrified. There was a big chance she'd get pregnant tonight, and if she didn't, she soon would be.

He could guarantee that.

But he knew in his heart that once she knew the truth, she'd leave him. And that baby would go with her.

He was cornered.

There was no way in hell he could tell her no and no way he could explain to her why he didn't want to make that baby.

～

THERE WAS AN ICY UNDERTONE TO COLTON'S COMPLEXION that hadn't been there before Lauren had mentioned getting pregnant, and his brown eyes, once dark and heavy with need, were now staring at her bleakly.

Uneasiness crept over her. "Colton?"

He didn't move or speak.

"Hey," she tugged at his shirt.

He blinked twice then, focused. "Yeah?"

She backed away and wrapped her arms over her midriff. "Are you having second thoughts about this? Us? Because if you are, I need to know."

"What?" He took her back into his arms. "No, I'm not having second thoughts."

"Then what was that deer-in-the-headlights look about?"

He shook his head, widened his eyes, and gave her a huge smile. "I was shocked, that's all. You really knocked me for a loop. It's not every day a man gets everything he's ever wished for."

Her hands went back to his shirt. "Everything?"

"Honey, you and Little Jack are my entire world," he

said, gazing deep into her eyes. "And there is nothing I want more than to make a baby with you tonight."

And there it was. That magic world that made all her doubts disappear.

Baby.

"In our bed."

"In our bed," he agreed.

Lauren led him up the stairs and into the master bedroom. There was something profoundly moving about making love with the intentions of creating life. It was a step beyond intimacy and a sharing of more than love.

The bedroom was dark and years ago, she would have been thankful. But she wasn't that shy young virgin she'd been the first time they made love.

"I want to see you," she whispered, yanking the shirt from his slacks.

He switched the lamp on, and the room flooded with dim light. "Now. Where was I?" he murmured, his breath hot against her skin as he kissed her neckline. He navigated the zipper on her dress quickly and effortlessly. It slid from her shoulders, past her breasts, and fell to the floor.

Standing nearly naked before him, she'd never felt more appreciated for her feminine form. He gazed at her with awe, hunger, and appreciation.

This wasn't going to be all about her. He'd get his satisfaction, but she wanted to please him in another way. A daring way. The dark dusting of chest hair had been tempting to her since that first night.

She started at his abs and worked her way up his chest, covering muscles and scars. The soft scrape of his chest hair was so arousing and brought back vivid memories of the first time they'd made love.

"You're overdressed, Cowboy." she said, kissing the valley between his pecs.

Eyes closed, head back, he answered with a groan as she flicked his nipple with her tongue. She slid the shirt from his shoulders, trailed her finger down his chest, and stopped at his belt buckle. She'd never been brave enough to touch him below this point. But tonight, she was fearless.

His head came up when she unbuckled the buckle. "Remember?" She freed the button and dragged the zipper down. "You said anything."

He swallowed. "I'm a man of my wor—ah."

She moved her hand up and down the length of his shaft, loving the sounds she roused from him. "Being brave has its rewards. The big, bad cowboy is putty in my hands."

His mouth twisted into a mischievous grin. "We'll see how brave you are."

Her body quickened. "Yeah?"

"Yeah." Placing his hands on her hips, he guided her over to the bed and sat on the edge. "Put your legs over mine."

That flush she thought she had overcome was back with a vengeance. "I don't think—"

"I thought you said you were brave." He tugged on her hips, urging her to take the position. "I promise the reward will be worth it."

Of that, she hadn't a single doubt. Heart racing, face burning, Lauren lifted her leg and straddled his thighs. Reaching around her, he unclasped the snaps of her strapless bra and unveiled her breasts. "Gorgeous," he said, taking her nipple into his mouth.

"Ooh—ah..." The pleasure jolt from his suck caused her to jerk.

"This is one of my fantasies." Her hair mussed, eyes dark and wanton, he kissed his way to the other nipple. He moved his knees, widening the space between her legs. "To have you spread out like this for the taking."

She could hardly breathe. The erotic position he had her in made her feel so sexy and braver than she ever thought possible.

Colton slipped his hand between her legs and caressed her through the crotch of her thin lace panties. The friction of the lace rubbing against her was wonderful. "Wicked," she panted.

"It's only the beginning." Holding the base of her head with his palm, he brought her lips to his and brushed aside the lace. As he explored her mouth with his tongue, his thumb stroked her sensitive nub while his fingers plunged into her.

Lauren was lost, soaring into a place she'd never been. Her body burned and coiled tighter until she was begging him to stop, but he was relentless. Her plea became a cry as her release came.

He eased her down onto the bed and slipped her panties off. Having reached her first orgasm in nearly ten years, she could hardly move. But she knew more pleasure awaited her.

Feeling him erect and knowing he wanted her outweighed the satisfaction he'd just given her. She'd never cried during sex, even when he took her virginity. But she was suddenly overcome with emotion of love, happiness, the expectancy of that baby...

Positioning his knee between her legs, he moved over her and rested his weight on his palms. He searched her face. "What's wrong?"

She waved his concern away with a hand, sniffed and smeared the tears away. "I'm fine."

"Then why the tears?"

"It's just—I finally have my husband back and we're

together in our home, in love and making babies." She cradled his face between her hands and smiled. "This is my dream, Colton, and I roped it."

Lauren could have sworn she'd seen regret in his eyes. But then he kissed her long, and passionately, soothing her emotions and transforming them into burning desire. He pushed into her slowly, provoking a moan from her throat. Tiny bursts of pleasure exploded inside of her. She arched, thrusting her hips into his.

His body shook with mounting tension, and his shallow breathing intertwined with a groan. Sliding a hand under the bend of her knee, he raised her leg and rested it on his shoulder. He palmed her bottom, lifted her hips, and pushed in deep.

"Oh!" Pleasure spiked through her

He went still. "Too much?"

"No." She raked her nails down his chest. The tilt of her bottom gave her a new pleasure. One she'd never thought possible. "Again."

The thrust combined with his rhythmic grunts drove her higher and higher. Lauren didn't want it to end, but her control was slipping. Those little moans he said she made when they made love escalated. When she went over the edge, they culminated in a hoarse cry. Seconds later, he flexed and grunted a release. Falling to his elbows, he tucked his head against her neck. "I love you, Lauren," he declared breathlessly.

She wrapped her arms around his shoulders. "I love you too."

Their new relationship had been beautifully and orgasmically consummated.

～

IT HAD BEEN A WEEK SINCE COLTON AND LAUREN FIRST
made love, and things between them had never been
better. She found a new level of bravery, pleasing him in
ways she never had before, and she took delight in making
him beg.

Mostly, Colton and Lauren had the ranch house to
themselves. Mia and Ian were no longer trying to hide
their relationship from Colton. Ian came and went from
Mia's cabin as he pleased, and she resumed her weekly
habit of restocking the bunkhouse.

Christmas was approaching. Sue, Lauren, and Mia
were communicating back and forth via texts and video
conferencing to make this holiday special. It was their first
Christmas as a family and Colton's first Christmas without
his dad. Having the others around would help fill that
emptiness caused by Jack Reid's death.

Lauren had told them the news about her plans to stay
at the ranch. Sue wept, and Little Jack was happy he'd be
permanently living at the Lucky Jack.

Today, she'd reacquainted herself with Church and
practicing her rope throwing skills from the saddle. Then
she'd hurried back to work for a conference call while
Colton returned the roping dummy and hale bales back
where they belonged.

He tossed the rope out in front of him to straighten the
kinks and twists. Then, he held the noose in his right hand
and looped the rope with his left, giving it a half turn each
time. Coiling a lariat skillfully and quickly was an accomplished he'd learned years ago as a young boy and a
grueling tasked he'd had to re-learn to use his disabled
hand.

He gave the rope a last turn and sighed, realizing time
had run out for him. Sue and Ed were flying in with Little
Jack on the twenty-second. There'd be no more procrasti-

nating about the new will. He had to tell Lauren the truth before the others arrived for Christmas.

Lauren was excited about seeing their son and having the whole family at the Lucky Jack. Colton was too, but unlike him, she projected that excitement with chatting nearly nonstop at breakfast.

He hadn't minded. He was in no mood to talk, so he'd nodded and smiled as he ate the crispy biscuits and rubbery bacon she'd prepared.

Like the will, that business card in his back pocket was searing a hole through his soul. Colton hadn't made a phone call. After they made love, he'd shoved the will and his guilty conscious to the back of his mind. He'd wanted to savor what time he had left with Lauren.

Darlene hadn't revealed Bill's location, only that he wouldn't be back until after the holidays. He was an adventurous man who loved to fish—in any weather or water. Sail fishing at Cabo San Lucas, bonefish fishing at St. Brandon's, ice fishing for walleye in Minnesota. Being nearly seventy hadn't slowed Bill down.

Colton walked out to the paddocks and leaned his back against the fence. From there, he could see Lauren sitting as she worked. He pulled out his cell phone and sighed. Ignoring the problem wouldn't make it go away, and neither would address it.

Lauren had put in her two weeks' notice and was making plans to sell her house. He'd done what he'd set out to do. He'd rerouted their path to a time before his deployment. But at what cost?

He slipped the business card from his pocket and pulled out his phone. He did not know what he'd say if Bill answered, but he had to start somewhere.

Colton had punched in the first three numbers when he heard Ian yell his name. He looked around and saw the ramrod walking towards them with Mia's cookie tin tucked in the crook of his arm.

Another embryo had been stolen earlier this week. Colton and Lauren had talked about Ian over the last couple of days. They'd tried coming up with solutions how they could catch the thief.

She was a superb listener who absorbed everything he said and could roll problems he thought to be complex around in her head and present a simple solution. His wife was an amazing woman.

She'd suggested hidden security cameras, but then stated that it might be hard to install them with Ian around. But cameras were easily installed, so Colton could do it by himself when he was sure Ian and the others were asleep in the bunkhouse.

Luke was sure he hadn't seen Ian in the store, so proving a key had been made would be nearly impossible unless Colton widened his search into other counties.

He didn't have rock-solid proof of the thief's identity, other than his theory about Mia's keys. Installing security cameras could solve the problem.

But until those cameras were installed, Colton couldn't do much except keep a close eye on Ian and Mia. If he was the thief, the Lucky Jack would lose a ramrod.

Seeing him stroll up to the fence with that damn cookie tin left a bitter taste in Colton's mouth. The container was a slap in the face because Ian carried it proudly like a trophy. He'd challenged the boss and won. The Golden Rule no longer applied to him. He was cavorting with the boss's sister and there wasn't anything anyone could do about it.

He didn't think Ian would physically hurt Mia, but if she was in love, learning he'd used her would crush her.

He feared that more than anything.

But if Ian was innocent and Colton accused him of the crime, his sister would hate him, and Ian wouldn't continue working for an establishment that didn't trust him. Either way, Colton stood to lose more than money and bovine embryos if he made a move without proof.

He walked around to the other side of the fence and met Ian just outside the horse barn. "Delivering cookies for Santa?"

Ian held the tin up and gave it a shake. Cookies rattled against the inside of the container. "Keeps up morale."

"I'll bet."

Ian rested an elbow on the top fence and looked up at the window where Lauren was sitting. "She's pretty good with a lariat."

Colton nodded slowly and tried swallowing that awful taste in his mouth. But it wouldn't budge. "Dad taught her well."

"He talked about her a lot." Ian said, still focused on Lauren. "I feel like I know her."

Colton knew this was more than a friendly conversation about cookies and Lauren's roping skills. And the way she'd been casually brought into the conversation was making him uneasy. "You don't know anything about my wife."

Ian scoffed lightly and dropped his head. "I know she wouldn't approve of what you're doing. The two of you are getting along so well. Mia thinks things might just work out this time. It'd be a shame if she found out you'd been lying to her."

Colton's blood went cold. "What the hell are you talking about?"

Ian raised his head and squinted against the sunlight as a cloud opened. "You're not the only one who's been eavesdropping. I know about the new will Jack Reid had made before he died. I know about Mia's share of the Lucky Jack, and I know Lauren's mandated time for fulfilling the stipulations of the will is a month, not a year."

If he had any doubts about Ian's innocence in the embryo thefts, this had just shredded them. The pompous ass was leading up to something. "What do you want, Ian?"

With his wrist resting on the fence post, he casually waved towards the building where the embryos were stored. "Three more."

Colton took a deep breath, trying to rein in his anger.

"Three more of those embryos and I disappear, and we both keep our secrets. Lauren will know you lied to her eventually, but she'll know sooner if you turn me in."

He wanted to knock Ian's ass in the dirt and beat the hell out of him with that cookie tin. But if there was an altercation here, the women would come running. Lauren would be on his side until Ian coughed up a few teeth and told her about the will.

Mia would be fit to be tied and demand to know why he'd beaten her boyfriend to a pulp. Ian would deny everything, and Colton didn't have proof to give her. It was Ian's word against his. Blood was thicker than water, but love was blind.

He wanted to call Ian's bluff, tell him to go screw himself and call the sheriff. But his ramrod had the upper hand. "And what about Mia? What happens when you disappear? What am I supposed to tell her?"

An unexpected wave of culpability washed over Ian's face. He dropped his gaze to the ground and scratched his nose. "I never meant for it to go this far between us."

"And just how goddamn far has it gone, Ian?"

His eyes showed regret. "Not as far as she wanted it to go."

Knowing there was a chance Ian and Mia hadn't slept together was a relief. Mia wasn't a young woman looking for a good time. She was innocent in the ways of a man like Ian and vulnerable.

But." Ian sniffed and straightened then, got a better grip on the tin. "She'll get over me. In time."

"You're a son of a bitch for hurting her."

Ian stared off into the distance with dull eyes. "Yeah, well." He ran a hand over his mouth. "That's my offer. Take it or leave it."

Colton didn't want Ian sitting at his table with his sister, eating turkey, and acting like he was a good guy. "I'll take it, if you're out of here before Christmas."

Ian shrugged, not caring that his disappearance would ruin the holiday for Mia. "Deal."

He caught hold of the ramrod's arm before he left. "Don't just disappear. Be man enough to end it face-to-face."

Ian jerked out of his grasp and headed for the bunkhouse.

COLTON SHOVED A HAND BEHIND HIS HEAD AND STARED AT the dark ceiling above him. It was nearly midnight, and he hadn't been able to sleep after he and Lauren made love.

The three embryos Ian took in return for Colton's silence were gone. Hopefully, the ramrod would disappear in few days, leaving Mia to salvage the pieces of her broken heart. Colton would hold her when she cried and do everything in his power to help her mend.

That was all he could do unless he confessed his lies to Lauren. She lay naked against him with her arm thrown over his stomach and her head on his shoulder, her breath steady and soft as she slept. He tightened his arm around her shoulders and drew her head to his lips for a kiss.

His life would be perfect if not for the lie he was living.

Lauren was in his bed, and they were trying to get pregnant. His heart overflowed with love. Throughout the day, he drifted off as he envisioned that future—that baby.

Birthing classes, doctors' visits, ultrasounds. He'd be there for it all. Holding her hand during labor, seeing their child born, holding it for the first time, rocking it to sleep, changing diapers, sleepless nights, story time... Those were moments he'd missed with Little Jack and treasures his heart happily expected with this baby.

But that future hinged on Lauren's forgiveness. Once Ian was gone, he'd have a long conversation with his wife. He'd confess his lies and his plan and pray she didn't leave him.

With a long sigh, Colton shifted his eyes from the ceiling to the window. Scant luminescence from the barn light shone against the house. It was snowing again. Small flakes with accumulation of three to four inches tonight.

The old house was quiet now, but when wind gusts hit, it would wail, creak and moan like it always did. Weather wise, this winter was off to a rough start and looked to be as bad if not worse than last year. A loud knock at the front door pulled him from reflections and roused Lauren from sleep. "What was that?"

"Someone's at the door?" he said, yanking on his jeans.

Her sleepy eyes found the clock beside the bed. "At this hour?"

He hurried down the stairs as the knock came again. "I'm coming."

"It's me, boss."

Why the hell was Punch Baker knocking on his door at

midnight? Colton unlocked the deadbolt and opened the door. "What is it?"

Punch wiped the snow from the brim of his hat and the cold from his nose. "Scrap, he, ah... There's been an accident."

Scrap was involved. Colton feared the worst. "Is he okay?"

Lauren wrapped a blanket around her nightgown as joined him at the door.

"He's fine." Punch hesitated. "Now don't get excited when I tell you this. She's okay."

"She?" Colton's heart stopped. He had three women in his life. Lauren, his mom and– "Mia! He hit Mia?"

Punch held up a hand. "She's a little banged up is all. Ian was driving and, well, you better have a look for yourself."

"What the hell were they–" Irritation clamped his mouth shut. Mia was hurt, and he had to get to her. That's all he needed to focus on. "Where is she?"

Punch pointed. "On the main road, just past the railroad tracks."

Colton bolted from the door and sprinted up the stairs, Lauren behind him. "I'm going with you."

Two minutes later, he and Lauren were shoving on outerwear as they ran to the truck. The main road ran parallel with Whiskey Creek, making it dangerous and, in bad weather, deadly. He switched the windshield wipers to high, cranked up the defroster, and drove at a turtle's pace.

"He said she was just a little banged up," Lauren reminded him. "Don't do anything you'll regret."

It was too late for that. Colton's list of new regrets nearly outweighed the old one.

"I, ah..." She paused to wince. "I should have told you sooner, but I thought I could talk Mia out of it."

"Out of what?"

"Leaving Crossfire Canyon with Ian."

He glanced at his wife, then back to the road. "You didn't think I needed to know that?"

She tilted her head from side to side. "I told Mia I'd talk to you about the Golden Rule and then you told me about Ian and…uhh, mmm… Well, I just thought it was best if I kept it to myself."

He faked a big smile. "Congratulations, you just passed Skirting 101."

# CHAPTER TWENTY-FIVE

A MILE AND A HALF FROM THE RANCH DRIVE, HE SAW RED and blue lights flashing through the thin curtain of falling snow. Driving closer, he could make out Ian's blue Chevy. The front was buckled and the rear-end was over the embankment. An ambulance and two sheriffs' cars blocked the road.

He recognized one deputy as Lance Baldwin, the officer who was working on the stolen embryos.

Colton parked in the middle of the road and got out. He spotted the top of Mia's dark head sitting inside the ambulance. Scrap was beside the door talking to Lance.

Rage rolled over Colton. Fists tight, steps wide, he hurried through the snow towards the ambulance.

Punch caught up with him. "Boss, there's something you should see."

"Not now, Punch."

When the young cowhand spotted Colton, his hollow-set eyes widened, and he started backing up. "It wasn't my fault, boss."

Colton grabbed him by the collar of his coat. "I told you to slow down."

"Colton, don't," Lauren pleaded, tugging at his arms.

"Whoa," Lance yelled, wedging himself between Colton and the cowhand. "Take it easy."

Colton made a grab for Scrap's collar. "I told you someone was going to get hurt!"

Scrap stayed behind Lance. "I wasn't driving fast. He was in my lane. I didn't see him in time to stop."

"Bullshit."

Lance shoved Colton back. "Calm down. He's telling the truth. The female involved in the accident verified Ian was on the wrong side of the road when the truck hit them."

"See," Scrap squawked.

Colton scrubbed his face and took a deep breath. "Where's Ian?"

"He took off," Scrap answered and motioned towards the tracks. "In that direction."

"On foot?" he asked.

"Yeah," he said.

Lance winced and turned his back to an icy gust of wind. "We'll get him. He won't make it far in this weather."

Punch climbed up the bank from Ian's truck, clutching Mia's cookie tin. "It looks like the Lucky J.'s ramrod was transporting more than cookies." He set the tin on the hood of the deputy's cruiser. Broken at the bottom, the container revealed a secret insulated compartment holding three stolen embryos. "It must have busted when it hit the floorboard."

Colton had his suspicions about the tin, but had let them go after Ian began blackmailing him.

"Case closed," Lance said.

"Yeah." Colton walked to the back of the ambulance, opened the door, and climbed in. Lauren was seated next to the gurney, holding Mia's hand.

Propped upright and huddled in a massive gray emergency blanket, without the frills of eyeshadow and lipstick, his sister was almost unrecognizable. She had the innocent face of an adolescent girl. Puffy eyes stained with tears, a pale face and a trembling bottom lip. A red mark bruised her left cheek.

He sat down next to Lauren and gently brushed Mia's cheek with a knuckle. "Did Ian do this?"

"No." Mia said, meekly.

"The paramedic said she has a fractured wrist, a bump on the head, and is a little shaken up," Lauren said, tugging the blanket closer to Mia's neck. "They're transporting her to County General just to be safe."

He eased a long strand of hair from her face. "What happened, Mia? What were you and Ian doing out here in the storm?"

She stared into space. "Ian came to the cabin around ten. He said he'd gotten in over his head and needed my help. I asked him to tell me about it, but he said he'd explain on the way, so I packed a bag and climbed in the truck."

Ian had waited until the snow hit to make his move. He'd figured the weather would slow down any effort to come after him, and he'd taken Mia just in case he'd needed leverage.

"Did you find the tin?" Mia asked.

"Punch found it."

Her lip trembled. "I thought he loved me."

Lauren hugged her. "Oh, Mia. I'm so sorry."

He was a bastard for letting things go this far. He should have stepped in when he first suspected Ian was the thief. He should've installed the cameras and been more vigilant at protecting his sister.

If the cold didn't get Ian, Colton vowed he would.

SUE, ED, AND LITTLE JACK HAD ARRIVED AT THE RANCH yesterday. Christmas was two days away, and the house was all abuzz. Sue had taken stock of the last-minute items needed for Christmas dinner, and Lauren had volunteered to do the shopping.

On her way home, she'd stopped by the pharmacy. Her menstrual cycle was a week late. That didn't guarantee pregnancy. Stress could have thrown her schedule off and the beginning of December had been more than a little taxing.

She'd even considered that her delayed cycle might be psychological and that her desire for a baby had somehow convinced her body she was pregnant. She supposed stranger things had happened. Though only a doctor could confirm it, she knew in her heart that she and Colton had conceived a baby.

After he'd showered, dressed, and gone downstairs this morning to make coffee, she'd hurried into the bathroom and taken the pregnancy test. It had been the longest three minutes of her life, but when the alarm on her phone beeped, there were two pink lines.

She'd covered her mouth to muffle her happy scream and jumped up and down. Then the tears came.

She was pregnant.

That baby she'd wanted for so long was growing inside her. She'd wanted to rush down the stairs and tell Colton the wonderful news first. But by the time she'd walked into the kitchen, Sue and Ed were at the table having their morning coffee. With excitement bubbling in her stomach, Lauren had tucked the positive pregnancy test into the pocket of her jeans and gone about her day.

Keeping her secret through dinner was hard, especially with Colton setting across from her. Tonight, when they were alone, she'd deliver the news. She imagined his face, ecstatic with a cheek-to-cheek smile and tears in his eyes.

Her heart was so full of love and happiness she felt like she might explode. After the holidays were over, she'd fly back to Texas to pack up their belongings and put her house up for sale.

The last few weeks had been heaven for Lauren. Her relationship with her husband had come so far, and she wanted to believe they were growing closer. He was sweet and affectionate, never frowned or tried distancing himself from her as he had before. They were finally a real husband and wife couple.

But she'd sensed a difference in him after the wreck. Deputies found Ian a few hundred feet from the tracks, alive and well. He was facing several charges, including leaving the scene of an accident. Mia's heartbreak and gloomy behavior after she was released from the hospital weighed heavily on Colton's mind. He felt partially to blame for what Ian had done, and he'd taken a significate financial loss.

It was plausible that either or both were cause for the change in him. But Lauren had a horrible feeling it was something else.

"Hey, Dad?" Little Jack spooned a helping of mashed potatoes into his mouth and swallowed. "Can we show Ed the horse barn?"

Lauren used her napkin to wipe away the potatoes left

behind. Little Jack pulled back with a frown. "I'm not a baby. I can do it myself."

"Sure," Colton answered with an amused grin. "We'll go after dinner."

Little Jack's eyes lit up. He told Ed about every horse in the barn. Their color, kind, and name.

Ed was attentive during the conversation. He'd never take Jack Reid's place. No one would. Those were big shoes to fill. But he was definitely grandpa material.

Sue tried taking Mia's mind off her Ian woes by saying she'd help bake the Christmas pies, but it would take more than baking to heal the young woman's heart.

When Lauren looked up from her plate, Colton was looking straight at Lauren with the same frozen expression he had the night they'd made love—when he'd asked her the what if question about getting pregnant.

Trepidation swept over her. What if Colton didn't want another child? What if that was the basis for the change? But there was no reason to think he didn't want the baby or that the change in him had anything to do with the possibility of her getting pregnant.

No.

She'd fabricated a mistress and assumed he was having an affair. She wasn't going to assume he didn't want this baby. Overthinking and doubts wouldn't ruin her baby celebration. With her heart and her head in agreement, the pregnancy high floated back.

Little Jack tagged along with Colton and Ed to the horse barn. It was, as Colton had said, a guy thing. A time of bonding between males. She didn't pretend to understand it. She was just thankful her son had two good men as examples.

Mia took a book from the shelf and curled up on the couch to read. Lauren helped Sue with the dishes. Then she went upstairs to wrap the smaller gifts she'd purchased while in town yesterday.

She'd bought Little Jack an antique finished belt buckle and had the initials J.D. engraved on it. Mia had wanted a new apron, so she'd purchased one from the Barn with cute little cows adorning the front. A travel pack for Sue and a sliver whiskey flask for Ed completed her gift giving.

The only person she hadn't bought for was Colton. She rummaged through bows and wrapping paper and found a thin piece of red ribbon. What better gift than to know you'd conceived a child with the woman you loved?

Smiling, she tied the ribbon around the pregnancy test applicator and shoved it back into her pocket. Gathering the gifts in her arms, she trotted down the stairs and was on her way to the tree when she heard Sue talking in the den. "Are you sure, Bill?"

Bill? Had he called? Lauren didn't remember hearing the phone ring.

"Of course, I am," a man's voice returned with a husky chuckle. "I was his lawyer, Sue Lula. I made the damn thing."

Bill was here. Better late than never, she mused, her pregnancy high growing bigger by the minute. Lauren quickly deposited the gifts under the tree and hurried to the den, where Sue met her at the door.

"Lauren, this is Bill Humphrey, Jack Reid's attorney."

The elderly man rose from the seat behind the desk and greeted her with a friendly smile. Then he shook her hand. "It's nice to put a face with the name. Nice to meet you, Lauren."

Sue pulled one of the straight-back chairs to the front of the desk. "Have a seat. I'm going to get Colton."

Bill took his seat and rested his arms on the desk, his smile holding strong. He was a thin man with silver hair and deep-seated eyes. A lifetime of wrinkles mapped his face, but there was a kindness in his gray eyes that reminded her of Jack Reid.

"So, Lauren." He paused to ask, "May I call you Lauren?"

She scooted to the edge of the seat and tucked her hands between her legs. "Certainly."

He unfolded a thick leather portfolio and eyed her amusingly over the top of his glasses. "I hear you've been taken hostage."

She chuckled. "It seemed that way at first."

Bill raised his bushy gray brows, leaned back in the leather chair, and laced his fingers together. "At first?"

"A year is a long time." She smiled brightly, the baby news jumping inside her. "But fulfilling the stipulations shouldn't be a problem now."

"A year. Yes. Well." He cleared his throat and proceeded to straighten the papers in front of him. "My grandson informed me you weren't pleased about Jack Reid's terms."

"No, sir. I wasn't," she admitted. "Colton talked to Darlene several times, but he was unable to persuade her into giving him your personal cell phone number."

"That's odd." His face was impassive. "When I'm away from the office, I check in with Darlene at least twice a week in case there's an emergency such as this. She didn't mention any phone calls from Colton."

"There must be some mistake." Confusion cluttered her mind. "He said he called the office."

Bill leaned his arms on the desk again. "Which is also odd because I gave Colton my cell phone number when Jack Reid changed his will."

"Wait a second," she said as a sinking feeling gathered

in her chest. "You're telling me Colton has your personal cell phone number?"

He reached inside his jacket and pulled out his cell phone. "I always have it with me, even bought a water-proof case so it won't get wet when I'm fishing."

Lauren rose from her seat as her mind tried absorbing what Bill had just told her. Colton had lied to her about calling Darlene and deceived her into thinking he couldn't reach Bill.

But he'd had his number since Jack Reid changed... his... will.

Hot prickly needles covered her body. "There's another will, isn't there?"

Bill picked up the legal-sized papers that were stapled together, licked his finger, and began flipping through it. When he found what he was looking for, he lay it down on the desk and spun it around so she could read the place he had marked.

She scanned the stipulation paragraph... A month.

That bubbly excitement in Lauren's stomach fizzled and floated away. She suddenly felt nauseous. Colton had deliberately lied to her about calling Bill and Darlene. He'd lied to her about everything and had been doing so for weeks. "A month. That's it?"

"Yes," Bill said regretfully. "I do apologize. The whole thing was a horrible mix-up."

No. It had been a set-up. A deliberate, well-thought-out plan to manipulate her into staying. Colton had known from the beginning that the will Martin read wasn't the most recent one, and he'd had the means to right that wrong and he hadn't.

"Given the state of panic Martin said you were in, I thought you'd be happier."

Hurt and anger tightened her chests. "Of course. Yes, I

am happy. My boss wasn't pleased about having a virtual assistant."

Her job.

She'd given her notice.

"I told Jack Reid it would be best to take out the whole stipulation. But he was set on giving you and Colton another go. Fortunately, I convinced him to change the time you had to spend at the ranch. A month was much more attainable and realistic." Bill closed his portfolio and stuffed it into his briefcase. "In a few days, you'll be free to go home."

Home. She'd thought this was home, but… Feeling weak in the knees, she leaned against the edge of the desk for support and bowed her head.

"Ah, Colton, there you are."

"Bill." Lauren heard him greet the man with a hollow voice. Her stomach rolled at the sight of his boots standing in the doorway. He'd been in the same spot when he'd told her the names of their babies. She'd been so moved that he'd remembered. That's how he'd hooked her. He knew how desperate she was for a baby, and she'd played right into his arms. How could she have been so blind?

Bill collected his briefcase and headed for the door. He gave Colton a pat on the shoulder. "I'll let myself out."

*I'll do whatever you want.* That's what Colton said about the divorce, but he'd changed his mind the next day. What if these last three weeks had been just as she'd thought, a plan to keep her at the ranch? What if he'd made love to her without protection just to appease her?

A rush of humiliation hit her. She felt so stupid and naïve for falling for his plan.

∾

COLTON RAKED HIS HAT FROM HIS HEAD AND WAITED FOR Lauren to throw books at him or shout curses at the top of her lungs. But she hadn't said a word since Bill left. She hadn't moved so much as a muscle either.

"Say something, please," he begged.

"Why?" she whispered despondently. "Why did you lie to me?"

"Would you have stayed if I hadn't?" With his hat in his hands and his heart on his sleeve, he tried justifying what he'd done. "I was desperate, Lauren. I tried for eight years to talk to you, but you wouldn't listen. You wouldn't even look at me."

"So you lied." Taking in a deep and ragged breath, she raised her head. But she wouldn't make eye contact with him. "And took advantage of Martin's mistake."

"It wasn't a lie. I just—"

"Skirted, right? To make be believe you loved me." The vulnerability and hurt in her eyes were tearing him apart.

"I do love you." She had to believe that, but why would she when he'd lied about so many things?

"I caught you off guard with the divorce papers, which is why you told me you'd do whatever I wanted," she speculated with a broken heart. "But you knew I'd never stay for the month needed to fulfill the will."

Colton tossed his hat onto the desk. "It wasn't like that."

"Then, after the wrong will was read, you saw your chance to swoop in and woo me with that let's-make-something-new garbage."

All she could see were his lies. "It wasn't garbage. None of that was a lie. I meant everything I said, honey, and we have made something new."

"Anything that was made..." Her lips trembled as she closed her eyes. "Was done so on a foundation of lies."

He plowed both hands through his hair. "Our foundation is love."

"And I made it easy for you, didn't I? I wanted babies."

Wanted. Pasted tense. "I want those babies too, Lauren."

"So you saw an opportunity to reel me in."

"Reel you in?" he questioned. "I lied. I admit it, but don't make it sound like I used you. We made love that night because it was what we both wanted."

The middle of her brows lifted. "That's why you were so worried about protection."

"No," he groaned.

"You couldn't refuse me when you'd been so gung ho about making babies. God," she scoffed. "That must have been awful for you. Knowing I might get pregnant."

He'd made love to her with the full intentions of getting her pregnant, and it had been one of the sweetest nights of his life. "Don't degrade what happened between us."

"I don't think I could say anything that would make it more disgraceful than it already is." She wrapped her arms around her midriff protectively. That hurt him nearly as much as her words had. "I quit my job and nearly sold my house because I thought you loved me. I've been so gullible."

He'd gone over dozens of scenarios as to how this would go. She hadn't questioned his love for her in any of them. "I do love you. What you saw that night after Claire's party was worrying. I knew if you got pregnant, when you found out I'd lied to you I'd lose you, our son, and that baby."

With her body shaking, lips trembling, and tears rolling down her cheeks, she dug into her pocket. On her way out the door, she shoved something into his hands. "You have."

Staring at those two pink lines lovely, decorated with a red ribbon, Colton knew he'd never breathe again. Not sufficiently, anyway. For the second time in a month, the person who made him whole was walking out the door, and she was taking his whole heart with her this time.

Little Jack would assume the same holiday and summer routine. Colton would see him at the airport. They talk by phone and send texts. Next summer, the child he'd said goodbye to would be closer to a man. Colton wouldn't be there for football games or school dances.

All those precious baby moments Colton dreamed about were gone. He'd never see that baby being born. If Lauren was generous, he'd get to see it, maybe hold it.

But that was it.

# CHAPTER TWENTY-SIX

LAUREN SAT IN A LARGE RUSTIC CHAIR AND GAZED OUT THE living room window of Mia's cabin. She'd watched the sun fade from purple to black last night and rise over the mountains this morning. Two squirrels leaped across the white powder and scurried up a pine. A red-billed woodpecker drilled into a dead spruce, dispelling chunks of wood and snow as he searched for his breakfast.

Tomorrow would be no different. The sun would rise and set. The wind would blow. Snow would fall. The world wouldn't stop spinning just for her.

After she'd given Colton his Christmas present, she'd walked out the door without her purse or coat, climbed in her Jeep, and started driving. She'd stopped at the Travelers Inn but remembered she hadn't any ID or money. Mia's was the only place she had to go.

Lauren hadn't taken a shower, brushed her teeth, or combed her hair since yesterday morning. Hurt and sadness had settled deep into her bones and taken root.

Mia shuffled from her bedroom into the kitchen,

rubbed the sleep from her eyes, and yawned. Then she shuffled to the coffeepot and sighed when she saw Lauren.

When the coffee was done, Mia poured two cups and bought Lauren hers. "Did you get any sleep?"

She took the cup, knowing it was the only way to appease her sister-in-law. "No."

Another sigh. "You have to rest and relax a little. Stress isn't good for the baby."

The baby. If Lauren had had any tears left, she would have cried, but those wells were dry.

There were ten days left in her sentence. After they were over, Little Jack would have his inheritance. She'd go home to Texas and try to get her life back. Things would be different, but the same. Maybe she'd be able to get her job back. Jonas wouldn't care if she was expecting. He'd push her just the same. Long hours, six days a week, until she went on maternity leave. Then she'd find a babysitter, juggle work and kids by herself, and fall into the same old routine.

Colton wouldn't be there when the baby was born. Sue probably would be. It would say its first words and take its first steps without him seeing it. When it was old enough, it would spend its summers at the Lucky Jack.

Lauren drew her legs up, rested her feet on the edge of the seat, and laid her head on her knees.

More sadness sank in.

"I'll fix some breakfast."

She set her coffee to the side. "I'm not hungry."

"Neither am I, but we can't stop living because love sucks and men are jerks."

Lauren had a bag full of better descriptions, but she was too tired to vent.

Sue and Major dropped by after lunch and brought Lauren her things from the ranch house. "I wish there was something I could say, something that would make all of this magically disappear."

"Not me," Mia said, scratching the dog behind its ears. "If it all disappeared, Lauren wouldn't be pregnant, and that baby is the only thing good to come from Dad's crazy plan."

Lauren brushed her hand over her stomach. The baby was worth every tear she's shed and every heartbreaking moment she'd gone through.

Mia wasn't angry with her brother for letting her think Jack Reid had left her out of his will or that he'd hadn't told her about Ian and the missing embryos. Her forgiving heart had understood why Colton withheld the information.

Lauren understood why he said he'd lied to her, but she wasn't as forgiving.

Sue took a seat next to the window. "I wish Jack Reid was here now. Maybe he could figure out a solution to this mess."

There was no solution. Colton had lied and manipulated her. He'd used her to secure the Lucky Jack and there was nothing Jack Reid or anyone else could do to alter that.

"The day he died, I sat there holding his hand, and I thought about how much I was going to miss him. And about all the time we wasted by being mad at one another." Sue looked woefully dramatic and near tears as she sighed and rose from the chair. "As he said, I wished we'd fought harder for our marriage."

Lauren knew her mother-in-law had said those things for her benefit. But there was no way she could simply forgive and forget because, damn it, this time around, she'd fought for her marriage. She'd stopped being angry at Colton and put her heart and soul into making it work. But he'd been cajoling and manipulating her the whole time.

Mia motioned Sue into the kitchen. "I have that roasting pan you wanted."

Lauren stared at the squirrels. Pots and pans banged, and cabinet doors closed. Then there was silence.

"I can't get her to eat anything," she heard Mia whisper. "And I think she poured the coffee I gave her into my ivy plant."

"Oh, dear," Sue replied in a hushed voice.

Did they think when she'd marched out of the ranch house, she'd left her ears by the door?

Major whined and laid his head in Lauren's lap.

"Have you heard from him?"

"No, we haven't seen him since the night she left." Sue had that worried, motherly tone Lauren knew well. "He saddled his horse and rode out. I'm afraid he's..."

"No," Mia gasped. "You don't think he—?"

"I don't know what to think. Punch and the others went out to look for him this morning."

Lauren wanted to tell them they were wrong. Colton wasn't trying to do something irrational. He'd simply taken a ride to clear his mind.

*Two days ago.*

That meant, when he'd left the house, forecasters were predicting the active storm front rolling across Wyoming would miss the Canyon. But it had shifted. Several more feet of snow were coming, along with winds that could reach blizzard-like conditions. Everyone was keeping a close eye on the weather system as it moved nearer. This one wasn't going to miss them, and residents of Crossfire Canyon were preparing for the worst.

The storm had started just before sundown, with light flurries. By sundown, it was expected to march across Montana, kicking up powerful wind gusts that were predicted to turn into blizzard conditions by morning.

A horrible picture of Colton motionless in the snow flashed before her eyes, causing anxiety to barrel through her numbness. What if he was hurt? What if he'd fallen from his horse or been attacked by a mountain lion? Okay, maybe the mountain lion was a stretch, but anything could happen out there.

"And why do you care?" she bleated and crossed her arms. *He lied to you. Skirted. Withheld information.*

*Like you did when Mia told you she might leave Crossfire Canyon?*

*No.*

*Yes.*

"Bah," she grumbled.

Colton was more than capable of taking care of himself.

*He's a Marine.*

*Tough as nails.*

"Right," she agreed with herself, unfolded her arms, and began tapping her fingers against the wooden chair arms.

Life had tried killing him—twice.

But he'd survived.

*Third time's a charm*, her heart whispered and reminded her of the phone calls. *Mrs. Ritter, your husband was wounded… McCrea found him in time…*

Helplessness and fear were two things she swore she wouldn't succumb to again. She couldn't handle another phone call. She couldn't bear the news that Colton had died because she'd been too stubborn to help.

There wasn't an ounce of fear in her now, and she wasn't helpless. She would not sit on her butt and let the father of her children freeze to death, even if he was a… jerk.

Marriage can't be all fun and games now, can it?

This wasn't the fun part.

This was the part of marriage that tested her resilience and forgiveness. She recalled all the times she'd been sure he loved her. The trip to Dawson's and the way he'd patiently waited for her to pick out a tree. The lights and decorations and the game he'd bought for them to play. Her burnt rolls, the yellow painted hall, and their photos. The emotional intimacy they'd built, the way he'd shared Ray's death with her. Those weren't things a man did to manipulate a woman.

And the way Colton made love to her.

She knew he loved her and the baby, a child that wouldn't have been conceived if he'd presented Martin with Jack Reid's last will.

Sometimes she hated when Colton was right.

"That stubborn mule of a man," Lauren muttered under her breath and tugging her boots on. She grabbed her coat and motioned Major towards the door. "Going off by himself to clear his mind."

≈

THE LUCKY JACK WAS PREPARED FOR THE STORM. Generators were fueled and firewood was stacked at the ranch house and at the cabin, and snowplows were mounted to the four-wheel-drive rigs.

None of those things would help Colton now.

The ranch was huge, and the chances of Punch and the others finding Colton weren't good. But Lauren knew where he was. On the way to the ranch, she tried to recall the exact location where McCrea had found him.

*There's a slot canyon on the other side of Whiskey Creek, just past Mars Falls.*

She'd been to Mars Falls once, but if she could find it

again, she knew she could find the slot canyon. Gathering camping gear from the storage room in the barn, she organized and packed a three-day supply of food and water and added a first aid kit and extra blankets. Then she saddled Church.

Major barked and wagged his tail.

"I'm going as fast as I can."

Within the hour, she was half-way to the falls. Another thirty minutes and she'd be there if she wasn't lost. She'd get to him in time, if it wasn't already too late.

Sue's words kept repeating in her mind. *I thought about how much I was going to miss him, and about all the times we wasted by being mad at one another... I wished we'd fought harder for our marriage.*

Lauren was so angry at Colton, but if something happened to him...

She nudged Church forward. Winds were picking up, and the temperature had dropped three degrees, according to her phone. She trudged on through the brutally cold wind and finally the cold, cutting waters of Whiskey Creek.

Major crossed the creek with minimal water damage by jumping from rock to rock. On the other side, he shook himself dry and took off.

Lauren was so cold by the time she found the slot canyon her teeth were chattering. Bends and twists in the rock prevented her from seeing more than a couple of yards in front of her. She dismounted and led the horse deeper in. On the third bend, she noticed plumes of smoke rising above the canyon. When she rounded the next bend, she saw Colton in his shearling coat and Dunn Resistol, warming his hands by a fire.

His handsome features were taut. Deep lines of thought and worry dug into his forehead, dark circles hung under his eyes, and days without shaving had given him a scraggly beard.

He looked awful, but he was alive and well.

Church whinnied, announcing their arrival. Colton's head jerked up, and those lines in his forehead deepened. "Lauren? What the hell are you doing here?"

"W—we were worried about y—you," she chattered and Major barked his agreement.

"Christ, honey," he swore, and hurried to her. "Are you wet?"

Her body shook. "T—the c—creek."

He led her to the fire. Taking a wool blanket from his bag, he flung it around her shoulders. "The s—storm turned. More snow. Blizzzarddd."

"So you, Major, and Church thought you'd venture out into it to save me?" he asked.

Major barked.

"Oh, shut up," he snapped. "I can't believe you let her do this."

"H—he's a dog," she explained.

Colton removed her gloves and rubbed her hands with his. "Your feet are soaked."

But they didn't feel cold anymore. "Punch is l—looking for you."

Moving quickly and efficiently, he saddled his horse, packed his bags, and kicked the fire out.

"W—what are you doing?"

"We need to get you out of the storm."

"I'm t—tough. Stick it out w—with you."

"Lauren, if your core temperature drops you could go into shock and lose the baby."

Lose the baby?

No. She wasn't that cold.

"Can you stay on Church?"

What had happened to her between the creek and the canyon? She was so confused and groggy and she was tired, so tired. "Don't know. K–kinda weak."

Scanning the sky and the churning clouds, he swore. "We won't make it back to the ranch before the storm hits."

She'd never seen him look so scared.

"Come on, honey." He picked her up, set her on the horse, and mounted behind her. He whistled a command for Church to follow and gave Major a nod. "Go on, git."

He secured the surrounding blanket and took off into the fusillade of snow, leading the horse in the opposite direction she'd come. There were parts of the ranch she didn't know, and the path they were on was one she didn't recognize.

The horse lost its footing more than once on the frozen snow, but they made the top of the ridge. There sat the cabin, shed, and corrals of cow camp.

When he stopped the horse and dismounted, he lifted Lauren into his arms and hurried inside. Homemade bunk beds made from rustic lumber sat on one side and a small sink and woodstove occupied the other. He placed her on the bottom bed and tucked the blanket around her.

He set about the task of building a fire. After it caught, he went to the door. "I've got to put the horses in the shed. I'll be right back."

He pointed a finger at Major. "Make sure she doesn't wander off."

The dog barked.

Feeling was slowly coming back to her fingers and toes by the time Colton returned.

"Warmer?" he questioned, dropping their bags by the bed.

She sat up and put her feet on the floor. "My hands are

but my feet are still frozen."

The haunted gaze returned to his face as he dug into his saddle bag for a pair of his socks. He wasn't done chastising Major. "You knew she was pregnant, but you let her come anyway."

The dog sniffed Lauren's midriff, barked, and laid his head in her lap.

She sunk her fingers into the fur at his neck and rubbed. "You really think Major knew?"

He briefly raised his brows. "Why do you think he's been following you around?"

"Who's my good boy?" she asked, scratching behind his ear.

"Ruff!"

"Yes, you are," she crooned.

Colton scooted a wooden chair in front of her and patted his knee. "Give me your feet."

The last time he'd patted his knee like that, they'd done some very naughty things.

Clearing her throat, she held her hand out. "I can do it."

He handed them to her, dug his boot heels into the wooden floor and scooted back. The chair legs scrapping across the wood floor made a screeching sound.

Major barked, then the cabin was silent.

After the socks were on, she checked her cell phone for service. "I don't have a signal."

"You won't until we get farther down the mountain. Get some rest." He stretched his legs out and crossed his arms. "We'll ride out the storm here and head back as soon as it's over."

Lauren was exhausted, but the moment she drifted off, the wind would beat against the logs, or the tin roof would rattle. Colton had fallen asleep a while ago and now sat sleeping in the chair, resting his chin against his chest. His chest rose and fell with each breath he took.

She was so relieved he was safe.

When she'd learned he'd lied to her, she couldn't wait to get away from him and the Lucky Jack. But now her heart ached to be with him. They'd only been apart a short time. How was she going to survive a lifetime of never being in his arms, never hearing him laugh or see his eyes darken with passion when he kissed her?

They'd both be alone again and this time, there wouldn't be a reconciliation. Jack Reid had given her a chance to rope her dream and she had.

But if she left...

Colton was hers. He was the husband she'd always longed for. The man who loved her, needed her, and made her feel wanted. He'd given her her heart's desire

There was no way she could leave him. She should wake him up and tell him the news, but he was sleeping so soundly. Tomorrow would be soon enough.

COLTON HAD WOKEN JUST BEFORE DAWN AND GONE OUT TO check on the horses. The storm had passed, dumping a fresh layer of pure white snow over the land. The sky was blue, and the sun was bright.

It was a beautiful Christmas morning. He should be watching his family, in their pajamas, opening presents and wading through piles of gift wrap. Eating that turkey his mom was making and feasting on Mia's pies.

Instead, he was in a dusty old cabin preparing to sign his name to a document that would bind him to a lifetime of loneliness and heartache.

But there was no way around it.

He'd taken a risk and lost.

He'd see Lauren safely back to the ranch, put on a smiling face for his son, and go through the holiday knowing after everyone was gone, he'd exist as he had before.

Alone.

Colton wasn't sure how he'd make it thought next September. He'd hear the news of the baby's birth and he'd have to learn how to live in a new kind of hell.

Lauren stirred in the bed behind him. He wiped the dampness from his face and sniffed. As he slid the papers back into the manila envelope, he heard the soft sound of her morning sigh and stretch.

God, he was going to miss her.

"It's stopped snowing," she said, raising to looked out the window.

He turned and leaned against the single sink cabinet. "We should head back. Little Jack will be waiting to open his presents."

She threw back the blanket, swiveled around in the bed, and placed her sock feet on the floor. Standing, she stretched and yawned again. Sleepy eyes, messy hair, and a rosy pregnant glow.

*Take a good look. A memory is all you'll have of her.*

Another yawn came as she stood and stretched. "I forgot about Christmas."

Colton shoved his arms into his coat, picked up the envelope from the sink, and stepped over to where she was.

She glanced down at it and back at him. He thought she'd snatch the papers from his hands and head out the door. But she just stood there, looking at them like he had her.

"When you handed these to me——" The pain of letting her go consumed him. Whatever he was going to say had to be done before they walked out that door. No rehearsed words or scenarios came to mind. The only thing he could to do was open his mouth and let his heart speak for him. "I knew there wasn't a damn thing I could do to get you back. It was over. You wanted what I had failed to give you."

Her eyes glistened with tears. "Colt–"

"I couldn't stand to see you so broken and miserable. I knew I had to let you go. I told myself that I could watch you fall in love and have babies with another man. But honey, I couldn't–" His voice cracked. "So when Martin read the wrong will, I had to take one last shot at it. I'd show you you were loved and wanted, and I did. Our baby is proof of that. I lied more than once and when I had the chance to tell you the truth, I didn't. I couldn't bring myself to do it because I knew you'd leave me. I've screwed everything up. I have to accept that. This time it's really over."

He hated seeing her cry, but she had to see that she was taking everything from him.

"I'm not above begging and before you say anything, I'm not asking you to forgive me or–or take me back. Just," he paused for a deep breath, "don't leave Crossfire Canyon. I'll stay out of your life and goddamn it, I won't say a word when you fall in love with another man. But please, let me be there when our baby is born."

She clapped a hand over her mouth. Was that a sign she'd have mercy on him?

"Let me hold that baby and be a part of its life. I want to go to my son's football games and give him advice on love and be a full-time dad to my kids."

Time ticked away and seconds seemed like hours.

Finally, Lauren looked down at the floor. "Is–ah, that all?"

Was that all? It was everything he had. Heart, soul, and tears. What more did she want? "Yeah," he said, dully.

"Are the horses ready?"

He managed a nod.

She took the papers from his hand and turned to the stove. "Let me warm up and I'll be ready to go."

Colton had his answer.

Lauren had no mercy.

He picked up their bags and went out the door. Hands shaking, heart barely beating, he walked to the shed, dropped the bags to the ground and fell back against a post.

She'd dismissed him and everything he'd said, and she'd accepted the divorce papers.

This was the end.

Tears froze on his face. How was he going to make it? She wasn't gone yet, and he already felt like he was dying.

Suddenly, the cabin door open and out walked Lauren with a flaming manila envelope in her hand. "You!" She pointed at him. "Are on such thin ice, Cowboy."

Huh? He pushed up from the post and wiped his eyes.

Major ran to the shed and took shelter. Colton wasn't the only one who was clueless.

She started stomping through the snow towards him. "I mean, like the thinnest ice in the history of marriage."

Had she gone off the deep end? "What are you talking about?"

Her mouth fell open, and her eyes nearly bulged out of her skull. "What am I talking about? You lied to me. You– you jerk."

Was that new news? "I told you I was sorr–"

"Oh, please," she said, rolling her eyes. "You're going to have to do better than that."

Do better than that? What the hell was going on? And

then it hit him. He'd been so worried about losing her he hadn't considered why she'd risked life and limb to save him from dying in a blizzard.

Lauren wasn't leaving him, and she'd accepted those papers so she could destroy them. He quickly scanned her face, looking for signs he was right.

And there it was. The hint of a smile tugged at the corner of her mouth. His lethargic heart jolted to life. But just because she'd come to save him didn't mean she had forgiven him.

He had nothing left to lose. If she set him on fire, at least he'd be warm. "What do you suggest?"

She sighed heavily and pooched out her bottom lip as she thought. "I don't know. Maybe a life of servitude?"

He wanted to grab her and kiss her. "I'm up for a little bondage."

"You wish." She snorted and continued. "Or I could use a new wardrobe."

"I like you naked." He liked her any way he could get her.

"I know." She held her left hand out and wiggled her fingers. "Or how about a big, flashy diamond?"

"I thought you said you didn't want a new ring," he said, closing the space between them.

"Ouch." She shook her hand when the flame reached her fingers. The ashes of their divorce papers scattered to the wind and blew away.

It was beautiful.

"I did say that." Her smile was flat. "But that was before you lied to me."

He drew her to him and eased his arms around her waist. "I get it."

She flattened her hands on his chest. "Get what?"

"Every time I lie, you get a flashy diamond."

She sobered and cocked an eyebrow, her expression as serious as that flaming torch smoldering in the snow. "If." She shoved her finger into his chest."

"Oww."

"You lie." Poke. "To me." Poke. "Again." Poke. "I will string you up by your bal—"

He hushed her with a kiss. "I won't. Does this mean you forgive me?"

"Yes. No." She narrowed her eyes. "Maybe."

"Yeah?" he whispered.

She smiled and wrapped her arms around his neck. "Yeah."

Colton kissed her softly.

She took his hand and placed it on her stomach. Desire and love filled her eyes. "You're going to be here there when our baby is born. You're going to hold it and watch it grow up. You're going to watch Little Jack play ball and give him love advice. You're going to be a full-time dad."

"I can't wait," he said, adoring every word she said.

"Marriage isn't easy," she reminded him. "But I'm willing to tough it out."

"Me too." He kissed her again.

"We'll talk through our problems."

He nibbled her earlobe. "Communication."

"Exactly, and we'll forgive each other."

"Always."

"Now." She patted his chest and headed for the horses. "Let's go home."

Home.

Their home.

The Lucky Jack.

"And," she cut him a heated glance over her shoulder, "no more going off to clear your head unless I'm with you."

"You mean, you, Major, and Church?" he questioned.

Major barked and jumped his way over to Lauren.

"We're a team. Now, come on. I haven't had a bath since yesterday morning and my teeth are fuzzy."

"Gross. I kissed you?" he joked, walking behind her.

"Thin ice, Cowboy." She unwrapped the reins from the hitching post and mounted Church. "Oh, and by the way. Don't think you're skirting your way out of your share of the baby work."

"Baby work? I thought I'd done my part." He shoved his boot in the stirrup, took hold of the cantle, and swung a leg over the saddle. "You know with the—"

"You call that work?" she asked, nudging the horse toward the east trail.

Colton grinned, brought his horse around and followed. He didn't have a clue what had just happened, and he didn't care. Lauren wasn't leaving him. He was going home to spend Christmas with his family. His wife, son, and unborn baby.

A few yards down from the cabin, the view opened, and he could see for miles. The ranch house, the barns and paddocks. Whiskey Creek and... the cemetery.

Jack Reid had a plan.

A plan so outrageous it had worked.

*Thanks, Dad. I couldn't have done it without you.*

Colton and Lauren had gone full circle, back to the days before his deployment. Back to the days when they were first married and in love.

Those essential pieces of their marriage he'd feared were lost had been found safely tucked away in the forgiving heart of his woman.

Made in the USA
Las Vegas, NV
31 January 2022

42701685R00194